WINE THIEF

MARY BILLITER

Wine Thief © 2018 by Mary Billiter

For information, contact the publisher, Hot Tree Publishing.

WWW.HOTTREEPUBLISHING.COM

EDITING: HOT TREE EDITING
COVER DESIGNER: SOXSATIONAL COVER ART
FORMATTING: RMGRAPHX

ISBN: 978-1-925655-59-9

DEDICATION

One of my favorite photos was taken at a winery in Napa Valley, California, in 2015. My sister, Suzanne, and her husband, John, took my husband, Ron, our son, Cooper, and me to wine country for the day. It was November, the trees had turned golden, and we stopped for a picture. I ran down the tree-lined road and playfully called to my husband, "Ron, do you see me? Can you catch me?"

He turned his camera on me and captured the spirit of love and happiness. Those photos appear on my website, and every time I see them, I am reminded of a wonderful moment between us.

On the flight home from my sister's home in the Bay Area to my home in Cheyenne, Wyoming, I wrote a letter to my family. We had just celebrated Thanksgiving at my sister's house with my little brother, Patrick, and our families. It was probably one of the most perfect holidays we have shared together. But I knew my breast cancer had spread to my ovaries—they didn't. I had kept that to myself.

So, on an evening flight between California and Wyoming, between sickness and remission, I put on paper everything I hadn't said, in the event I didn't win my battle.

It was the hardest letter I've ever written because thinking of life without my husband, children, and family was unimaginable. But I knew that I had one wish, and it was that their lives not stop. Cancer had already stolen so much. So, in writing this letter, I left it all on the page—my hopes, my dreams, and the future I wanted for my husband and children.

That letter became the turning point for this story. And it all started in Napa.

ALSO BY MARY **BILLITER**

RESORT **ROMANCES**

(Standalone Series)

Do Not Disturb Book 1

Escape Clause Book 2

Rule Breakers Book 3

Spirited Away Book 4

Wine Thief Book 5

The Changeup Book 6

CHAPTER **ONE**

CHLOE

"Drive it like you stole it, Chloe. Drive it like you stole it!" He drummed his fingers on the dash.

It didn't matter who sat behind the wheel, my brother-in-law, Coach, was the consummate motivator. His go-to line for any driver, in any car, was to, "Drive it like you stole it."

My hands gripped the black leather steering wheel like they belonged there. With the hardtop down, the Napa Valley sun kissed my head with heat that brought sugar to the vines and a thirst to wine lovers. Coach grinned like a willing accomplice.

"Come on! Come on! Let's go. Let's go."

I pulled out of the Oakville Grocery lot, the cup of coffee in the sleek beverage holder barely moving when I punched the accelerator. Gravel spun beneath my tires as the large Coca-Cola sign on the side of the brick building quickly vanished in my rearview.

Highway 29 stretched out before me with vineyards on both sides of the two-lane road. With only twelve miles between Oakville and Napa, there were a handful of stoplights. Not that I had to worry about a red light. When Coach had knocked on the guest bedroom door this morning, I think the moon was still out. Now, there were more flashing yellow lights giving me the go-ahead than cars yielding.

I paddle shifted into first, and felt the pull of the engine. I raised an eyebrow at Coach, who along with my sister had convinced me that the price the dealer finally settled on for the Mercedes 350 SLK was a steal, but what did I know about cars? I was still learning to operate my new ride, which was less than a week old. And I was still in shock that I'd cashed out my 401K to purchase the car. Not a house, or condo, or something that would appreciate in value. Nope, I put all my stock in a car. *What was I thinking?*

I shifted into second, running through another blinking light, and felt like I was breaking the law. My pulse pounded and my clasp tightened around the wheel. All I knew about cars was that this little two-door coupe looked like a mini Bond-mobile, replete with a two-seated leather cockpit, a voice-guided navigation system that I set to a British accent, and a retractable hardtop that could bring the sky to me with the touch of a button. That's what sold me. It was badass, which was 180 degrees away from who I used to be. If you are what you drive, I'd just become a far better version of myself.

I hit third hard; the gears ground, and I cringed. *Gotta work on that.* I corrected by paddle shifting from third to fifth in under five seconds. The V6 hummed beneath me like a panther. The red needle on the odometer spiked to seventy.

"Let that baby fly!" Coach encouraged.

I glanced in his direction, and his blue eyes were almost as majestic as the metallic silvery blue that coated the car and shone like a rare diamond in the sun.

A cool breeze coming up from San Pablo Bay blew my hair across my face.

"Damn. I knew I forgot something. I should've put my hair back." I reached toward the glove box that was in front of Coach, and he moved as if to do it for me. "No!" I snapped. "Don't!"

Startled, he pulled his hand away as if it had been slapped.

"There's…. It's just…." I shook my head and waved my hand as if that would explain my sudden outburst. "I just…. Let me get it."

"You're driving."

"I'll pull over." My tone stayed sharp. I glanced in my rearview. A blank canvas of road greeted me. There was something about the vacantness in front of me and the nothingness in my rearview that was oddly reassuring. I drove for a moment in silence.

"Chlo, isn't your scarf in the glove box?" Coach's voice was reassuringly calm.

I nodded.

"Should… I get it for you?"

I rapped my newly manicured thumbs against the

steering wheel. "Uh...." The pop of tangerine polish bounced in the sunlight. "Yes. Please."

Coach pressed the silver button on the console and the lime-colored Hermès silk scarf my sister had given me slid forward. He reached for it, and was about to close the glove box when he paused.

I kept my focus on the road, and my hands steady around the steering wheel. Maybe it would ground me.

"Oh, Chloe." The words caught in his throat.

I swallowed hard.

"Was this...."

I nodded and felt my throat ache. *Why now?* The little statue of Buddha was Ben's way to keep things light. *So why is it dampening my mood?* As a psychologist, I knew that grief came in waves, that even three years after my husband's death it would occasionally overtake me. But this was supposed to be my new beginning, a chance to leave the worst of it behind.

"Well, what the hell is this doing stuck in here?"

I almost got whiplash turning to look at him. "What?"

Coach gently reached for the yellowing figurine that was on top of the owner's manual, and placed it beneath my rearview. "Girl, you can't hide a piece of art like this."

I looked at the faded, smiling Buddha that was as fat as he was happy, and my chest felt heavy. But the weight of sadness didn't last long. Laughing Buddha's charm was that it was impossible to be unhappy when he was in front of me.

"He belongs right up there." Coach leaned forward and centered the chunky statuette. "Right up on the dash."

"My dashboard decoration."

Coach sat back in his seat hard. "Man, I haven't heard that expression in…."

"Three years?" I glanced at my brother-in-law. *Shit. This isn't any easier on him.* I drew a deep breath of California air, which reawakened the reason I had uprooted my life, placed most of my belongings in storage, and moved in with my sister and her husband. Buddha was about the only relic from my past that I'd brought to Napa.

"See." I paused until I had his attention. "This is how it begins." I pointed toward the front console. "First, a Buddha on the dash. Next, I'll be working as an Uber driver right here in Napa."

Coach wagged his finger. "Nuh-uh. Not with this car. And your sister would *never* let that happen."

I shrugged. "Okay, a beat-up Toyota and Bangkok it is."

Coach handed me my scarf and held the steering wheel. "Don't be knocking Toyota. You know I love my 4Runner. And Bangkok was never *your* dream, Chloe."

"Eh, at this point what does it matter." I wrapped Hermès silk around my head and loved how soft and smooth it felt on my skin when I tied it behind my neck. Shorter, dark waves of hair slipped past the fine silk. I tucked the renegade locks beneath the scarf.

"A fat and happy Buddha on my dash just may bring me the luck and income the Bangkok taxi drivers believe it generates," I said, regaining control of the wheel. "Who knows? Maybe the hotel will offer me free housing. It's a long shot, but so was buying this car. And taking a job in a hotel. So, anything's possible, right?"

It oddly felt natural handling my new set of expensive wheels. "What do you think?" I glanced at Coach and playfully cast my head up like I was some famous movie star and not one of many new wine educators hired at the Napa Valley Point Resort and Winery.

"Looking good, girl."

"Now if I only had tucked my jean jacket in the glove box." I raised my shoulders to my ears as if that would suddenly take the chill out of the air. Cloud cover splotched the sky and played peek-a-boo with the sun. Combined with the morning mist, I was beginning to rethink having the top down.

Coach reached across the center divider and pressed a button on the console. Within seconds, a concentrated flow of heat hit my neck, and cascaded down my back and across my shoulders, warming me. I looked at him.

"Luxury has its perks," he said.

"No kidding."

The sun shone on the Vaca Mountains on the eastern side of the valley. The light dappled on the full green leaves of the vines, rows upon rows of bountiful fruit waiting to be made into delectable nectar greeted us as we drove past each winemaker's backyard. Bottles and bottles and barrels and barrels of the Point's signature—and extremely guarded, I was told in my phone interview—red wine danced in my head like sugar plums. *Working in wine country will soon be a reality.* A familiar pang tugged at my heart, but I quickly redirected my attention to the dash. *No sadness around Laughing Buddha.*

I glanced at Coach, whose head was tilted down. *Is he asleep?* A ring of graying hair circled his head like a wreath. When he held up his iPhone, it made sense. Coach was reading his phone. "Charlotte's there. Come on! Can't keep her waiting," which was his code for *faster, faster.*

I pressed on the gas pedal and let the V6 shift us into another dimension.

"Hell yes!" *This thing has speed.* But as soon as the wine train came into view, sun gleaming off the golden chain of cars, my nerves caused me to suddenly come to a halt. My foot lifted from the accelerator.

I shook my head. "I can't do this."

Coach slowly nodded. "Okay. I can call Charlotte and tell her that I'm taking your place. She'll understand."

"Yeah, let's do that. I'm not ready for this."

"Sure," Coach said. "I get it. New car. New town. New job. It's *a lot* going on."

I slowly exhaled so I wouldn't puke and ruin that new car smell, which, really, no air freshener could replicate.

"I get it. Not everyone can handle so much at once."

What? "I can handle it," I said, pressing back on the gas. "I'm just not sure I *want* to go on some four-hour wine train. I mean, what is this? Gilligan's Drunk Island?" I elbowed him with a laugh.

"Oh, sure. Yeah, that's funny," he said without laughing. "Charlotte and I had a great time on the Wine Train and we thought you would too. And with your new job, it wouldn't hurt to learn more about wine. But I understand. You have the keys to the house, so you can go let the girls out. They'll need to be taken care of."

"The dogs?" I took my eyes off the road and looked at Coach. "I have to take care of Zoey and Lana?"

He nodded.

"Coach, they *hate* me. They chase me around the house, nip my heels, and when they aren't tormenting me, they eat the soles out of my shoes."

"Well, if you're not going on the Wine Train…." He shrugged. "Someone's got to take care of them. I was going to, that's why we had a friend drop Charlotte off after boot camp at the gym, so we'd have only one car to deal with, but now…." He trailed off.

"Oh, fine!" I downshifted hard into third. *What the hell is it about that gear?* "I'll go, but only because my sister has demon dogs."

His laughter made me smile. "Chloe, they're not demons."

I held up my right hand while I drove. "Yes. They are."

"This'll be good for you, Chlo. You're getting back in the game of life. I wasn't sure you were ready."

"Huh?" I glanced at him, but he was staring out the side window. "Oh, I'm ready to get back in the game, Coach." *What else would this move and career change be about?* He still wasn't looking at me. "Coach?" I waved my free hand at him, but his sights were set somewhere else.

I redirected mine to the road ahead of us. "I just don't know if a *wine train* is necessarily the best way to get back in the game." I waited a beat. "Now maybe a church social."

I chuckled. "Kind of more my speed."

Coach looked at me and grinned. "Chloe, I get it. When you're ready to do this, you will. So, consider today a warm-up."

My stomach flip-flopped. "Ah, Coach. It's not that I don't *want* to do this. I'm just not sure I *can* do this." Vulnerability caught in my throat. "Or that I even remember how."

His blue eyes locked on to mine. "Girl, you've got this. You just turned thirty, you're not some old goat like me."

I shook my head. At forty-five, Coach was ten years older than my sister, but their age difference had never been an issue. Coach was Coach. He oversaw the high school football program, drove a truck for the local union, and was the blue collar to my sister's white collar. They contrasted, yet complemented each other. Every yin needed a yang, and Coach was my sister's.

"Look, it'll all come back to you. And besides," he said, "Charlotte will be with you. What could go wrong?"

I smiled to hide the laughter ready to erupt. I didn't want to tell my unsuspecting brother-in-law that my older sister and I had gotten into *a lot* of trouble when we were young, stupid, and single. Once our dad used his contacts on the police force to get us out of jail. Charlotte was locked up because she had ordered bottle service for us, not realizing it was outrageously expensive, and then couldn't afford to pay the tab. When I grabbed her hand and bolted us out of the bar and into a cab because we were both too drunk to drive, the taxi driver drove us directly to the Orange County jail. *Of all the cabs in California, I had to get in his.* We were held until my father paid our tab and the cab fare. It was why my sister now went on four-hour prepaid wine trains.

Yeah, some things were just best left unsaid.

As I slowly pulled into the parking lot and spotted my sister with a glass of wine already in her hand, I looked over at Coach. "Yeah, what could go wrong?"

CHAPTER **TWO**

TONY

Nice wheels. The only thing hotter than the Mercedes SLK roadster that pulled into the lot was the driver. Something about a woman handling a fast car revved my engine. It was lame, but with her bright green scarf blowing in the wind, and dark Ray Bans covering half her face, she carefully navigated around the potholes in the parking lot like a pro. Then I noticed the dealer plates on the back of her car. Her careful maneuvering wasn't an attention grab, but a move toward preventing a trip to the car wash. *Smart.* When she parked as far away from the crowd gathered by the train as possible, I'd bet money it was from a lack of experience parking the new ride. Her car was flashy, but something told me she wasn't. But what did I know? Probably wishful thinking.

"Fifty bucks says she checks herself in the rearview before she exits." Ty stood beside me. We were already into our first glass of wine, and about to claim the caboose.

"I'm in on that action." Dan shouldered his way past us to stand on the top step. Taller and leaner than both of us, Dan didn't need the extra leverage, but his years playing basketball made him position himself wherever he went. We all played ball together in high school and college, but Dan was the only one who had recruiters scout him out. He'd opted for an education over a basketball career, which I never understood. But that was Dan. A locked door prevented him from entering the tail end of the train and the ultimate center post.

"What about you?" Ty elbowed me. As our former point guard, he hadn't outgrown his misuse of swinging elbows and causing personal fouls.

I shook my head. "No, my money says she won't."

Dan gripped my shoulder hard, like he was palming a basketball. "Oh, sweet Tony, always wanting to see the best. Look at her. Mercedes. Scarf. Big glasses. She reeks of conceit and money."

"We're in Napa, about to board a semiprivate wine train for your *four-hour* bachelor party," I said. "It'd be hard to find someone in this crowd who *doesn't* reek of money." I paused and looked at the woman in question. The scarf, while loud in color, didn't scream of conceit, but rather class. "It gets windy in a convertible," I said absently.

"I think Tony likes her," Dan said.

I shrugged him off me.

The woman we were stalking, I hoped from an appropriate distance, reached behind her head and untied her scarf. I hated to admit it, but I felt a bit of an adrenaline spike waiting for the reveal. With the green scarf, I think I was expecting a ginger, but instead smooth black hair that hit her chin shone in the sunlight.

"Short hair?" Ty said. "Why would she need a scarf?"

Dan laughed. "That girl has a hell of a lot more hair than me." His black hair was thinning, and we knew it'd soon be gone like his father's. But until then, Dan spiked it forward. He stood with a shit-eating grin on his face that made me shake my head.

When a tall blonde sipping a glass of red glanced over at us, I politely smiled in her direction. I shot my two moronic friends a stern warning glare, but that didn't stop either of them from laughing. And despite myself, I grinned, but added, "Nothing wrong with short hair. And from where I'm standing she wears it well."

"Ah, get over it, Mahoney, you're just trying to win the bet," Dan said.

"What I want to know is whether the carpet matches the drapes?" Ty said. "'Cause that could be some serious bush."

"That's what I'm talking about." Dan slapped Ty on the back. "Let's keep this shit light." He raised an eyebrow at me. "Especially since this isn't where I expected to have my bachelor party. Vegas—yes. Napa, not so much. But when you called about some business deal—"

I held up my hand, cutting off the rest of what he had to say. Despite being six feet to his six nine, my position as a former small forward gave me experience thwarting big men. "I know, I know," I said, lowering my voice. "You changed everything to come here. And if I could have done my research and reconnaissance anywhere else, I would have."

"So, what's your R&R on this time?" Dan asked quietly.

My voice was barely above a whisper. In my line of work, I couldn't afford prying ears. Dan knew, so it wasn't a surprise when our conversation turned to low tones. "I'm working for Old man Winters again. He wants me to collect as much information as possible about a wine coming out of the Point Resort. It's got a rare, rich taste and it's already an award-winning vintage. But it can only be found at the Point's winery. So I've got to get friendly with someone in the Point's vineyard."

"Which is why you got us rooms at the Point," Dan said softly.

I nodded. "Yeah, this new cabernet is really eclipsing Winters Summerset collection."

Dan seemed to absorb my new assignment with interest.

"Anyway," I said, "I *really* appreciate that you were willing to come to Napa."

"Listen, I'd go to Chuck E. Cheese with you just for the shenanigans."

"Sure. Chuck E. Cheese," I replied, smiling.

"Oh, oh, hold up," Ty said, oblivious to our conversation. "I think the moment of truth is about to be revealed."

We both returned our attention to the blue coupe.

"Scarf's off. Key's out of the ignition. And the dude she's with is *clearly* ready," Ty said.

Yeah, who is that guy?

"Okay, here's the money moment. Will she or won't she?"

I held my breath. *Come on, whoever you are. Don't do it. Don't do it.*

But instead of reaching for the door handle, she reached behind her seat for something, a purse? *Oh, God. Is she getting a makeup bag?* I didn't have any sisters, but Ty did, and I still remembered all the makeup crap they left in his car. My heart raced. I casually leaned forward to get a better view of what she was pulling from the nonexistent back seat.

"What the hell did she tuck behind there?" I asked the question we all wanted to know.

"In a car that expensive, the only things people stash behind the seat are drugs and weapons." Ty's years of working as a parole officer surfaced. "And she doesn't look like a felon to me." He paused. "Or a stoner or shooter, either."

"Maybe she's reaching for a fistful of Franklins?" Dan mused. "Not only is her mattress stuffed with money, but so is the interior of her car."

"Yeah, that's it," Ty said drily. "She's driving her own personal ATM."

Suddenly a big pink-and-black polka-dotted handbag slung over the seat and practically knocked her in the face.

"Yes!" I pumped my fist in the air.

"Don't go counting your money yet," Ty said.

I tapped my foot on the metal train step. *How long does it take her to exit a damn car?*

Suddenly her hand went for the sun visor, and it felt like my heart plummeted to my gut.

"Uh-oh, Tone," Dan said. "Looks like your girl may be going to check herself in the mirror."

I spun toward Dan. "You said rearview." My finger pointed at his chest.

"Wow. Defensive much?" Ty said.

I withdrew my finger, but not my position. "He said rearview. You heard him." I sounded as junior high as when we all met.

Dan slowly shook his head. "Tony. Tony. Tony. And you wonder why you're still single."

"This whole thing is stupid." Yet I couldn't stop looking toward her as I spoke. The visor was down, but from my vantage point, I couldn't tell if there was a mirror or not. And from the lack of response from my buddies, neither could they. "What does it matter whether she checks her makeup or not? Unless she exits the car and suddenly we discover she's a cyclops, she looks pretty damn good to me. She just didn't seem like the kind of girl who needed a mirror or *relied* on a mirror, but," I shrugged, "if she does, well, I've been wrong about women before… so big shock. I missed the mark." I reached into my back pocket and withdrew my wallet. I grabbed two fifties and was about to hand them to my best friends when the blonde I'd noticed before walked by.

"Put away your money."

I looked up. "Excuse me?"

"My sister is many things, but vain isn't one of them."

Heat rose to my cheeks. "I wasn't…. We weren't…. It was just…."

The blonde waited for me to complete a full sentence or be coherent. I wasn't sure which. I was about to reconstruct my thoughts, when the roof to the Mercedes rose.

"You have to drop the visor to put up the roof," the blonde said.

When the roof was sealed, the brunette aimed her remote toward her car and I heard the beep of the alarm activating.

"And there's no mirror in the visor," the blonde added with an arched eyebrow.

I quickly glanced at Ty and Dan, who reached into their wallets.

I turned to look back at the blonde. She raised her glass toward me. "To cyclopses and lasting first impressions."

CHAPTER **THREE**

CHLOE

My sister walked away from three men who seemed very amused by something she'd said. Or done. Who knew with Charlotte. Still, I tilted my head and raised an eyebrow as she joined us. "You know none of Dad's old friends work on the force here, don't you?"

"Uh, should I be worried?" Coach pecked her cheek.

Charlotte waved her hand, and the flash of a two-carat Tiffany diamond was impossible to miss. "Those guys? They're harmless. Cute, but harmless."

"Cute? Men aren't cute, Charlotte. They're rugged or handsome, but never cute." Coach shook his head.

"Or ruggedly handsome," I said with a laugh.

"Right," Coach said. "I think I'm going to get a glass of wine. Can I get you one, Chloe?"

"Red, please." I casually snuck a peek at the ruggedly handsome men as Coach walked past them.

"That guy's got to be close to seven feet," I said.

My sister had her back to them and knew better than to turn around.

"I know, he's tall. He looked familiar, too. I think he played college ball."

"Hmm. He doesn't have the best hair, but his minimal beard and mustache has this Chris Pratt feel, and that always works."

"Yeah… I think he's getting married."

I winced. "I don't even know why I'm looking."

"Chlo, three cute guys hanging out on the caboose is kind of hard to pass up."

"True." I continued to hide behind my sunglasses and my taller sister as I studied them. "The other guy in the T-shirt, jeans and… what is that slung over his shoulder?" I felt my shoulders tighten. "Oh, my God. Is that…?" I glanced at my sister for confirmation.

"A very loud plaid sports coat?"

I gasped. "Doesn't he know Dad's rule?"

She slowly shook her head. "Apparently not."

My shoulders dropped. "He just doesn't know. The guy's built like a wrestler, and short, stocky people should just avoid plaid. I can't imagine that even looks good on him."

My sister nodded. "Plaid. It was Dad's curse. He loved plaid, or anything checkered, but it made him look as broad as a barrel."

"Wow. I see that now. It's just not flattering, and he's only got it draped over his shoulder." Even though I knew I shouldn't stare, I couldn't help it. "Other than the yellow, green, and pink jacket, he's kind of cute."

Charlotte shrugged. "He wasn't my type, but he wasn't ugly. But the other guy…."

There was one man we hadn't dissected. The sleeves on his dark jacket were pushed up, his jeans were the right shade of faded denim, and even though his dark hair was cut short, it didn't look lacking. Not that I was opposed to bald—at all. Bald was hot. But it wasn't his hair or clothes that made me really take notice. It was his posture. The guy stood with a quiet confidence that was alarmingly attractive. *Ben stood like that.*

Charlotte repositioned herself beside me while I stared at the last of the three men. *What is wrong with me? I don't even know him.*

"Oh, hey, I think it's time to get on the train. Get us a seat." Charlotte grabbed my arm and all but slung me away from her. I stumbled in her four-inch Christian Louboutin leopard-spotted peep-toe pumps she insisted I wear. I could barely walk in them, but they did make my shorter legs look super long and thin, so I managed. Coach was walking toward us in the distance, balancing three glasses of wine. I glanced over my shoulder. *What the hell?*

She smiled in the direction of the caboose where the last of the three men boarded the train.

CHAPTER **FOUR**

A bold streak of red popped on the soles of her shoes with each step she took down the narrow train aisle. I couldn't stop gawking at those shoes, which reminded me of a matador's cape flashing at a bull. But instead of making me angry, the spiky heels and her short yet shapely legs stirred longing. *What I could do with her legs wrapped around mine.*

Her black tank top swayed like silk against her jeans when she walked. A silver chain draped her cleavage, just the right amount of breast revealed. Not too much, not too little. Our paths were about to intercept, and my hands became sweaty and my tongue felt two times its size.

She smiled with her eyes and said, "Hey," as she passed.

All I could do was utter a tongue-less version of the same word. The guttural utterance, "Aa-ay" came out of my mouth just as my foot hit the seat in front of me. I stumbled awkwardly, but at least didn't face-plant in the aisle. *How's that for meeting a gorgeous woman?* Incoherent mutterings coupled with inebriated-like walking—could there possibly be a worse combination for a first impression? I probably would have made a far greater impression on her if I had just farted instead.

Dan raised an eyebrow.

I shook my head, took a seat beside him, and glanced over the back of the seat toward Ty.

"Smooth," Ty said.

I smiled through gritted teeth. "You saw that?"

"Dude, what the hell? It's not like you to lose your shit, let alone balance, around a woman," Ty said.

"I told you Tony liked her," Dan said.

I rolled my eyes. "I don't even know her."

"Yeah, but you already placed money on her," Ty said.

"And I'm a hundred ahead," I reminded him with a grin. "If we *were* in Vegas, the safe bet would be to walk away, which is what I'm doing."

"There's a difference between walking away from a dealer's table and a girl," Dan said.

I shrugged. "With a Vegas bet, all I'd lose is money. But with *Strangers on a Train* involving a *Single White Female* it could end up being a *Fatal Attraction* that leads to *Murder on the Orient Express*. And if for some tragic reason you don't understand any of these movie references, you need to bone up on your classics. Besides," I elbowed him, "once you get married, you'll have plenty of spare time on your hands, not having sex again. So, for your wedding gift, I'm thinking of getting you a subscription to the Fabulous Films channel." I paused long enough to grin like I was about to verbally dunk on my buddy, which I was. "I mean, I figure since you're not going to have any *Carnal Knowledge* after marriage, at least you'll know about the Jack Nicholson film."

Ty laughed as I wrapped my hands on the back of my seat. "Dan, buddy, you did say to keep it light."

Dan slowly nodded as the wine steward appeared with a tray of drinks. "I did." Dan carefully took a red, Ty reached for a white, and I stuck with the red.

"But?" Ty asked Dan.

A sly smile spread across Dan's face. "But just like when we're choosing teams in a pickup game, no one wants to be the last one selected." He shot me a look, and I knew our basketball captain was about to slam me. "So, unlike you single losers still waiting to be picked for a team, I'm the first one to be joined forever. While you guys are hopelessly scoping the bars and endlessly swiping right on your phones to check the latest text or group chat, I'll already be home with the best woman out there. It's game over, boys, and as usual, I win!"

I raised my glass toward him. "Indeed, you did. Lori's a great gal."

"To Lori," Ty said.

When our glasses clinked, it caught the attention of curvaceous. I smiled in her direction, and when she returned the smile, I was grateful that I was still waiting to be chosen for the right team instead of tripping myself up by falling for, and being tied down to, the wrong woman. Of course, I'd already been embarrassingly tongue-tied and nearly fallen on my face at the mere sight of the raven-haired beauty. Yup, like it or not, there was something about her that made me lose my footing.

CHAPTER **FIVE**

CHLOE

"Welcome to the Wine Train and your trip back in time." His name tag read Martine, and his glass was filled with a hearty-looking red wine.

"The Wine Train has seven cars that were originally used in the early 1900s as part of the Northern Pacific Railway. But as you can see"—Martine extended his glass toward the caboose and the rest of the train—"great cost was spent to restore the cars."

I glanced at the knotty pine paneling, silver accents, etched glass partitions, and the rich red-and-gold tapestry that covered the armchairs. It *was* like stepping back in time, and I couldn't believe I'd almost missed it.

"The Wine Train is equipped with a fine dining car where chefs prepare every entree made-to-order right here on the train. There are no microwaves or food lamps warming your food."

Everyone that had gathered laughed, including the nameless hot guy who had practically tripped over himself to say hello. I glanced in his direction. He leaned on the edge of the armchair with his arms loosely crossed over his chest. His jacket was gone, and in a cream-colored short-sleeved Polo, the definition in his forearms was impressive. He didn't look like the weight-lifting type, but muscles like that didn't lie. *My, my, my.* I quickly looked away before he caught me staring.

"Trains are part of our American history. Long before planes, people traveled by train. In fact, train travel was considered a smart, sophisticated way to see the country," Martine said.

"Martine, we bought a lifetime ticket, and we were wondering where we will be going?" an elderly woman asked. She was surrounded by a gaggle of old people. *Are these the original passengers who never left the train?* Perhaps they thought that a lifetime ticket meant having to spend their lifetime on the Wine Train. *Maybe I should buy a lifetime ticket and just ride the rails.*

"That's an excellent question. We will go through all thirty miles of Napa Valley, which offers remarkable views of the crops, vineyards, and overall agriculture of wine country," he said.

My stomach fluttered like I was about to buckle up for a monster roller coaster ride and not a train trip. Or maybe it was the effects of the second glass of wine, but as I stood beside my sister with Hot Guy in my periphery, I suddenly didn't see a downside to the day.

"All wineries have their own story about how they got started," Martine said. "As we pass wineries, I'll shout out information about the different vineyards. And I did say 'shout.'" His laughter was as contagious as the smile that broadened across his olive skin.

"The Wine Train can get a bit loud, and what that means to me is that you're having a good time." He glanced at the passengers gathered around him. "Which is why it's helpful if you gather in groups. It makes my job easier—if you miss something, there's usually someone in your group who will have remembered."

"We'll stop at a winery, right?" a guy about my age asked.

"Yes, we'll be making one stop. We'll explore one cave and one winery."

"Sounds like a movie title," he said with a laugh, and I chuckled. This seemed to get the attention of Hot Guy, who smiled.

Martine surveyed the number of people in front of him. "I think three groups would be great. And each group will have their own train car." He nodded toward the section of train that extended beyond the caboose where we had gathered.

I glanced at my sister, who quickly stepped toward the three men she thought were cute.

"Martine, is five enough for a group?"

He grinned. "Now, Ms. Sparks, you know the rules."

My sister's fair face ignited with color. "Yes, but Martine, when the groups get too big it's hard to make new friends."

Martine waved his finger back and forth. "Ms. Sparks, you are trouble."

Charlotte shrugged and playfully rolled her eyes. "Yes, but perhaps we can have smaller groups this time?"

Martine rubbed his smooth chin. "It will be a lot more walking and talking for me—I'll probably be hoarse afterward, but I cannot refuse one of my favorite guests." He again shook his finger at my sister. "You are a troublemaker."

She grinned. "Totally worth it." Her knobby elbow hit my side. "And so is my sister." I was pretty sure she directed that comment to Hot Guy. *WTF?*

I nervously laughed, but thankfully wasn't alone. The majority of newbies like me who had no idea what to expect from a four-hour wine tour laughed.

"We'll begin here in the caboose, and then as you form into groups of *five or six*," Martine glanced at my sister, "please find a car to claim as yours. The same tour will be provided to each car, so there's no reason to feel left out." He tilted his head. "Ms. Sparks, you know the drill, so if you see any stragglers, kindly direct them to a section of the train. Or allow them to join your group."

"Yes, sir." My sister saluted him, and I shook my head.

"Sorry, Martine, she can't help herself," I said.

"I am well familiar with Ms. Sparks," he said, which made me laugh. I was sure he was well familiar with her generous tips, too.

"There will be a lot of information provided on this tour, however"—Martine made eye contact with the clustering groups—"if you remember anything from today's trip, I hope it is this—wine is about a place. So ultimately, wine is about a landscape."

He paused, and I quickly texted myself what he'd said. I whispered to my sister, "Why didn't I bring a pen and some paper? This guy is golden. Part of my job is to come up with things to say to guests about wine."

She smiled and reached into her leather handbag, which probably cost as much as my new car, and handed me a silver pen and small pad of paper.

"And since wine is about a landscape, you'll see how the landscape changes as we travel through the valley." Martine raised his glass toward the groups. "To my favorite three words."

"Which are?" Hot Guy asked.

"Let's drink wine!" Martine said.

And with that, I finished the last of my second glass of red wine. The crystal had barely left my lips when my sister replaced the empty glass with a full one from the traveling cart of wine. She glanced at the three guys and raised her glass toward them.

"To drinking *lots* of wine!"

"Cheers! Cheers!" The tall guy and plaid-wearing man who were closest to my sister toasted.

Hot Guy looked at me, and for a moment hesitated.

I said nothing.

His bottom lip was pouty and pursed, like he was thinking. When he finally spoke, his voice was much deeper and stronger than his first attempt at hello. "To discovering new wine country," he said.

I didn't miss a beat. I held my glass toward his and cunningly grinned like I knew something he didn't, which was true. This guy had no clue how terrified I was to talk to him. All I let him see was what I wanted to project in my new job, new community, and new life—confidence. I'd told more patients than I could remember that sometimes the façade of confidence would help real confidence develop. So, as I tucked my hair behind my ear and smiled toward him with my glass raised, my intent was crystal clear. "To *many* new discoveries."

CHAPTER **SIX**

CHLOE

"So, what are we celebrating?" My sister was sandwiched between two of the three guys, who raised the armrests on their chairs so she could straddle the center. Only Charlotte could fit in the small space between the two armchairs and look elegant in the process. With crossed legs, a silver necklace shimmering against her blue silk blouse, and just the right amount of perfume, she drew a crowd—even the stragglers we were supposed to help find a car and a group.

"Our buddy Dan's getting married," the one with the plaid jacket draped behind his seat said.

Dan was on my sister's right side, next to the window, and nodded. "Hi. I'm Dan Shay."

"Hello, Dan, I'm Charlotte, and that beauty over there," she smiled toward me, "is my baby sister, Chloe."

"My groomsman Ty Masters is sharing a seat with you, and my best man, Tony Mahoney is—"

My sister held up her hand. "Hold up. Your name is Tony Mahoney?"

"It's Anthony. My mom's Italian and I'm named after her father, and my dad's Irish. So my name is supposed to take each culture to heart, but it's been nothing but a pain in the ass for me."

My sister offered an encouraging smile as if that would improve Tony Mahoney's rhyming name. *Poor guy.* And he was so cute, too.

Dan tilted his glass toward his best man. "As I was saying, the infamous Anthony Mahoney is sitting next to your beautiful baby sister."

If I wasn't already working on my third glass of wine, I'd have said something smart, but my hand-eye coordination was getting worse by the sip. And while I was having a difficult time guiding the wineglass to my lips, it would take absolutely no effort for a slip of the tongue and I'd end up putting my foot squarely in my mouth—especially with hotness sitting beside me. Nope, saying less was more.

"It sounds like you've been on the Wine Train before," Ty said to my sister.

"My husband and I have a few memberships at select wineries, and they often hold private events on the train to showcase their latest reserve. Martine is currently"—she raised a professionally threaded eyebrow at me—"one of the best wine educators in Napa, so he's hired a lot."

Oh, that's right, I'm a wine educator. And Martine had to be my sister's less-than-subtle attempt to improve my wine knowledge for bigger paying gigs. *Crafty.* So, these bottles and glasses were merely continuing education units. At this rate, I may even earn my PhD before the train stopped.

"Wine memberships?" Ty raised his glass and dropped the tone of his voice. "Swanky."

"Nah, my husband and I just like wine," she said, and clinked his glass.

Maybe it was the wine, but I couldn't stop staring at my sister's eyebrows. She spent more money threading her eyebrows than I did on my threadbare wardrobe. Although who was I to throw stones, or even grapes. I just cashed out for a car. *A car.* I was cash poor, but now had a rich ride. And if I didn't start earning a decent paycheck soon, I'd have the finest ride to the poorhouse. I watched my sister effortlessly arch a single eyebrow, while all I could do was furl the fuzzy caterpillars above my eyes, which I repeatedly did until I could feel my eyebrows. *There they are.*

I suddenly felt Tony staring at me, and I raised what I thought were my eyebrows at him. I was sure my overture looked like an enormous unibrow or caterpillar dancing across my forehead. *Oh, my God, what am I doing?* Granted, I hadn't dated in a while, but I was pretty sure acting like someone who either had a severe nervous tic or didn't realize that sign language was supposed to be performed with hands and not eyebrows wasn't a draw to a guy.

"Seriously, wine memberships?" Ty said before the wine passed my sister's lips. "That can't be a cheap hobby."

Hobby? Oh, no he didn't. I held my breath. My sister didn't regard wine lightly. Shit, the woman had bought her house because it had its own wine cellar.

She gently set down her glass, reached for the carafe, which seemed bottomless, and refilled everyone's glasses. The merlot left legs on the wineglass that she studied with her cool blue eyes. She was either stalling or avoiding, I wasn't sure which. Charlotte wasn't someone who backed down from a fight. And hobby and wine in the same sentence were fighting words.

When her gaze lifted from her wineglass, she turned directly to Ty, tucked her white-blonde hair behind her ear to reveal dazzling diamond studs, and politely smiled. Her looks alone could bring a guy to his knees, but when she killed them with kindness, it was a double punch.

"My husband and I work hard, and we like to enjoy the finer things in life," she said.

"To finer things." Dan raised his glass.

I tilted my glass toward my sister, who I knew held back from tearing Ty's face off with a well-crafted defense on wine's behalf.

"To finer things, like wine and women." Tony paused and smiled toward my sister. "Which everyone knows simply get better with age."

"That's what I'm talking about," Dan said.

Tony was almost as smooth as the rich merlot that went down way too easily. If I kept drinking at this rate, I'd be inebriated, infatuated, and in over my head.

"So, bachelor party then?" Charlotte said.

"Yes, ma'am." Dan's broad smile revealed large, straight teeth that strangely reminded me of a set of dominos. I couldn't stop staring at his teeth. If he lost one, would the rest topple? I was keenly aware that the wine was doing my thinking, but it was so yummy, who could stop? And why? I wasn't driving.

"Yes, my bachelor party consists of a four-hour wine train tour." He glanced toward the caboose we had commandeered as our group's car and nodded. "Which isn't too shabby."

"Dan, I would've taken you for a Vegas or Palm Springs kind of guy," my sister said while she refilled our wineglasses.

Yet it was the best man who rubbed the shadow of a beard on his chin and placed his hands on the table that separated our seats.

"That's my bad," he said. "I had some work to do in Napa that conflicted with the only available weekend for my buddies."

"Oh, so you're not from Napa or Sonoma County?" My sister's inquisitiveness rivaled interrogation techniques outlawed by the Geneva Convention. Instead of waterboarding her captive audience, she merely went overboard with the wine to extract their secrets and confessions.

"No, Southern California," Tony said, and suddenly I felt empty inside.

"Chloe just moved from So Cal," Charlotte said.

I tried to smile, but no matter how cute or seemingly nice this best man was, I promised myself the next time I went to Orange County it would be to empty my storage unit. It was just another sign that, three years or not, I had no business even contemplating a dating life.

"Where'd you live in So Cal?" Ty asked.

"Huntington," I said, and realized that was what locals called it. "Huntington Beach." I pursed my lips hoping he'd get the clue that I didn't want to talk about Huntington, HB or—

"No way!" Ty said. "Surf City, baby."

Or Surf City. *Great.*

"What are the odds?" Dan said.

I glanced at my sister and then to Tony.

"We grew up in Huntington," Tony said.

I blinked, hoping it'd improve my hearing. *How many glasses have I drank? Or is it drunk?* My sister reached for the carafe, which thankfully was nearing empty, and before I could put my hand over the mouth of my glass— the universal gesture for "no, stop, I'm about to hurl,"— she poured the remnants into my glass, and any chance of a graceful, and sober, exit from this train died. It would require me to suddenly develop an iron will to stand up to my sister, or an iron stomach to keep the wine down. Barring either, I wouldn't be riding this train to more employment opportunities with Martine, but a brief layover at the local police drunk tank seemed highly likely.

"Do you still live in HB?" my sister asked Tony.

For the love of God, why? Who cared where he lived?

"Indianapolis Avenue and Magnolia Street," he said, and I immediately knew where he called home. There was a subdivision across from Sts. Simon and Jude church where I attended Catholic school. My best friend had lived in the tract of houses and walked to school. The neighborhoods by the church were older, but well-established. Owners took pride in their homes, so it became real estate that was always in high demand.

"So, you went to Edison," my sister stated of our rival high school.

"Go Chargers," Dan said, and raised his fist.

"Yeah! And keep going, and going and going…."

All three guys looked at me in stunned silence.

"We went to Huntington Beach High School," my sister explained.

"And keep going and going until you run out of train and fall on the tracks!" I slapped the table when I burst out laughing. No one joined in—not even my sister, who usually provided a courtesy chuckle.

What did it matter anyhow? The best man of the group lived in Orange County, I lived in Napa County. He'd gone to Edison, I'd gone to Huntington. It didn't matter how much time had passed since high school, Chargers and Oilers didn't mix. Besides, aside from my sister leveraging us into their group, I was probably never going to see him again.

CHAPTER **SEVEN**

TONY

"What could possibly compel someone to leave Huntington for Napa?" Ty looked at Chloe, waiting for an answer. "I mean, I get that Napa is beautiful. But there's no beach. I couldn't survive without the ocean." He continued to stare at her.

"Excuse me." Chloe stood. "I need to find the ladies room before, uh, I float away." Her voice was upbeat like she was trying to keep it light, but it didn't feel real.

When she left, we sat, and Ty turned to her sister. "Was it something I said?"

Charlotte slowly shook her head. "No, Chloe's been through a lot."

"So, Napa's a fresh start?" Ty said.

"Something like that." Charlotte reached for the carafe, which we'd collectively drained, and she frowned. "Well, this won't do."

I stood and nodded toward the decanter. "I'll see about a refill."

"Wonderful," she said. "Would you like to try something that's a bit more toasty and oaky in flavor?"

"Sounds good," Dan said.

Charlotte's blue eyes were impossible not to stare into—they were such a watery shade of blue that it looked like the sky after a rain. But this woman was all thunder. "Tony, perhaps ask Martine for a cabernet."

"From?" I said, holding the carafe.

Her eyes narrowed in on me as if I'd dared challenge her knowledge of wine. I quickly recovered. "I read in a magazine on the plane something about fruit from each vineyard yields, uh, gives it a different taste. So, one cabernet might not taste like the other."

Dan stared at me, but thankfully kept his mouth shut.

"That's true. I think Stage's Leaf has a distinct flavor."

"Stage's Leaf then," I said.

"You really know your wine," Ty said.

"Wine geek and beer snob," she said with a pleasing smile.

"Okay, then, I'll find Martine." I turned, and when I was out of sight, exhaled. *Fuck, that was close.* I was successful in my career as a competitive intelligence gatherer because I purposefully stayed under the radar and didn't draw attention to myself. This allowed me to familiarize myself with the business climate and clientele, and systemically gather, analyze, and manage information on our competitors without anyone the wiser. I was in Napa to gather information on the Point Resort's private reserve. Revealing I had any knowledge of wine, albeit limited, wouldn't just hinder my objective, it'd downright blow my cover. *Fuck, Mahoney, get a grip.*

I spotted Martine in the far distance and walked toward him. The sixth and fifth railcars connected through an extremely tight passageway. I waited for an older woman to pass before I stepped inside. In the distance, Chloe walked toward me in her spiked shoes that looked dangerous in so many ways—and all of them included me grabbing the heel in one hand while her leg was stretched against me. I couldn't get the image out of my head. *Ga-damn.*

When she passed the group in car five, the men glanced in her direction. She wasn't as striking as her blonde, blue-eyed sister, who a guy immediately checked out. But there was something about Chloe that radiated energy and sex appeal, and just made a guy smile. Her chin-length hair framed a face that wasn't spoiled by heavy makeup. She had a bright, clean, girl-next-door look that radiated purity. But her dark brown eyes hinted at something less than neighborly. Chloe seemed like a woman who would whisper naughty things in the dark or giggle under the covers. She was someone I knew nothing about, but her quiet reserve made me want to know everything.

I stood in the passageway waiting for her.

"Hey." She waited for me to move forward or take a step back. I did neither.

She raised an eyebrow and tentatively entered the passageway. I was taller than her, but not by much. Her heels probably had something to do with her increased height that she used to her advantage when she looked at me directly. But just like in basketball, I didn't back away from her stare down. The train vibrated the accordion-like walls in the passageway, wind whistled through the seams, and wine country blurred past us. To reach the caboose, she'd have to squeeze past me, but neither of us moved. Our bodies practically touched, and the heat between us was insane. *Who is this woman? And why Napa?*

I was about to say something, anything, when her fingers faintly trailed down my arm to my hand. It was the smallest amount of touch, but it felt like the tactile version of a whisper.

I almost dropped the carafe when she reached for it and swung it between us.

"Empty?" Her eyes wandered up to mine. They were slightly glassy, and I remembered that she'd already had two—no, three… or was it four?—glasses of wine.

"Uh-huh." I could barely put two words together, let alone a cohesive sentence.

"That's not good."

"That's what your sister said."

"We tend to do that when we're together," she said.

"I bet." A strong scent filled the air between us. "Is that peppermint?"

A striped mint stuck out from her lips. "Martine's got a bowl of candy," she said with a grin that would melt the most hard-hearted bachelor. "I may have grabbed a handful."

"Got any more?"

She nodded.

"May I have one?"

She tapped her chin with a finger, which involved her elbow pressing into my abs, which I quickly tightened.

"I don't know," she said. "Why should I share?"

"Because sharing's nice."

She shrugged. "Maybe I'm not nice."

I laughed. "Sure. You're not nice. Says the girl that looks like Jennifer Garner and has hardly said two words."

She playfully rolled her eyes. "Yes, but the two words I said were memorable: Chargers suck."

"Easy there," I said. "Those are fighting words."

"Like you're a fighter." She flaunted the candy on her tongue, provocatively moving it in and out of her mouth like a game of hide and seek. If anyone else did the same thing, it'd probably gross me out, but this woman's playfulness was sensually flirty.

I leaned toward her, braced my arm against the side of the passageway, and went in for the steal when she popped the candy back between her front teeth and bit down.

Our eyes never left each other. Suddenly, she cupped her mouth with her hand, her eyes watered, and she tried to lean back, but there was no room.

"Oh my God. Are you okay?"

She lowered her head. "I don't know. Something cracked." She continued to cradle her mouth with her hand.

I gently tipped her chin toward me. "Let me look."

She hesitated. Her brown eyes stared into mine, and it was like being bathed in a warm sunset.

"Chloe, it's okay. Let me take a look."

She flashed her teeth, and I practically had to grit mine to prevent from laughing. I swallowed hard. Her front tooth was chipped in half and the other half was missing. At best, she looked like a rugged hockey player. At worse, straight-up hillbilly. Within a matter of seconds, she went from innocent, sexy girl-next-door to scary toothless girl. *Oh, fuck.*

"It's not that bad." I tried to sound as helpful as possible because no one likes the bearer of bad news.

"Really?" Her tongue felt its way to her front tooth and I cringed.

This won't be good.

"Oh, no! My tooth." Her finger gently touched the jagged edge and her eyes widened. "You lied!" She frantically searched the space between us. "Where's the rest of my tooth?"

I looked down just as she looked up, and we bumped heads. Tears streamed down her face as she rubbed her head. "Don't hurt me!"

"I'm sorry, it was an accident. It's really tight in here." I sounded like a complete buffoon. Of course she knew it was tight. That's why I hadn't moved to get closer to her.

"Do you see my tooth?" Her voice was panicky.

"Uh…." I glanced at the small area between us and all I saw was metal flooring.

"What happened to my tooth?" Her brown eyes pleaded for an answer. I wished like hell I'd never trapped her in this passageway. The only possible explanation for her missing tooth was obvious to me, but apparently not to her. And I had to be the dick who told her.

"I think you may have, uh, swallowed it?" I tried to sound as hopeful as possible. "If there's a silver lining, I'm sure you didn't have a filling there. Most people don't have fillings in their front teeth. I thought about being a dentist once." She may not kill the messenger, but my chances with her could very well be dead on arrival.

"Swallowed it?" Her smooth complexion drained of color, and I thought she was going to faint. Not that she could fall far. "Why should I believe you? You already lied and said my tooth was okay. You're a horrible liar," she said.

"Chloe, I'm sorry. I'm not a horrible liar." *I'm actually quite good at it.* But I silenced the urge to tell her all my secrets.

She dropped the carafe into my hand, covered her mouth, and walked away.

CHAPTER EIGHT

TONY

If wine was the magic elixir that turned nice girls naughty as Dan always claimed, I hoped it'd soften Chloe. I doubled down and brought two carafes back to our table. Everyone's wineglass was empty and parked in front of Chloe, who sat beside her sister. Ty and Dan were across from them. There was no place for me to sit, so I leaned against the side of Dan's seat.

Charlotte took one carafe and seemed about to place it between her and Chloe, but her sister grabbed it and began drinking directly from it.

"Right on," Dan said.

"Chlo, easy," her sister said.

Chloe raised a finger and wagged it back and forth. When she came up from guzzling, she didn't hide her semi-toothless grin. "When you have a hag's tooth instead of a tooth, you can judge, but until then"—her finger rotated around the table until she had pointed to each of us, including her sister—"zip it."

"Chlo, by Monday, or actually Tuesday because of Memorial Day weekend, your dental implant will be repaired. I've got a great dentist. He does cosmetic dentistry all the time," Charlotte said.

But Chloe's finger remained wagging. "And I'm sure as far as dentists go he's better than being a toothless hag, but until then, to numb the physical and emotional pain, I may still need another bottle or two." She shook the carafe, which she was putting quite a dent in, and looked in my direction. "I'm sure you won't mind serving as my barkeep, will you?"

I grinned. "Not at all."

"Wonderful. Thank you." When she tilted her head and smiled, her slight imperfection made me like her more. Her improved attitude didn't hurt either.

"Dental implant? What happened to your tooth?" Ty asked, and if he was closer to me, I would have smacked him.

"I killed the tooth on a sledding accident," Chloe said, before taking another chug from the carafe. Despite the sizeable mouth on the jug, she handled it like a pro without spilling a drop.

"In Huntington?" Ty said.

Chloe tilted her head. "Now we both know it doesn't snow in Southern California."

He grinned. "Yeah, so...."

"So, my dad took us to Lake Tahoe after Christmas

one year. The streets were icy and all the kids were taking sleds, running with them, jumping on, and riding them. I overshot the sled and skidded over the ice on my front tooth and ended up with a root canal," she said, so matter-of-fact it was adorable.

Charlotte tentatively smiled at her sister, and reached for the other carafe and filled our glasses.

"Remember when we were at Disney World in Florida and you got a Mickey ears chocolate-covered ice cream and you didn't know it was semifrozen?" Charlotte took a sip, and Chloe took another slug.

"What happened?" Ty asked.

"Like my sister said, I didn't know it was semifrozen, so I took a bite and broke off *this* tooth, which is the one with the root canal," she said. "It was an ordeal I never wanted to repeat. I almost went a year with no front tooth. And I don't care what dad said…" She looked at her sister. "No one looks good with a missing front tooth."

"So, it happened by biting into something?" Ty said.

Chloe nodded into the carafe that she drank from like it held grape juice and not wine.

"Seems like you have a thing for biting?" I raised an eyebrow toward her.

She returned the raised eyebrow and added a sly, closed-lip grin before she handed me the empty carafe. "More please."

I slightly bowed. "My pleasure."

CHAPTER **NINE**

CHLOE

"Napa Valley is one of the most perfect regions to grow cabernet," Martine said.

"Why?" I asked with my carafe tucked against me like a security blanket. I had a warm, fuzzy feeling. I had passed the stage of tipsy and was headed toward toasted.

"Napa has hundred-degree days, fifty-degree nights, and the hillside soil is rich and plentiful, which provides for quick growth. Napa is a warmer region for vine growth. But if the vine feels stressed, then the vine will focus its energy on protecting itself and not producing fruit," he said.

"A vine can feel stressed?" I glanced at the guys at the table and my sister, who didn't seem surprised by this revelation. "Maybe it just needs wine."

My sister shook her head.

"Remember how I mentioned that each winery has a story?"

Everyone at the table nodded, including Tony who stood beside Dan.

"The winery we're going to visit is the Napa Valley Point Resort and Winery, which was started by two people with big dreams and little money," he said.

Big dreams and little money. Ben. His blue eyes surfaced in my mind like icebergs that sank my mood. *Nope, not today.* I took another sip from the carafe. Drinking straight from the jug may be in poor manners, but my hag tooth would only look better with wine goggles.

"However, these two dreamers were smart and realized that to keep their dream alive their best option was to franchise with the Point Resorts, which gave them the necessary capital to expand their operation to include a hotel and wine tours of the cave and vineyards for a glimpse of their coveted Napa cab," Martine said.

"The Point Resort has a cave?" I glanced at my sister. All my interviews had been conducted on the phone; I didn't know anything about this hotel or winery. For all I knew it could be a Zagat-rated wonder or a roadhouse with rotgut. "Did you know we were going to the Point Resort?"

She smiled. "Yes, goober girl."

"Did you know they had a cave?" I asked.

"I did," my sister said.

"Wicked," I said, and shot a look at Tony, who seemed very interested in our conversation. "The Point Resort has a cave."

"Yup, heard that," he said, less than thrilled.

Whatever. Caves are cool.

"The Point Resort's cave is full of cab that's stored in barrels that are chilled to forty-eight degrees," Martine said.

"And we'll see these barrels?" Tony asked.

"In a matter of moments, we'll enter the caves in groups," Martine said. "The Point is our only stop today, but as I mentioned you'll tour both the winery and cave. The Point keeps winning awards for their cab, which has been featured in every wine magazine as the best vintage since Winters Summerset cab in 2012," Martine said.

"What was so special about Winters 2012 cab?" Charlotte asked.

"Perfect conditions," Martine said. "It was a bumper crop year with an overage of grapes—the weather maintained perfect temperatures with an early morning sun that provided a longer growing season."

"But if perfect conditions existed for Winter's vineyard, wouldn't it have applied to all the vineyards in Napa?" Charlotte asked, and I mentally entered the wine cellar in her house. She housed bottles of the wineries she was a member of, but I didn't think she belonged to Winters Winery. Their label was extremely memorable with winter and summer blending—almost looked like something from Game of Thrones. *Oh. That's why she's pissed. She doesn't have a 2012 Summerset cab.*

"Wouldn't every cab produced in 2012 be award-winning?" she pressed.

"It would seem that way, wouldn't it, Ms. Sparks." Martine gently navigated my sister's disgruntlement. "But Winters Winery hit gold with the three wells they dug in

2010. The lake beneath their vineyard was like hitting the sweet spot in Napa. They were able to grow on the slope of the mountain and pull new flavors from the soil," he said. "Winters 2012 Cabernet Sauvignon was award-winning because of the aroma of summer berries with just a hint of cocoa, which lead to a rounded, yet restrained finish. If you haven't had it, it's one to put on your wine bucket list."

"What makes the Point's 2016 cab better or rather more desired than Winters 2012?" Tony asked casually, but it seemed like there was an undertone of contempt. The trained therapist in me never turned off.

He probably doesn't have a 2012 Winters cab either. Sheesh, people were like parents or pet owners about their wine. No one wanted to hear that they had an ugly child any more than they wanted someone to kick their dog. And both my sister and Tony acted like Martine had done both.

"Excellent question," Martine said. "The Point Resort's 2016 Napa Valley Cabernet Sauvignon has concentrated flavors of mocha, cherry, ripe raspberry, and nutmeg that lead to a rounded finish, like Winters Summerset, but unlike Winters's 2012 cab, the Point's cab has rich, silky, velvety tannins that highlight the flavor profile. It's truly an artisan wine," Martine said.

Tony seemed to make mental notes of everything Martine said.

I elbowed my sister. "Where's my notebook?"

She reached between us and handed me the notebook and pen. I released my hold on the carafe and made a quick note. I knew why I was interested in Martine's presentation, but what was Tony's interest?

"When we get into the caves, you'll see the barrels," Martine said. "I'll let your cave guide, Chris, explain the barrel and racking process. However, most wine is placed in barrels for six to eighteen months, depending on the type of wine."

"What kind of barrels are used?" I asked.

Martine spent a few minutes discussing wine barrels and the chemical changes wine underwent. He spoke so fast with so much information, that I reverted to my college days and jotted the key points: Tight barrel = no leaking, Dry & oaky = yummy. I smiled. *I'm gonna be a great wine educator.*

The train braked with the sound of air being released from a steam kettle. I smiled, and for a moment forgot about my front tooth.

"Cave time!" I quickly stood. Wine rushed to my head and the caboose began to spin. I grabbed Charlotte's arm and leaned toward her. "I may need some help on the tour."

She leaned her head against mine. "You think, goof?"

I giggled and thought I was using an inside voice when I said, "I've had *a lot* of wine."

The men in our group laughed.

I glanced up and Tony was looking at me. "If you need a hand, I've got one to offer," he said.

I quickly looked away from his penetrating gaze.

"The caves are dark and some guests find it chilly," Martine said. "The winery has jackets you can borrow, if you don't have one."

I didn't, but the heat from Tony's smile could be all a girl needed to keep warm. And if I was in a different head space, I'd probably cozy up to his surplus of energy, but I wasn't, so I wouldn't. I'd rely on my sister's warmth, who I followed out of the caboose into the blinding sunlight. I raised my hand to shield the glaring sun from my eyes, which suddenly felt very light sensitive.

"Do you want to hold my hand?"

When I didn't answer, my sister looked at me staring at Tony, who walked slightly ahead of us.

"Chlo, you should probably hold *someone's* hand."

Tony turned around. If eyes are the windows to the soul, this guy's light brown eyes were more than mere windows. They were access to a whole new world.

He held out his hand. "I won't bite, that's your thing."

I knew he was a deep well of charm, but I felt like diving in and getting wet. I could blame the wine, but I knew if I slipped my hand in his I was delving into dangerous territory. Despite how much I liked the view and I did, there were some things best left alone. I walked past his outstretched hand and gently smiled.

"Thanks, but I've got it," I said.

My sister caught up to me, wrapped her arm around my shoulder and pulled me into her. Her voice was in my ear. "You know it's okay to move on, right?"

I looked into her crystal blue eyes. "Is it?" I quickly flicked away a tear. "It doesn't feel okay. In fact, it feels *really* not okay."

"Even with all that wine?" Her laughter made the

heartache hurt just a little less.

"That's it." I grinned. "I just need more wine."

Martine walked toward us with a silver tray. "Did someone say they needed wine?"

My sister gently placed her hand on his shoulder. "Martine, where would I be without you?"

"Thirsty," he said. "Very, very thirsty."

CHAPTER **TEN**

TONY

A light rain fell and seemed to awaken faint fumes of asphalt, which from the looks of the winery's smooth, black front drive had recently been resurfaced. In the distance, an older estate, which had to be the hotel, was tucked on a knoll behind the winery.

"Nothing like the smell of asphalt in the morning," Ty said.

I chuckled. "Yeah, I never minded the smell. If anything, it reminds me of summer."

"Shooting hoops down at the beach." Dan shot an imaginary three-pointer. I knew his stance as well as my own.

"You know it." I feigned dribbling behind him and dunked on the trees that lined the walk.

"We'll gather around the entrance to the cave, which is just up the walk." Chris, our wine guide—or educator, as he called himself—wore a red pullover and khakis. He looked like a worker at Target and not someone employed by one of the best wineries in Napa. I quickly took a picture of him walking beside Chloe and Charlotte.

I picked up my pace and followed closely behind the sisters, telling myself it was to hear everything Chris had to offer on the tour, but it was hard to concentrate with Chloe navigating past each puddle like a game of hopscotch. With each jump, she lightly shrieked as if the water would burn her, which made me laugh. I wondered if sober Chloe was as exuberant as drunk Chloe. Based on how she'd been before we all started drinking, probably not. But her sister had said she'd been through a lot—maybe drunk Chloe was the inner Chloe, the real Chloe, and the more serious Chloe was just a result of life dragging her down.

She glanced at me over her shoulder, her dark eyes connecting with mine, and then just as quickly she looked somewhere else. *Come here, go away.* I was all too familiar with that dance and it was one I wouldn't repeat. Not for anyone—not even someone as bubbly, effervescent, and quirky as drunk Chloe. I offered her my help, she'd declined. Logically, I knew the signs of trouble, but physically anytime she even hinted a peek in my direction my body responded. My palms got sweaty. My mouth got dry. And my stomach tightened like I was about to compete in the biggest game of my life, and I was ill-prepared.

I rolled my shoulders and cracked my neck, like I did during a warm-up. *What the fuck?*

Dan gripped my shoulder. "Hey, buddy."

"You enjoying yourself?" I asked.

He took his umpteenth glass of wine off Martine's traveling tray and shrugged. "Who knew wine from a bottle tasted so much better than from the box?"

Ty heartily laughed beside him, and I chuckled.

"Box wine? Seriously?" I said.

Dan brushed his hand across his thinning hair. "Hey man, no judging. Lori likes box wine."

"Lori doesn't know better," I said. "I wasn't kidding about getting you a subscription to the Fabulous Films channel. And while I'm at it, I'll throw in a membership to your favorite winery. So when you find the one you like, let me know."

"You do the same," Dan said with a nod toward Chloe.

I rolled my eyes. "Yeah, she's cute, but she's *not* interested and I'm *not* interested in chasing a dead end. Or being the rebound guy."

Dan slowly nodded. "I get you, brother, but maybe it's not a rebound. Her sister said Napa was a fresh start—that could mean a lot of things."

"And none of them are any good. Lost her job, had a bad breakup, or let's even go the extreme of Witness Protection. 'Fresh start' is just a polite euphemism for 'old baggage,'" I said.

The sun broke through the clouds, the drizzle stopped as quickly as it had started, and my head felt the warmth. I knew technically it was spring, but it felt like summer. The sun shone on the vines that lined the hillside. We walked past the well-kept vineyards where the leaves looked greener, the grapes fuller, and the soil richer. The only disruption to the Point's vineyard system of perfect rows and equally perfect spacing were the tendrils that crept this way and that, reminding me that wine was its own mistress. It took orders from no one—not even old man Winters.

The landscape of the winery was manicured to perfection. Hedges curved around the entrance to the caves, and a row of trees with bright yellow leaves was on either side of the narrow drive leading to the winery.

"What kind of trees are those?" Chloe asked with a pen and paper in her hand.

"Ginkgo trees," Chris said. "In fall, the leaves are even more vibrant, if you can imagine that."

I pulled out my phone and took a picture of the trees that stood like sentinels welcoming guests to the private enclave. I understood why Ty didn't want to live away from the ocean because surfing was his jam after working with criminals all day. But if I had to live anywhere besides Huntington, Napa would be hard to pass up.

"We're passing our cover crop, which is a cocktail of different seeds. And to answer your next question," Chris said, politely cutting Chloe off. "Cover crops or weed farming have everything from wheat to clover and fava beans with the intent of rebuilding the soil each season."

"Wine and weed? The modern version of the land of 'milk and honey?' This must truly be the Promised Land!" Ty said.

I sensed the wine was catching up to my buddy.

"No, you, idiot! 'Weed' as in the unwanted growth that

competes with plants. Don't you know anything about horticulture?" Dan said.

"I know you can lead a whore to culture, but you can't make her think. And you may end up with an unwanted growth on your junk that needs a shot of penicillin," Ty said, and I knew the wine was talking.

Dan, Chris, and I laughed, and so did Chloe. Charlotte didn't look as amused.

"We have a crew of twenty-five, and during the early part of the season the vines grow one foot per week—that's how fast they grow. Our crew does the best they can to keep up with the growth," Chris said.

"Like trimming?" I asked.

"Pruning will increase fruit growth," Chris said without being a dick about correcting me. *Trimming? WTF? Vines are pruned. Trees are trimmed. Dumbass.* The upside was that there was no way he'd ever think I was there to gather info on his vineyard.

"But the most important decision in the winemaking process is the grape picking time. Wineries want to ensure they pick when the sugar and acid are at the right balance," he said.

"So what's the difference between the grapes we get at the grocery store and the grapes used in wine? Or is there any difference?" Chloe asked. It was a legit question. She was either slowly sobering, or the girl could handle her grapes.

"Sugar," Chris said. "A table grape contains 15 percent sugar, a wine grape has 25 percent sugar. In red wine, you use the whole grape, and with white wine you only use the juice."

"I did not know that," Chloe said, and wrote something in her book.

I quickly made a note on my iPhone, when I should be taking pics of her little book.

"In Napa, we're always able to find and build good grapes," he said, and I was literally banking on it. So was Winters, who had made it his mission to beat the Point's cab and reclaim his title.

Chris held the door that led into the caves, but prevented our party of five from entering. "Some of the first wineries didn't have caves so they had to store all their wine in air-conditioned warehouses," he said. "It took one winery to begin slowly digging underground to change the way wine was stored."

"But caves?" Chloe said.

"Caves pay for themselves because there is no property tax underground," Chris said, and there wasn't one of us that didn't have a reaction.

"For real?" Ty said.

"Yes. Wineries are taxed on everything else, but there is no property tax on caves," he said.

"Wow," Chloe said, and then turned to her sister. "I need to look for a cave to buy."

We all laughed, but it was Chris who approached her. "At first caves were built for utility, and when they dug as far as they could, they used dynamite to excavate through rock. But over time, decorative rock walls were added to bring a design element to caves."

"So our early ancestors chose their living spaces to avoid the *most deadly predator* of all"—I glanced at Chloe, who turned from Chis and looked at me with captivating eyes—"the IRS."

She threw her head back and laughed, which caused me to stand tall.

Dan walked beside me as we entered the cave. "See, maybe her fresh start has nothing to do with her having old baggage."

CHAPTER ELEVEN

CHLOE

As soon as I walked into the entrance that led to the cave, the temperature dropped, and I wished I had taken Chris up on his offer of a jacket.

"How far down are the caves?" my sister asked.

"The cave is 130 feet underground and a mile and a half long," Chris said.

"And me without my breadcrumbs," I said.

Chris, who was probably my age, smiled in my direction. "I'll make sure you stay with the group."

I gave him a quick once-over. Short blond hair, hazel eyes, and lanky build. Nothing muscular like Tony, but he also didn't seem as intense about wine. And his name tag didn't rhyme. Chris Staple was a pretty generic name, but his looks weren't. Nothing that immediately turned my head, but, eh, I'd seen worse.

"Don't shit where you eat," my sister said in my ear.

"What?" Now my tone was defensive.

She chuckled. "Uh-huh."

"Where's the hotel?" I asked as my eyes adjusted to the dim lights.

"This is the winery, and the Napa Valley Point Resort is up on the hill," Chris said.

"Swanky," I said to my sister. "A hotel on the hill. Like Nob Hill in San Fran."

"You goof, Napa is surrounded by hills," Charlotte said.

"It can still be swanky."

She tried not to smile, I know she did, but nevertheless grinned at my merriment. Who wouldn't? Wine was the great equalizer. It allowed my straitlaced sister to relax and see the humor in life. Wine was magical. And I was drunk on its magic.

"More please." I looked for Martine, and instead was greeted by a twentysomething holding a tray of glasses. I stuck with the red.

"Before we descend into the caves, we'll take a look at the fermentation room." Chris extended his arm toward silver vats that rose to the vaulted ceiling. "This is where our winemakers work to blend new grape varieties, so it's part laboratory and part cellar."

The air in the fermentation room felt thick like I was walking through humidity, but instead of a suffocating heat, the rich smell of grape juice spiked with vanilla and nutmeg infused my senses and made my mouth water.

"It takes a lot of good beer to make wine," Chris said, and I shook my head.

"Did I hear that correctly?" I asked, almost choking on my merlot.

His face was easy to look at. "When the wine is being made the whole valley smells of grape, like what you're smelling in here. During harvest, you're working twelve- to fifteen-hour days, and you don't want wine. So, you go home and have a beer."

I must have still look confused.

"Imagine if you worked at a Twinkie factory. Would you go home and eat a Twinkie?" Chris's lips flattened across his face. "No. I'd have a HoHo."

"I'd have a HoHo *and* a Twinkie," I said, laughing, and Chris smiled.

"The Point's 2016 Napa Valley Cabernet Sauvignon swept the wine awards," Tony said with his arms crossed over his chest. His forearms rippled with definition. "So, what's the secret?" Tony raised a single eyebrow the way my sister did, only when Tony did it, my stomach fluttered.

"When you're spending up to fifteen hours a day working a harvest and repeat that for three back-to-back harvests, you're going to have success," Chris said.

A grim look crossed Tony's face. "Yeah, but that could be said of every vineyard in Napa."

Chris shrugged. "Mother Nature's in charge of most of it."

Tony slowly nodded.

"And UC Davis. Every vine goes through UC Davis for analysis," he said, laughing.

"Why would a vine be analyzed?" I asked.

"Wine is a sixty-billion-dollar industry," Chris said without blinking an eye. "The Foundation Plant Services at UC Davis keeps a database of all plant material it analyzes. They perform a DNA analysis on all our vines."

"DNA analysis? Like fingerprinting vines?" I asked.

"Exactly," Chris said, grinning. "That's actually a great way of explaining it."

I felt so good, I wanted to bow, but opted not to.

"And just like fingerprints, a DNA-based grape analysis identifies the grape variety by comparing the DNA profile to the ones in the UC Davis database. The profiles range from raisins to rare varietals," said Chris.

"What would be an example of a rare variety?" Tony asked.

"Just a few years ago UC Davis did a DNA analysis on vines at Olvera Street in downtown Los Angeles, and the results were mind-blowing. The vines they analyzed matched what has become known as Viña Madre, which is from the San Gabriel Mission."

"Oh-kay?" I said. "I don't get the importance."

"Think about it. The Olvera Street plant was probably a clipping from the Viña Madre vine at the mission, and the mission dates back to the Spanish missionaries in 1769. The vine at Olvera Street, in the heart of LA, was probably planted in 1818. We wouldn't know this without DNA analysis of the vines," Chris said.

His enthusiasm was almost overwhelming. *How in the hell will I ever learn all this, let alone remember it?* I took another sip of wine to release the vise on my head. *What was*

I thinking? I can't be a wine educator. But a wine drinker, yes, yes I could do that.

"That vine at Olvera Street is older than the state of California," Ty said.

"Exactly!" Chris said. "DNA analysis is everything. It allows us to identify the grape variety, profile, and the mother vine."

"The mother vine?" Ty said.

"It's the heart of the vine, and for a winemaker, the best way to preserve the characteristics of a grape variety is through cloning a piece of the mother vine, either by cutting off a piece of the plant directly from the soil, or grafting it onto another vine," Chris said.

"So, if someone wanted to replicate the Point's award-winning Cabernet Sauvignon, all they'd have to do is cut off a piece of the mother vine and they could claim it as their own?" Ty's question seemed odd to me, or maybe it was my wine buzz.

When Chris didn't immediately respond, Ty spoke again. "I'm a parole officer. After years on the job, I guess my thinking has turned criminal. My apologies."

"No need to apologize," Chris said. "I was just trying to figure out the best way to answer. And basically, any offspring from the mother vine will produce the same grapes, so a piece from any vine in the vineyard will work."

"For real?" Ty said. "I could just cut a piece of the vines out there and go to my garage and start fermenting award-winning wine?"

Chris volleyed his head back and forth. "If a person

could get past our cameras and security, they'd still have to find where we keep the mother vine and its offspring. Only our wine educators and winemakers know where it's located." Chris paused. "Folks, wineries guard their vines like Fort Knox protects gold. If you're caught wandering a private vineyard with a pair of pruners, you'll probably end up fertilizing next year's crop."

We all laughed.

"Okay, now that we've soaked in the fragrance of the fermentation room, let's go tour some caves," Chris said.

"Wow. The mother vine sounds like the secret formula for Coke," Charlotte said. "I knew about the mother vine, but I guess I never put much stock into how hard it would be to access."

"Or someone could just get friendly with a wine educator," Dan said under his breath to Tony, which I heard but I'm not sure Charlotte did.

Didn't matter. Besides, why would three guys from HB be interested in the mother vine? They were here for a bachelor party. *The only thing they want to cut loose are the binds of convention and common sense.*

CHAPTER **TWELVE**

TONY

Could it really be that easy? All I needed was a clipping of the Point's mother vine, and old man Winters's wine crew could clone or graft it onto another vine. *Winters is a winemaker—he would have known about the mother vine, so what's he really after?* We entered the caves, where a curved ceiling and arched walls reminded me that we had descended 130 feet underground. A row of lights on the curve of the ceiling and along the walls kept it well-lit, even cheerful.

Old man Winters didn't have a cave. His winery was a small parcel in Oakville, but as Martine had pointed out, the wells allowed him to tap into a rich source for his slope-sided vineyard. Winemaking was supposed to be his hobby—a break from his corporation. But when he won big with his sophomore year Cab, the bug for more victories bit him hard. It was one thing to investigate competing products he produced like toothpaste, dog food, and detergent, but wine, as I was discovering, wasn't solely produced by corporations, but by individuals. I knew from my research that the Point was started by two regular guys who had a passion for wine and the sense to buy land when it was presented to them. I didn't know all the details, only that Rob Chambers and Rich Erickson were co-owners in the Napa Valley Point Resort and Winery.

Barrels stacked on top of other barrels lined the long-tunneled entry into the cave. The cards that Martine had mentioned that identified the wine and aging process were stuck to the center of them.

Chloe suddenly stopped, turned her sister around, held her phone high and snapped a selfie. The light from the flash illuminated her face that looked carefree and fun. Whatever her fresh start was about, it was hard to imagine anything or anyone that could cast a shadow on her. She radiated light.

At the end of the tunnel, two candelabras were positioned beside the entrance of a banquet-style room. A massive circular wooden table consumed the majority of the room.

"Damn, it's like King Arthur's round table," Ty said.

"Right," I said, and suddenly felt rather knightly. We waited until Chloe and Charlotte sat before we took our seats across from them. Four wineglasses and a serving plate with cheese, nuts, and crackers were placed in front of each chair.

"Lunch," Dan said.

"Actually, it's the appetizer before lunch," Chris said.

"Nice," Ty said.

"I'm told these aren't the most comfortable chairs, so if you need a pillow for your back"—Chris pointed his thumb toward the corner—"there's a decent stack over there."

Chloe leaned her head on her sister's shoulder. She whispered something in Charlotte's ear, and then quietly excused herself from the table.

"You'll see dried fruit, cheese, and nuts," Chris said. "The chemical composition of wine is complemented by certain foods that are sweet, tart, or salty."

"Are you a sommelier?" Charlotte asked, sitting across from us alone.

"No," Chris said. "But I am trained to *educate* you about wine. *And* since we discussed security earlier, I wanted to mention that this wine cellar room is the only area in the wine cave that is *not* monitored by security cameras." He pushed his hands down in the air to suppress the questions I was sure he knew were pending. "Since the Point rents this space for private functions, it adheres to our privacy policy for our guests. So eat, drink, and act like we're in Vegas because no one will ever see what's happening in this part of the cave. And," he dropped his hands and a smile broadened across his face, "be free from worry because no one, not even Santa, can see you in this area of the cave, so no matter what happens, you still won't land on the Naughty list."

Naughty list? Vegas? Hell, yes. I glanced in the direction Chloe went, but that didn't make her materialize. She hadn't returned.

Chris walked us through tasting the wine, and I could tell

my buddies were as surprised as I was by how the different foods brought out different flavors. All these years, I'd been enjoying the alcoholic content of a wine bottle more than the taste, but now I could pick out flavors of cherry and chocolate.

The only damper on my enjoyment was that every time I looked across the table, I saw Chloe's empty chair. *Where is she?* And what was she doing?

CHAPTER **THIRTEEN**

CHLOE

A chair? I told Charlotte I needed a bathroom break when really, I just needed a break. That's the thing with wine, or really any alcohol. The initial peak was amazing, but the drop—not so much. I knew alcohol was a depressant, which was what I often reminded my clients. And I also knew my mood swings ran the whole gamut of emotions when I was drunk. *Still, a chair?*

When Chris mentioned the uncomfortable chairs and the need for a pillow, I was instantly reminded of my first apartment with Ben. That's all it took.

"Those stupid, annoyingly stiff dining room chairs." I walked beneath the arched walls in the cave. "God, they were awful." I spoke to the barrels beside me with my back to the cameras positioned in the far end of the cave. I didn't need my future employer to see or hear my temporary break from reality. *When furniture can tank my mood, it's time to disappear and regroup.*

I was halfway between the room where Charlotte and everyone were eating and I think the entrance to the fermentation room when a wine educator found me.

"Lost?" he said.

I shrugged. "No, just kind of finding my way."

"Maybe this will help."

I accepted the plaid wool blanket he offered. He was leading the next group from our train to the fermentation room. The group had already had their wine tasting and lunch. Apparently, we did get the same tour, just in a different order.

"If you want to park yourself beside the barrels, Chris will get you on the way out," he said. The guy didn't seem at all surprised to find a drunken woman wandering around looking for a place to sober up.

When his group left, I leaned against the side of the oak barrel and pulled the gray-and-blue plaid around me. Drinking wine on an empty stomach had finally caught up to me. If I could just calm my stomach, I wouldn't risk embarrassing myself by getting sick.

As if I hadn't already embarrassed myself enough. I finally decided to get back in the game, took a chance, and flirted with a man… and fate punished me with a broken tooth.

My tongue rolled across the jagged edge.

"Brilliant job, Dorsey."

I knew the wine was blowing my reaction all out of proportion.

"Okay, what would you say to a client?" My rational self struggled to break free.

As my tongue continued to play with the gap in my mouth, I thought about the clients I'd help rationalize their dramas. When I sobered up this would probably just be a funny story. But right now with the wine clouding my brain and the memories of Ben swamping me, I felt like nothing in the world could ever get better. I wanted to cry, but instead I closed my eyes, and as I drifted away I looked for Ben, who stood before me.

"Hey," I said.

His blue eyes were bright and full of life. Wisps of blond hair looked like a halo on his head. I fell asleep with the thought of him.

I was in a strange hotel with a maze of staircases that led nowhere. I climbed to the top only to find a door that led to more stairs.

"Where's the exit?"

I followed the slices of light on the stairs, hoping they'd take me outside. When the last door opened to the street, I searched for my car. The blue Mercedes shone. I hopped in, and drove away from the hotel and toward the freeway.

The freeway entrance was a ramp that rose high above Orange County and gave me a bird's-eye view of the freeways below. There was a hodgepodge of intersecting on-ramps. It was like a heap of spaghetti, only it was multiple freeways converging, with cars going left and right trying to jockey their way onto the interstate. With so many cars constantly lane switching, combined with the curves as the highway broke away and rose even higher above the city, I felt stuck in this nightmarish maze.

My palms gripped the steering wheel, but no matter how slow or careful I drove, I couldn't find my way home. I knew Huntington was somewhere up ahead, but where? Cars came to a screeching halt and in the next instant, the freeway was at a near standstill as cars crawled for miles. I was in the midst of the chaos, searching for a way out of the labyrinth of interchanges. Panic seized my chest, and a sense of dread overwhelmed me. Why can't I get home?

The freeway had three lanes on either side and still there was no room to breathe. Carpoolers suddenly merged from their lane and wove across the freeway to exit. I looked for my exit, or a straight road that would lead me home, but all I found were more curves, more detours, and more confusion.

My body jerked awake like someone had shaken me from the nightmare, but I was alone in the tunnel. *It's always the same dream—I'm lost and I can't find my way home.* Feeling lost now seemed like a permanent ache that resided deep inside of me, yet lived so close to the surface. And like the familiarity of the dream, so was the bleak emptiness that followed. It wouldn't matter if my stomach was full of food, I'd still feel hollow. Intellectually I could rationalize my reactions, but emotionally I couldn't. When it came to body, mind, and spirit, my intellect was the only nonfractured component.

"What am I doing? I don't belong in Napa." I glanced at the twinkling lights that lined the ceiling of the curved tunnel. It was beautiful, even romantic, but there was no one to share this romance. I felt lost, alone, and terrified that this was how it'd always be.

CHAPTER **FOURTEEN**

I pushed away my plate. There wasn't anything left of the grilled steak and salsa verde, which left a gamey taste in my mouth. I probably needed gum, but I didn't want to lose the flavor of beef.

"I could never be a vegetarian," I said.

Ty raised his glass. "Amen, brother."

"Were there any new flavors you discovered with the cabernet sauvignon and the seasoned steak?" Chris asked.

"The red fruits brightened up an already hearty and rich dish," Charlotte said.

"Wonderful." Chris smiled at Charlotte. "Before you leave, you'll get a few recipes from the Point's Bar & Grill that are tasty, easy to prepare, and they're paired with the Point's award-winning cab," Chris said.

"Nice," Dan said.

"Will today's salsa verde be in the recipes?" I asked.

Chris smiled. "Absolutely. The grilled steak and salsa verde drizzle is one of our signature dishes here at the Point."

"And to think I missed it."

I turned to find Chloe standing beneath the archway with eyes that had a sleepy glaze to them. Her raven hair looked messy and tousled. She had a just-been-fucked look, and I glanced behind her to see if anyone was with her.

She tucked her hair behind her ear, something her sister also did, and softly smiled in my direction.

"Where'd you go?" Ty asked.

She shrugged. "Nowhere in particular." She walked past us and sat beside her sister, who had eaten a quarter of her steak. Chloe reached for her sister's fork and pierced a piece of the meat.

I was sure it was the massive amount of wine influencing me, but there was something sexual and primal about how Chloe didn't hesitate to polish off the rest of the steak. She was carnivorous, and I liked it.

When she emptied her wine glass and reached for the carafe in the center of the table, I grinned.

"What?" She caught me staring at her. "Food absorbs alcohol, right?"

We all laughed.

I'd noticed that whenever something clicked with Chloe her face brightened.

However, being surrounded by all these bottles of wine was making me all too aware of my need to find a men's room to make my bladder gladder. I tapped my foot, hoping we'd exit soon.

Chris made eye contact with each of us. "I hope you've enjoyed your lunch at the Napa Valley Point Resort. It was a pleasure serving as your wine educator today. Also, the restroom facilities are just outside the caves we'll hit on our way out. It seems to be a regular stop for most guests." He chuckled.

Charlotte reached into her purse, and when she stood, she placed a fifty in his hand. Chloe simply shook his hand, which made me grin. She was just who she was. No pretense.

Ty glanced at me, and I withdrew the two fifties I'd won betting on Chloe, which I gave to Chris. I wasn't about to be out-tipped by Charlotte.

As we left the cave, I turned and asked Chris one last question. "How many cases of the cab does the Point Resort produce each year?"

"Before it won big, we were producing two thousand cases a year. But after our 2016 cab hit gold, the demand became so great, we produce thirty thousand cases a year," he said.

"Thirty thousand cases?" I had to ensure I'd heard him correctly. Winters Summerset produced double that amount.

"It's still a low number compared to other wineries, but Rob and Rich don't want to grow too fast, too soon, and lose the quality that made them award winners," Chris said.

"Rob and Rich?" Chloe said.

"Rob Chambers and Rich Erickson are the owners and founders of the winery," Chris said.

"And they joined with the Point Resorts?" she asked.

"It was a merger of resorts and reserves for the best of both," Chris said.

The guy was good. He didn't miss the opportunity to upsell the wine or the resort. But I wasn't quite buying the quality over quantity spin.

"I'd think with the merger, they'd be able to produce more wine," I said.

"We could, but then we may lose quality. A lot of wineries use their wine clubs to move wine they're not selling. We don't do that. We also don't ship in the summer, because it's too hot. Anyone who becomes a Napa Valley Point Resort wine club member will receive shipments directly from our cave collection. We also waive tasting fees. The benefits of our winery far exceed the cost of membership," Chris said, making a valid argument for quality and one of hell of a pitch for the wine club.

"How much is a wine membership?" Ty asked.

"Our wine memberships began at four hundred dollars per shipment for our exclusive wines from our vineyard. Our signature membership starts at $1,400 per shipment for our limited-production Napa Valley wines," he said.

"Signature wines like the Point's 2016 Napa Valley Cabernet Sauvignon?" Charlotte asked.

"Absolutely. Our signature membership is geared toward the wine collector and connoisseur of fine wines," Chris said.

"How many shipments are there in a year?" Ty said.

"Four automatic shipments—in March, May, October,

and December," Chris said.

"And each shipment costs four hundred dollars?" Ty worked for the state, which didn't pay well for the thankless job of working with criminals all day.

Chris chuckled. "Yeah, it's a bit rich for my budget, which is why I work here," he said.

"Do they have any openings?" Ty said, and he sounded serious.

Chris smiled. "The Point just hired some new wine educators." He glanced at Chloe, whose cheeks reddened. "For any other job openings, you'd have to check with human resources."

As we left the winery, he handed each of us a glossy pamphlet. It contained the recipes he'd promised, and the back page was a tear-off enrollment card for their wine club. Charlotte sat outside the winery and filled out the request card, which she handed to Chris.

Chloe elbowed her sister. "Why are you joining the Point's wine club? You know I'll be able to get—"

"No." Charlotte held her hand up and shut down the conversation. "You didn't uproot your life to get fired from the Point before you've even begun."

Hired? At the Point? For what?

Dan grabbed my elbow and held me back from following too closely behind them. When we were out of earshot, he spoke. "Chloe may just be the weak spot in the vineyard's defense. If you're going to make a play on the mother vine, you may need to make a pass at her."

"Uh, I don't know about that," I said, heading toward

the restroom.

Dan's glassy eyes were all I needed to see to know he'd drunk his fill, and that the wine was probably talking. "Buddy, when have you ever let someone or something come before your career? Fuck, we're in Napa and not Vegas because of your job. Besides, all's fair in love and corporate war."

I didn't reply because it would only egg on a conversation I didn't want to have. The only way I lived with myself in my career was that I didn't take advantage of people. What was the expression? You get more flies with honey. Well, honey worked. Ask the right person the right question in the right way, and the answers materialized. And it allowed me to sleep at night.

"Did you know hugging releases endorphins?"

Chloe no longer smelled like a fresh peppermint breeze wafting through the wine train, but now strongly emitted the scent of a boozing hobo hitching a ride on a freight car. When she returned from wherever she'd ventured in the caves, she began drinking again, and heavily. I sat beside her and almost wished I hadn't.

"Did you know that, Tony?" When she smiled, her partial tooth looked like the before picture in either an advertisement for capped teeth or a campaign for fluoridated water.

"I did not," I said.

"Yup, a good hug is the fastest way to get oxytocin

moving in your body."

"Oxytocin?" Ty said.

"It's the love drug," Chloe said. "But actually, it's a hormone."

"Oh, right. I'm thinking of oxycodone, which isn't."

"No, one is a natural hormone and the other is an overprescribed opioid," she said.

"Sounds like you know your stuff," Dan said, and I knew he was on a fishing expedition. The bottomless glass of wine in front of him wasn't helping either.

Chloe's reply consisted of a shrug. Her silky tank top rose up and down against her cleavage. *The things you discover on a wine train. Dan drinks wine and gets combative, I get horny.*

"So, what industry are you in?" Dan pressed Chloe like he did an opponent on the court.

But it was Charlotte who spoke. "Education."

"Cool." Dan slowly nodded, and tossed the conversation back to Chloe. "Do you teach?"

"I did at one time," Chloe said.

"So, from the interaction between you and Chris and all your questions, I'm guessing you must be one of the new wine educators at the Point."

When Chloe didn't correct Dan, he continued. "Before Napa. What'd you teach?"

"Psychology." Chloe's energy shifted beside me. She seemed to perk up at the mention of her career.

"Chloe earned her doctorate in psychology," Charlotte said. "She was a counselor, and taught at the collegiate level."

"So, what, you stopped teaching psychobabble because you made everyone suddenly alive and well?" Dan wore a smile even though his tone was sharp.

Her energy shifted. When I turned toward Chloe, she seemed to be contemplating her next move. She glanced at Dan from beneath her eyelashes, and her stare was enough to make Dan shift in his seat.

"I stopped teaching when my husband suddenly died and I went numb."

Fuck. The woman may not be able to handle her wine, but for sure she had already handled a lifetime of grief. And what I planned on doing at the Point, regardless of how much honey I served up, would probably just add more grief in her life. There had to be a way I could get what Winters wanted without involving Chloe. But how?

"They say there's truth in wine," Ty said. "But I sure as shit wasn't expecting that."

Chloe and Charlotte had excused themselves and moved to another car. I couldn't blame them. Dan had pushed too far.

"Yeah, me either." Dan brushed his thinning hair with his hand. "I feel like a major dick."

"You should," I said. "What happened to keeping it light?"

Dan shrugged. "Buddy, I don't know." He swirled the rest of the wine in his glass. "Well, one thing's for sure.

Chloe can't be your 'in' at the winery."

"You think?" I shook my head. "You guys are only staying the weekend. I'm booked at the Point for a month. If she doesn't call security on me, I may have a fighting chance to get what I need for Winters."

"Why would she call security?" Ty said.

"I don't know, because my friend was a prick?" I said. "It doesn't have to make sense. The only memory she'll have of me is telling us that her husband died. I can't even imagine."

"Me either," Dan said. "Lori means everything to me. If she died…."

"She's got to be our age," Ty said. "What could cause a guy our age to suddenly die?"

I blew out a mouthful of air. "Fuck. Where do you begin? He could have had a heart attack or been hit by a car. Shit, do you think he killed himself?"

Dan shook his head. "No, I didn't get that impression. Someone who loses someone by suicide quickly learns the language, which is usually 'died of suicide.'"

"Fuck. Buddy, I wasn't even thinking," I said. Dan's brother died of suicide when we were in college.

"I blame the vino," he said with a weak attempt to laugh.

"Yeah, and suddenly all I want to do *is* drink," I said.

Dan nodded.

"We have one more hour on the train. Let's make it count." Ty pushed the carafe toward me.

I filled our glasses, leaned back, and watched vineyards stream past our window.

CHAPTER FIFTEEN

CHLOE

"So, if this was supposed to be my fresh start, I don't think I'm starting off too well." The merlot slid down my throat, coating raw emotions.

"I don't know about that, Chlo. You just told three complete strangers that Ben died. I chalk that up to progress."

When my sister wasn't acting like a swan—someone smooth and serene on the surface who refused to show any cracks in her appearance—I saw the girl I'd shared a bedroom with. The girl who'd tell me stories about our beds floating above the city to help me fall asleep and keep the bogeymen at bay. The girl who explained genetics so I understood why I had boring brown eyes while she had magnificent jewel-like blue eyes. I wasn't impressed by her oversized house, showy cars, or wine memberships. I had a new flashy car that I liked, but it didn't make life better, just faster. What drew me to my sister was her heart that she guarded so well. God forbid anyone ever see who she really was. Coach was probably the only man, besides our father, who knew that Charlotte might look like a swan, but she paddled like hell to stay afloat—just like the rest of us.

"I don't know what happened, but that guy pissed me off. As if I don't realize the only reason the hotel hired me, despite my *total* ignorance of wines, was because of my educational background?" I said.

"That's not true. You've also got a great bod and a decent memory. No, wait, that's me. For you it's the other way around."

A good hug may get oxytocin flowing in a body, but laughter was never awkward or clingy. And no one made me laugh like my sister.

"Look, being a wine educator may not have been the job you ever imagined. But sometimes a shift, albeit new and scary, brings renewed purpose. And it wasn't too long ago, Chlo, that you spoke about that Greek and his link between purpose and happiness."

I rolled my eyes, but my sister was spot-on. "It was Aristotle and his study of ethics. His writings recognized the connection between Eudaimonia or happiness and a sense of purpose."

"That's it." My sister slapped her thigh. "A sense of purpose leads to happiness."

I shook my head. "It's not quite that simple. In fact, Aristotle's work focused on answering *one* simple question— what is the ultimate purpose of human existence?"

"To drink wine?" Charlotte said.

"Well, that's a good start." My brain wasn't as fuzzy, which I attributed to the steak. "But Aristotle's writings focused on identifying what the end goal was that we should work toward. Most people believe money and success will make us happy." I overtly waggled my bushy eyebrows at my sister, who ignored my less-than-subtle cue.

"But Aristotle believed happiness was not something that could be gained or lost. Happiness was the final end or totality of one's life." I paused and slowly took a sip of wine. *Maybe I should have drunk wine when I presented my dissertation.* The shit I'd learned in my doctoral program just flowed out of me.

"Anyway, if what Aristotle believed is true, then a genuinely happy life is how well someone lived up to their full potential. When Ben died, saying he lived a happy life would align with Aristotle's beliefs. Happiness is an activity of the soul that gives us purpose, it's not a fleeting moment in time. Although I wish it was, because for a moment in time I was really happy."

"And you will be again." Charlotte softly smiled. "But having a sense of purpose won't hurt, and the Point will give you that."

"You didn't hear anything I said, did you?"

My sister's white-blonde hair swayed. "Not all of it, but I was impressed with how well you explained it."

"Great. So my teaching skills aren't as rusty as I thought."

"Nope, Professor, you did a fantastic job boring me."

"Har har."

Martine approached our table. "Ladies, if I could get you to return to the caboose, I have one last presentation for our group."

Charlotte's arm draped protectively across my shoulders when we approached the guys, who stood and offered us their seats. We declined, which was when Dan remained standing.

"Listen, I opened my mouth and prodded into your personal life when I had no business there. Chloe, I'm really sorry." Dan looked at me, waiting for forgiveness.

If I believed Aristotle's definition of happiness, whose basic tenet was to do the right thing, even in difficult situations, then the right thing to do was to accept his apology.

Despite my hag's tooth, I broadly smiled in his direction. "Dan, it's forgotten."

While it was Dan to whom I extended compassion, it was Tony who looked astonished.

"What?" I stared at him. "I hold grudges about as well as I do alcohol."

This made him laugh, which thankfully softened his piercing gaze. I turned my attention to Martine.

"This morning at the station, you may have noticed a small footbridge that connected the train station to the boarding platform," Martine said.

My sister was the only one in our group to nod.

"The footbridge is dedicated to lovers all over the world. In fact, it's called Love Lock Bridge," he said.

"Love Lock Bridge?" Ty said.

"The idea is that lovers can take a lock decorated with their names, initials, or perhaps a date, and hook it to the bridge fence. Once the lock is locked, the key can either be tossed below the bridge or saved as a keepsake." Martine reached into his pocket and presented each of us with a heart-shaped lock and key.

"What if you don't have a lover?" Ty asked, causing everyone to laugh, which returned the caboose to the carefree place we'd boarded nearly four hours ago.

"You can still leave a token of your love for Napa on the bridge," Martine said, clearly prepared for this question. "But I have heard many stories where someone has left their lock and a message for their future love, and within the year their lock was linked with the love of their life."

"Well, I've chipped and probably swallowed my tooth, I told three strangers about my dead husband, who I never speak of, so really there are worse things than placing a heart-shaped lock on a bridge," I said with a toothless grin.

"Yeah, why not," Ty said.

"Nothing says love quite like vandalism and lack of originality," Tony added, and we all booed him.

"Nuh-uh. No negativity," I said. "We're leaving this caboose the way we came on it—"

"Drunk?" Dan said.

"No." I giggled. "With the spirit of adventure. And if I can get on, or rather off board with that, then you can too."

Tony waved his heart-shaped lock. "Fair enough. You have been a great sport."

I tipped my head. "Thank you, Tony Mahoney."

Laughter erupted again, and it was a wonderful sound.

Martine placed an assortment of permanent markers on the table. "Now remember," he said, "this is Love Lock Bridge, and more importantly Napa—the land of dreamers and believers."

Which was exactly what I wrote on my heart. *To Napa, the land of dreamers, believers, and second chances.*

CHAPTER **SIXTEEN**

TONY

Chloe departed the train station less dramatically than she arrived. The older guy who had been the passenger in her convertible greeted her and Charlotte at the platform, but he only kissed Charlotte. *Must be her husband.* I grinned.

The convertible wasn't in the lot. Instead, I watched Chloe hop into the back seat of a dusty, older black Toyota 4Runner. The tip of her red-bottomed heels rested on the silver running board while she waited for her sister to get into the truck.

"Listen, just because I was an asshole doesn't mean you shouldn't get her number." Dan's voice was in my ear.

I shook my head. "Nope. I'm here on business, and she's been through enough. Now that I know what her fresh start is about, she doesn't need a one-month fling, which is as long as I'm in Napa."

"That's probably exactly what she needs," Ty said with

a hearty pat on my back. "There's nothing wrong with a good old-fashioned short-term hookup. It's longer than a one-night stand and not as serious as a commitment."

"Nope. Dan had it right when he said Chloe wasn't my 'in' at the winery," I said.

"Which is even better. Then there won't be any hang-up or bad feelings when you leave," Ty said.

"Or you could just be her friend," Dan said. "I mean what's the harm in that? Like you said, you'll be in Napa for a month anyway. Might as well have someone fun to hang out with. And Chloe was fun."

"Yeah, no. I hate to quote another movie, but Harry had it right in 'When Harry Met Sally' men and women can't be friends because the sex part always gets in the way. And if we just have sex, then feelings come into play. It's a lose-lose proposition. I'm here for a job – plain and simple. There's plenty of women in So Cal that I have as friends."

"Granted, I don't know all your other female friends, but from what I've seen today your interest in Chloe seems to extend past friendship," Dan said.

There wasn't anything I could say to block him. I had watched Chloe. *Who wouldn't?* She was a magnet who drew people toward her. Even with a chipped tooth and smelling like the fermentation room, Dan was right, she was fun. And flirty. But the timing just wasn't right.

We walked toward the Napa Valley Point Resort and Winery, which looked exactly like the label on its wine bottle. The two-story stone estate reminded me of one of the fairy tales my niece demanded I read to her every time I visited my brother. Nestled on a little bluff in Napa, the gingerbread-colored stone cottage had frosted windowpanes and a chimney that I was sure piped smoke in the winter. It was a tucked-away haven. Rob Chambers and Rich Erickson weren't just selling wine, they were selling an experience. I didn't even have to set foot into the resort to know it was the perfect pairing to their award-winning wine.

CHAPTER SEVENTEEN

CHLOE

The dentistry was called Napa Valley Dental Aesthetic & Orthodontics, and run by the poorly named Dr. Randall Payne. Dr. Payne was probably Coach's age, but with more hair. And it looked perfectly kissed by the sun. Blond highlights popped in his shaggy brown locks. He reminded me of a surfer, and anytime he moved his head, his hair swept across his forehead like an incoming wave. His forearms were tanned, his eyes were an interesting shade of hazel, and his smile revealed perfectly straight teeth. It was hard to remember what I was doing there. And the heated dentist chair relaxed my mood.

"So, what does the other guy look like?" he said.

With my mouth open, I muttered, "Ha."

"Let me guess, you were crunching on ice?"

I shook my head.

"Piece of hard candy?"

I nodded, and when he removed his hand from my mouth, I asked, "How'd you know?"

"Occupational hazard. I've seen the results of too many butterscotches," he said with a smile.

"Peppermint," I said.

"Restaurant?" he asked.

"Wine Train."

"Of course. I put myself through medical school working at a winery. In fact, didn't your information sheet say you work at the Point?"

"Start tomorrow," I said.

"Good for you. My first introduction to wine was with one of the owners, Rob Chambers. We worked at a winery together. Not the Point, that came later for Rob." Dr. Payne reached for an intimidating pointed tool from the paper-lined tray beside me. He began to gently scrape what was left of my tooth. "Even though enamel is the hardest tissue in the body, it has its limits." He glanced down at me. "And peppermint seemed to be the limit."

I grinned as best as I could.

"I'm glad you came to see me," he said. My furrowed eyebrows must have conveyed my confusion. "Your tooth could have been damaged further or become infected," he said, wiping what I can only imagine was plaque on a gauze.

"Not sure how I could have made this any worse," I said.

He chuckled and stared at my tooth. "If this ever happens again and you end up with a jagged edge, until you can get in to see me, you can cover the sharp edge with a piece of paraffin wax or sugarless gum."

I burst out laughing. "You're kidding, right? Sure, next time I lose my tooth over a long holiday weekend, I'll stick a Chicklet on it and call it good?"

"Not a Chicklet." He chuckled. "But a soft piece of sugarless gum will protect your gums." He gently pulled my lower lip out. "Ouch, that looks like it hurts."

I shrugged. "It was more painful looking like a toothless rube, or inbred."

He laughed.

"Nope, the sooner I'm rid of this ugly eyesore the better. Hopefully, Doc, you'll never have to see me again."

He paused, like he'd been going to say something and opted not to. Instead he picked up an instrument with a circular mirror on the end and dipped it in my mouth.

"Since such a large piece of tooth broke off, I won't be able to fill or bond the damage. What I suggest is that I file away the remaining tooth and cover it with a porcelain crown." He stood back and waited for me to answer.

"How 'bout just the latter part, and we forego the filing part?"

His hair swept across his eyes. With a quick shake of his head, his hair realigned. "The tooth's already dead, you won't feel anything."

"Yes, but I'll hear it."

His face lit up and he raised a finger. "Not if you have earphones on while I work."

"Doc, you've got a deal."

A dental assistant placed a pair of plastic-covered cushioned earphones over my head. Tracy Chapman piped in my ears. Not what I would have chosen, but only because her songs were usually too sad for me. Still, as her smoky voice sang in my ears, I closed my eyes and imagined my next stop: uniform shopping.

The Point didn't care what I wore when I clocked in tomorrow for my first day of work as long it was khaki and red, which pretty much limited my choices unless I wanted to go on the hunt for red jeans. I visualized myself in khaki pants and a red top, and no matter how many scenarios I conjured, none of them looked good. Even though I'd lost weight when Ben died, which the grief counselor called the "death diet," my thighs were still too thick and my ass was way too round for khakis. I imagined looking like a middle-aged mom who just gave up even trying to look good.

But then something Tony had said on the train surfaced during Tracy Chapman's version of "Stand By Me." If there was a silver lining, it was that there hadn't been a silver filling, and I'd have all my teeth when I started my new job.

Dr. Payne gently touched my shoulder, and I opened my eyes. When he handed me a mirror, his dental assistant removed the earphones. I leaned to look in the mirror, and two full front teeth shone in my reflection.

"Perfect." I smiled. "Thank you."

"My pleasure."

He offered me his hand and helped me out of the heated chair I had come to appreciate.

"Alice will give you an instruction sheet when you check out, but basically no food for a couple hours. And if you must eat, eat soft foods and avoid biting down on anything."

"If I could avoid biting down, I'd be half my size and at least double my dating prospects."

He laughed.

"Not that I'm dating," I quickly clarified, and then shook my head. "Uh, I'm not sure why I said that. Although my death therapist would say my reaction was somehow tied to grief. For three years, all she focused on was grief, which prevented either of us from recognizing even the remotest chance of happiness. It's like even if Mr. Future Happiness stood right in front of me, I doubt I'd know." I paused, lost in thought. "I mean, there was this guy on the Wine Train, but all I got out of that remote encounter was a chipped tooth and an emergency visit to the dentist. You know, to come see you."

He slowly nodded.

I was sure he was wondering if he'd given me too much Novocain.

"Charlotte tells me you've moved to Napa?"

I was grateful for the redirect. "That's right."

"You like it?"

"Sure, what's not to like. Wine trains. Cosmetic dentistry with heated chairs…."

His grin made me smile.

"Well, if you ever need a break from the wineries, I know a really good beer pub."

Huh? "Uh, okay, thanks." I grabbed my purse, nodded with a smile, and headed toward the exit. *What was that?*

CHAPTER EIGHTEEN

CHLOE

"I trust you all enjoyed the long holiday weekend. Starting a training session on a Wednesday is not the norm for us at the Point, but with some of you relocating for this position, Mr. Chambers thought it wise that we extend the holiday weekend."

The woman was a bit older than me, but seemed better put together. Her rich, beautiful burgundy dress hugged her slender body, which looked like it never saw the inside of a convenience store. A cream-colored sweater with midlength sleeves hit her waist and accentuated just how tiny she was. *What the hell is it with women who look like they don't eat?* I grinned with a belly full of cinnamon spice oatmeal, a toasted bagel with cream cheese, and a tall glass of orange juice. Nom. Nom. Nom.

"My name's Victorine. It's like tangerine, only with a *V*."

I scratched my head and casually glanced at the guy

to my left. He didn't seem surprised that our training supervisor was named after fruit. Or vruit.

"In our industry, connecting with our guests is vital. The Napa Valley Point Resort and Winery is, after all, more than just a resort. It's also an award-winning winery. So we ask all our wine educators to not only inform our guests about the winemaking process, but to make a *real* connection with them," she said.

I inhaled and slowly nodded on an exhale. *I can do this.*

"We've found that one of the most effective approaches toward connecting with our guests is by giving them a way to remember you!" Enthusiasm flashed in her blue eyes, and when she smiled, she revealed really little teeth. It was like she had a mouthful of baby teeth. *Ew.* Not that I was one to cast stones or caps about anyone's teeth, but at least mine were full-grown and thankfully all present and accounted for.

"Can anyone tell me how I explained my name?"

Everyone's hand shot up, but she pointed to the guy on the edge of the fray.

"Your name's Victorine, like tangerine, but with a *V.*"

She smiled again, and I wished she hadn't. I couldn't stop staring at her baby teeth.

"Name association is one of the best tools for guests to remember someone," she said. "We've realized from popping in on a few wine tours that our wine educators aren't taking that moment to really connect with our guests. So, we'll go around and introduce ourselves, but before we do I'd like you to take a few moments and think of something creative or clever you can say about yourself that will create an association for our guests to remember you." She paused and tilted her head. "It's always helpful when guests leave a tip and they know who it's intended for."

"Tips?" The guy on the end of our semicircle asked.

"Yes, besides your generous hourly rate, wine educators are in a tipped position."

I stopped myself from laughing. *Generous hourly rate? For real?* I only took the job because it didn't require as much of me as teaching. But generous? No. Twenty bucks an hour? After an hour on the clock, I could possibly afford a hamburger in Napa.

Victorine's hair was pin-straight, flat and dull brown. It looked as lifeless as her waiflike body. I didn't know why I was hating on her. She hadn't done anything, but something about her made my counseling Spidey sense ping. I couldn't place it yet, but there was something that didn't sit right. My counseling experience had taught me to always trust my gut, and in the presence of Victorine my gut tightened.

"Is everyone ready?"

"Huh?" I said.

"To introduce yourselves," she said with a touch of aggravation.

"Right," I said. *Fuck.* Now would be a great time to have a name like Tony Mahoney.

"Let's start to my left and work our way to the right," she said.

The guy on the end, who had been the only one to speak, spoke again. "Hey guys, my name's Barry, like Barry Allen in *The Flash*, and like my alter ego, I enjoy science. So, if at any time during our tour I *flash* through anything, just slow me down! That's Barry DeLorme at your service."

Victorine clapped, and we followed suit. "That was wonderful." She glanced at the next guy, who I had to lean forward to see.

"I'm Chris Staple," he said.

How did I not see him?

"Oh, my gosh, he was our wine educator," I blurted, and Victorine politely grinned at me like I was an annoyance she had to tolerate.

"Hello again." He smiled in my direction. "So, I'm Chris Staple, and like the office superstore, hopefully you'll find that learning about wine will be *that easy.*"

We all laughed.

"That was easy," Victorine said, with a homage to the store's slogan.

Lame.

The next wine educator, who stood beside me, was a gal about my age. "I'm Rebel," she said. "My mom wanted a girl who would rival any boy, so she named me Rebel Jean. You can call me Reb. Or Rebel. But if you call me Rebel Jean I'll think I'm in trouble."

It was simple, but worked. As did the khakis and red polo shirt she wore well. Combined with her long dark hair that was pulled into a low ponytail, a small silver nose ring, and the camouflage backpack slung over her shoulder, Rebel was my people. No-nonsense and real.

"That's wonderful, Rebel Jean," Victorine said, and my

gut radar pinged.

Really? She just said not to say that.

Victorine turned her focus toward me. "Okay, your turn."

"Hi! My name's Chloe, and it's spelled just like 'chloride,' except you get *rid* of the R-I-D. Of course, you really don't want to get rid of any part of chloride because it's one of the most important electrolytes in your blood. It helps digest food and does all sorts of great stuff. Anyway, my name is just like it." I quickly swiped my hands through the air as if I could erase what I had just said.

"I mean, my name's not important like chloride, just similarly spelled. But of course, it doesn't rhyme with chloride. Or really much of anything." *Fuck.*

"Maybe," I tried to recover, "Chloe is derived from the Latin root word for 'rambling,' so I'll just stop now." I flashed my new tooth at Victorine.

Rebel threw her head back and laughed, which was when I knew we'd get along.

"Uh, I don't think chloride is the best approach." Victorine eyed me like I was bad fruit. Her head slightly swayed from side to side without her hair moving. "Why don't we try—"

"She could say her name is like the popular pig call, 'sooey!' and when any guest needs her they could loudly call out, 'Chlo-ee!' Here, 'Chlo-ee! Chlo-ee!'"

The only flashy thing about Barry was how quickly he got on my nerves.

"Or," Rebel said, "She could introduce herself as Chloe

or Chlo." She smiled. "And then remind her guests, Chloe or Clo, either way, I'm good to go."

"Thank you." I made eye contact with her.

She shrugged. "Us girls have got to stick together."

The last person in our group was a guy to my left. "I'm Emerson, like the poet."

We were all waiting for more, but that's all he gave us. Emerson the poet seemed to challenge Victorine with his eyes, and damn if it didn't work. The Tangerine didn't utter a word.

"All right." She clasped her thin fingers together. "We'll descend into the caves where you'll learn or refresh yourself," she raised a disapproving eyebrow at Chris Staple, "on the winemaking process, so that all our guests get the tour they have come to expect at the Napa Valley Point Resort and Winery."

Ah, that's why he's here. I thought his tour was great. *What's her problem?* I clearly did not like her, and I really couldn't pinpoint why.

CHAPTER **NINETEEN**

TONY

"Sir, there are ninety vineyards on the Point property that get broken into 180 different sets that are assigned to a taster, who has to try each variety when it's made into wine." I leaned against the cobblestone side of the Napa Valley Point Resort and watched the train in the distance.

"I don't care if there are a million vineyards at the Point, if getting a clipping of the mother vine is what we need, then it's your job to find a way to get that clipping."

Winters was living up to his reputation of being a first-class prick.

"Actually, I was hired to discover what made the 2016 Napa Valley Cabernet Sauvignon unique and distinct from the Winters Summerset 2012, and it's their grape variety," I said, holding my ground.

"With that failed logic, I could have sent Ginger to the Point Resort and had her go on the wine tour. Do I need to send Ginger to Napa?"

I closed my eyes, but it didn't block his daughter's nakedness from my memory. The last time Winters had sent his daughter to accompany me on an assignment, I returned to my hotel room to find her naked in my bed. I still didn't know if it was a test, only that I'd left my room before I could find out. Ginger was a pain in the ass, but she arguably had a fine ass.

"No, sir, there's no need to send Ginger. I will do my utmost to locate which vineyard of the ninety contains the mother vine."

"Tony, you find the vine and I'll have my guy do the rest."

Guy? I was his guy. *Who else does he have?*

"Okay," I said.

"Excellent. We just need a location and he can do the rest."

What the fuck? "Sir, I'm not sure it'll be as easy as you think."

"Tony, nothing worthwhile in life is easy—that's what makes it worthwhile." I could practically hear him smile. Winters was like that when he was smug.

"Understood. But unless you have someone on the inside…."

When he didn't counter my assumption, I knew. He had some guy working on the inside. *Fuck. What's the point of having me here? What does he really want from me?*

"All right, I'd better go, the concierge said all the wine educators were being trained today, so if I'm going to locate the mother vine this would be the time to do it."

"Didn't you say that only select personnel knew the location of the vine?"

"That's correct, and the wine educators are part of that select few. I was curious why that was so I talked to Martine, the wine educator on the train, who said part of the Point's wine educator training is to learn viticulture with real-world grape farming. The idea is that they go back and forth between the concept of wine and the actual vineyard to be more informed of the wine-making process."

"Excellent. I look forward to your next report." The call disconnected in my ear.

Excellent? He wasn't even listening. I could have told him I struck gold in the cave and he wouldn't have cared. Winters's only objective was to ruin his competition. He didn't care what it took or who it hurt as long as he came out ahead. When I started in the business, it was like basketball where all I had to do was outmaneuver the competition. The intel I gathered, like why and how wine educators at the Point were trained, mattered. My intel allowed companies to strategically improve their process and get a leg up on the competition. But Winters and other clients continually raised the stakes until I no longer felt like I was sent to outmaneuver the competition with the intel I gathered—I was sent to demolish them. My stomach tightened and it wasn't from hunger. The job was beginning to eat at me. Deceiving people all the time and basically contributing to the ruin of businesses was *not* what I signed up for. *Hell, it's not who I am.*

I tucked my phone in my jeans pocket as the employee entrance to the back of the hotel opened. It was too late to disappear without drawing more attention to myself, so I casually grabbed the pack of gum from my front shirt pocket and withdrew a piece. I wasn't a smoker, so gum would have to be the reason I was lurking behind the hotel.

A sickly thin woman glanced in my direction. "Sir, may I help you?"

"Sorry, force of habit. Or force of bad habit, I should say. In high school, I always had to sneak behind the gym to smoke." I lied as naturally as I spoke. "But now that I chew gum instead of smoking, I still feel the need to hide my shame. Like my mom is going to pop out of nowhere and catch me, kind of like what you just did." I grinned with a piece of minty gum in my mouth. "So be cool and don't tell my mom," I said laughingly.

A hearty laugh and warm smile could rectify just about any awkward encounter. And I'd learned early in my intelligence-gathering career that if I sold it, people bought it.

"I won't tell." She smiled and held the door while four individuals fell in behind her. She seemed about to close the door, but instead tucked her head into the back hallway and then looked at the three men and one woman gathered behind her. I glanced at the guy in the far back. *Chris?*

"Where is she?" Her voice sounded as annoyed as the strained look on her face.

"She had to use the ladies' room," the only other woman in the group said.

"I suppose we should wait," the woman in charge said, and I wanted to say something to knock the superiority off her face, but drawing attention to myself was the kiss of death for my assignment. She closed the door sharply, as if it were punishment for a bathroom break.

"So, what are you all up to this beautiful morning?" I said while I tucked my gum back in my pocket.

The woman turned on her thin heel and smiled. "These are the newest Napa Valley Point Resort and Winery's wine educators."

"Right on." I glanced at them again and gave a nod toward Chris, who had been our wine educator.

He nodded back.

"Refresher course," he said sheepishly by way of explanation.

If you're Winter's inside guy—a refresher course would not bode well with the boss. A wine educator would have free access to the vineyards but not if they're stuck back in training. Still, Chris could be the guy. Maybe he's just not so great at his job? Great, I'm beginning to see conspiracy all around me. All I needed now was an aluminum foil hat and blog to spout all this conspiracy nonsense.

The door swung open and almost knocked Miss Bossypants all the way to Winters Winery in Oakville. The missing wine educator emerged with flushed cheeks and a harried look in her big brown eyes. Her khaki pants fit snugly across her ass, accentuating one of her best features. The three buttons on her red polo were open, revealing tanned, glistening, come-to-papa cleavage. *Chloe.*

"Sorry," she said. "I didn't know that employees weren't allowed to use the restrooms on the main floor. Then I wanted to get a jacket from my locker." She waved a black jacket with the gold Point emblem. Her black clogs looked like standard server footwear, but when she kicked the dirt it revealed neon pink-and-green-striped socks that were probably not uniform-approved attire. *Rebellious.*

"It's stated clearly in the employee handbook," a guy in the group said.

Chloe flashed him a forced smile. "Thanks, *Barry.* I'll have to bone up on that tonight."

That's right. *Fuck you, Barry.* I'd downloaded an illegal copy of the employee handbook, and restroom breaks were buried in the back section—if a person didn't fall asleep from boredom before getting to that little tidbit.

Chloe glanced over her shoulder, and when she spotted me her face seemed to soften, and her smile was no longer forced.

"Hey," she said.

"Hello."

She smiled.

"Nice tooth," I said, and her cheeks, which had just returned to normal, flushed again.

She stepped away from the group and seemed to be looking for someone. I turned, but no one was behind me.

"Just wondering where your posse was?" Her smile was playful.

"When the holiday weekend ended Dan and Ty had to get back to Huntington. I didn't," I told her.

She slowly nodded.

"I decided to take some time off, and Napa seemed like the perfect escape for a little R&R," I said.

"Nice," she said.

The woman in charge had exercised her patience while a guest spoke to her staff. But as soon as she saw a break in the conversation, she jumped in.

"Well, I trust if you need anything while you're at the Napa Valley Point Resort and Winery you won't hesitate to contact any staff member or the concierge desk," she said.

"Actually," I said, stepping into the door she'd unknowingly opened for me. "My buddies and I took a four-hour Wine Train tour, but by the time we got to the winery here, well," I purposefully rolled my eyes, "we were feeling the effects of the wine. How could I get another tour of the winery without having to board a four-hour train?"

Her face lit. "The concierge desk schedules all the wine tours for our guests."

I feigned disappointment, which wasn't too hard with Chloe about to walk away. "Is there any way I could tag along on your training session?"

The woman seemed to contemplate my request. And from my research and reading of the employee handbook, I knew why. One of the golden standards at any Point resort was that a staff member couldn't deny a guest request. It didn't matter if the guest wanted organic vodka at midnight, the Point was the leader of five-star resorts because they delivered. It was why the Hollywood elite, political powerhouses, and billionaires like Winters stayed exclusively at Point resorts. It was also why my single room cost Winters eight hundred a night. The Point never said no, which was an adult equivalent to an overindulgent parent spoiling their children.

"Normally," she began, and realized there was no way to avoid saying no in the direction she was headed. "Actually," she corrected herself, "we'd love to have a guest accompany us today."

"Wonderful." I pushed the sleeves on my white shirt up and smiled. "I'm Tony Mahoney." I shook her hand.

"Excellent name," she said. "I'm Victorine, like tangerine only with a *V*."

I clenched my teeth and forced a smile. *Does she actually think that works?*

"And this is our newest class of wine educators or returning wine educators, refreshing their skills on the winemaking process. It may seem a bit repetitive, but part of the Point training process is to have each wine educator practice their pitch and performance," she said, extending her thin arm to the group of five.

"That's probably a plus. By the fifth time I may actually understand all the intricacies to the process," I said. *And hopefully find where you have the mother vine stashed away.*

"Excellent," she said, and I knew it was a Point platitude. The staff were encouraged to respond with an adjective after a guest placed an order or made a request. I wasn't sure it was intended to make the guest feel like they'd won both an Olympic gold medal and the Nobel Prize by asking for an additional roll of toilet paper, only that I was told

"Outstanding" when I did.

"You won't even know I'm here," I said, falling in line behind Barry.

When Chloe put on her jacket, she glanced at me over her shoulder, made quick eye contact, and then returned her focus to Victorine.

It wasn't a come-here-go-away peek. It seemed different. Chloe genuinely appeared happy to see me.

CHAPTER **TWENTY**

"So, who's the guy?" Rebel cut out of line to walk beside me. She was either appropriately named, or overcompensated to try to live up to her moniker.

"That's Tony Mahoney," I said.

"I caught his name, but who is he?"

I shrugged. "Some guy I met on a four-hour wine train over the weekend. We were in his group."

"And…."

"And what?" I avoided her hazel eyes when she reached for my arm.

"Nuh-uh."

"What?" I looked at her. "Even if there was something to tell, I don't know you."

She chuckled. "True. But since we're the only two women on this education tour, we can either bond now, or later when they start pouring wine down us. It's entirely up to you."

"More wine?" I cringed. "I just stopped having it seep out of my pores from all I drank on the Wine Train, and that was three days ago."

"Uh, you know that drinking wine is part of the *experience* the Point is selling, don't you?" Her nose ring glistened beneath the twinkling lights of the wine cave.

"No, I didn't know that, because clearly I haven't read the employee handbook." I crossed my arms over my chest and knew my body language was clearly shutting her out, but I felt ill-prepared for this job.

"Get over yourself. Do you think Emerson has read the handbook?" She hip-checked me, knocking me off-balance. I unfolded my arms and smiled.

"Probably not. He's Emerson the poet, he doesn't have to read anything," I said.

"There you go," she said. "Put it in perspective. We're wine educators. It's not like we're expected to graduate these guests to sommeliers."

"Good point," I said, and casually glanced behind me. Tony walked behind Barry.

"Just a guy, huh?" Rebel's raspy voice was in my ear. "Sure, and the Point is just another hotel."

I was about to say something when Victortine snapped, like we were dogs she was herding, "All right, if I could get everyone to gather around this barrel." She stood beside an oak barrel.

One good snap on two of the barrels and Victorine would end up like an uncooked strand of spaghetti colliding with a giant meatball.

"Barrel tasting is an extremely popular and entertaining experience for the guest." Victorine nodded toward Tony, who returned her nod with his own.

"Barrel tasting?" Emerson said. "How do you get the wine from the barrel?"

"Excellent question, Emerson." Victorine flashed a smile, and her teeth looked like mini Chicklets. I thought of Dr. Payne and grinned.

She reached behind the barrel and withdrew a long, clear glass cylinder that looked better suited for a laboratory than wine cellar. One end of glass tube funneled into a narrow tip and the other end was twisted into a knot with an open hole. Victorine slipped her hand into the center of the glass knot, which allowed her to hold the tube while she pressed her thumb over the wide-mouthed opening.

"It's called a wine thief because we are stealing wine out of the barrel." It was the first thing she'd said all morning that captured my interest.

"But just because it's called a wine thief doesn't mean you can't use it to test your beer. It works just as well," Barry said.

"Asshat," Rebel said beside me.

"Yup," I said.

"We use a wine thief because unless you have very long, skinny fingers it's hard to test the wine." I think that was Victorine's attempt at a joke, but no one laughed.

The barrels were positioned on their sides and Victorine removed what looked like a cork from the center of the broad oak barrel. She gently placed the tip of the glass test tube into the cork hole.

"The wine thief lets you drop into the barrel and pull out wine. So—" She glanced at us. "You take the wine thief and put it down into the barrel as far as it will go." She showed us as she held the end of the long glass tube and the rest of it disappeared into the barrel. "After you insert the wine thief into the barrel, roughly to the middle of the wine, put your thumb on the top to hold the liquid inside the wine thief."

She slowly withdrew the wine thief, which was filled with a rich, burgundy-colored wine. "Chloe, would you please pass out the wine glasses?"

I carefully lifted the silver serving tray beside her and approached everyone, who took a glass. When I reached Tony, I looked up at him. "Sir, may I interest you in a glass for a taste of our barrel wine?"

He tipped his head. "Yes, you may."

This seemed to please Victorine, who grinned when I turned around with the last wine glass in my hand.

"This wine thief is large enough to serve about eight people." As she placed the wine thief over each of our glasses, she slowly released her thumb and wine flowed from the narrow tip into the glass. She placed her thumb back over the top as she moved from glass to glass.

"The sample doesn't have to be an entire glassful," she said. "You don't need that much."

"What happens if you take too much wine?" Emerson asked.

"Uh, you drink it," Barry said, and even Victorine laughed.

"If you take too much wine you can put the tip back into the opening of the barrel, release your thumb, and let the contents of the wine thief pour back into the barrel. We always replace what we don't use." Which was exactly what she did with the wine remaining in the wine thief.

She raised her glass. "This is one of my favorites. It's a red, but it has a fun twist."

I swirled the wine in my glass because it was what my sister always did, and took a sip. The wine had a vanilla and chocolate taste to it.

"Is this a dessert wine?" I asked.

"Excellent, Chloe."

I gestured toward the glass with my eyes. "Chocolate and wine combined should just be called a bottle of Viagra for women."

And just when I was making headway, she grimaced. But Tony and Rebel laughed. *Yup, my kind of people.*

"I'd like each of you to use the wine thief positioned beside the barrels to extract a couple samples." She pointed toward the tray of glasses stationed beside each barrel.

"Mr. Mahoney, this part may be a bit boring for you," she said.

"Unless you need someone to serve as the guest?" he said, and Victorine lit up.

"Brilliant idea," she said. "Why don't you start with Rebel and work through the group, ending with Chloe, if you don't mind."

Tony stood beside Rebel and while I could see him in my periphery, I focused on the task at hand. I had to master drawing wine from the barrel, which Victorine made look super easy. It wasn't.

My thumb kept slipping, and wine kept spilling over the side of the barrel. I glanced, but Victorine hadn't noticed. I stuck the tip of the wine thief into the barrel and quickly took off my jacket to wipe up what I'd spilled.

Once I finally conquered drawing the wine from the barrel, I couldn't seem to get it into the glass. The sample was proving to be the challenge. Instead of holding the glass, I placed it on the barrel and positioned at an angle over the hole, so if I spilled the wine would go right back where it belonged. Only that didn't work and wine went right back into the barrel. *What the fuck is wrong with me?*

When I went to retrieve more wine, the cork opening in the barrel suddenly appeared abnormally small, like I got a bad barrel. *That's probably it—I got a bum barrel.* I knew from my counseling experience that I was justifying or worse rationalizing my poor performance. But what the hell, stealing wine wasn't as easy as it looked. Add to it, the hole I had to cover with my thumb was ginormous. *Why can't I get this?*

I closed my eyes and thought back to how I prepared for a counseling session. The college filled every opening in my schedule, so I created a routine between each client to reset myself and it worked. *Get grounded.* I stepped out of my clogs and stood on the cold wood-planked floor. *Relax.* I rolled my shoulders. *Center my breathing.* I took a long, slow deep inhale through my nose, and evenly exhaled. The deep breathing brought oxygen to my brain. I felt calm, relaxed, and centered. I opened my eyes, dipped the point of the wine thief into the barrel, and withdrew an ample sample. I smiled and then approached the glass on the barrel. The wine slowly leaked into the glass, but didn't spill. When the sample reached the midway point on the glass, I closed my thumb over the pressure gap and the wine stopped. *I did it!*

I was so elated that I didn't see him approach until I felt him. I steadied my hand on the wine thief without looking at Tony—or his heated stare that seemed to follow me in the room.

"You're doing great," he said.

"Not really. If they deduct all the wine I've spilled from my paycheck, my entire career earnings at the Point will evaporate before my first day on the job is even over." I still didn't make eye contact with him. Or even glance in his direction. I couldn't—not if I wanted to master this, and I did.

"Okay, Chloe's the last one to serve Tony." Victorine's announcement did not help. "While she's serving him, I'm going to go around and check your process one last time."

Thankfully Tony stood with his back to Victorine and my fellow wine educators. It was like he purposefully blocked me from seeing them. I wasn't sure if it was intentional, but it was appreciated.

I carefully pulled the wine thief out of the barrel with my thumb sealing the top to hold the expensive liquid at bay. I held my breath as I held the tip of the wine thief over Tony's extended glass and gently removed my thumb. The wine began to slowly fill his wine glass, but then it built speed and my thumb seemed detached from my body. I knew what to do, but I couldn't seem to do it.

The top of Tony's glass was nearing full, and my thumb was not cooperating. I couldn't press it firmly enough into the top of the wine thief to create a seal. And without a seal, I had eight samples worth of wine that were about to release.

"Uh…." I panicked.

"Just press your thumb over the top," Tony said calmly and evenly.

"It's not working," I said frantically. "My thumb's dead or something's wrong, but I can't hold it."

Tony began to back away, but it was too late. The roaring rapids of merlot shot out of his glass and onto his white shirt, which now looked like the final toga worn by Julius Caesar.

"Oh, no. *Et tu, vinum*?" My Latin hung in the air like a bad joke waiting for a laugh that would never arrive.

"Dude! Check it out! The guy's soaked," Emerson said from behind Tony.

"What?" Victorine's heels tapped across the cave's planked floor.

With Tony's back to Victorine and the rest of the group, he grabbed the wine thief out of my hands and gave me his glass.

"Wh… what are you doing?" I stammered.

His brown eyes softened into a smile. "Trust me," he whispered.

"What have you done?" Victorine stood posed in front

of me with her hands on her hips and a stern expression.

"Uh, I…." I didn't know what to say.

"It wasn't her fault," Tony said. "I actually asked her if I could give it a try, and she didn't deny my *absurd request*." He raised his broad shoulders, and his shirt clung to his chest. "Yeah, this one's on me. I'm really sorry about that, Chloe." He looked past Victorine's disapproving stare to me. "Thanks for letting me have my hand at it, but clearly I'm no wine educator."

He handed me the wine thief, which I accepted, still trying to wrap my head around his gracious save. I placed the wine thief and the glass back on the serving tray.

"Uh, so what's up next?" Tony asked.

"The fermentation room," Victorine said.

His shirt stuck to him and his forearms were slick with wine.

"I'd want a shower," I said without thinking.

Tony laughed. "Yeah, I had hoped to catch more of the training, but perhaps another time?" He glanced at Victorine who nodded.

"Mr. Mahoney, you are welcome to accompany us during any of our training sessions," she said.

"Excellent. I think I'll end up calling it a day," he said.

"Actually, wait." Victorine's voice was as sharp as her chin that she tipped upward. "I'd appreciate it if you'd wait."

"Sure," Tony said.

"This is a great teaching moment," she said, and I wanted to gag. Whenever anyone used popular education catchphrases—like teachable moment, student-centered focus, or learning lessons—for basically tossing in random info when the shit hit the fan, annoyed the Freudian slip out of me. Anything that was said after one of those buzz words was just crock full of crap.

"If you ever find yourself in the unfortunate position of having spilled wine on a guest"—she looked at me as if she hadn't bought Tony's cover—"it is the Point policy to—"

"Offer to have their clothes dry cleaned and returned to them the same day," Barry said, and I wanted to steal another vial of wine and shoot him with it.

"Excellent, Barry. That's correct." Victorine turned to Tony. "We can have housekeeping return your soiled clothes to you before day's end."

"It's not necessary," he said. "As I said, this one's on me—literally. That'll teach me to try and be a wine thief." He held up his hand. "Correction, *use* the wine thief."

I waited for Victorine's next move. "We have nearly a dozen barrels for barrel tasting, but as I mentioned I think we'll move on to the fermentation room."

I stood motionless, not sure if I should follow the group or clock out for my first and only day at the Point. Victorine glanced over her shoulder.

"Chloe, you need a new uniform. There are wine splatters on your slacks. Why don't you escort Mr. Mahoney to the resort and get him a housekeeping laundry bag, and afterward you can change into one of your other uniforms. When you are Point presentable, you can rejoin us."

Other uniforms? I'd been lucky to find one pair of khakis that weren't too long for my short legs, yet ample enough to cover my ass. I did have another red shirt, but I'd left it at my sister's house. If I didn't already feel in over my head, I did now. The cave began to feel extremely small, and I was finding it hard to breathe. *This is a mistake. I don't belong here.*

His hand gently touched my shoulder. "Have I ever told you about my first college basketball game?"

He actually made me pause and look at him instead of the group of wine educators proceeding to the next phase of the training. "What?"

"Basketball. I played for UCLA."

"Oh."

"Yeah, I was way out of my league. Dan wasn't. It's one thing to play for Edison, but UCLA? I think I was given a mercy scholarship. Anyway," his focus never left my eyes, "it was our first game. I get the ball, and the first time I dribble, it hits my shoe instead of the floor. The ball goes flying to the side, and there's a mad scramble for the loose ball."

He paused long enough for me to imagine the scene. My dad had taken me to Pauley Pavilion, the home court of the UCLA Bruins, where the late John Wooden, the Wizard of Westwood, reigned supreme. It was as impressive a court to basketball fans as the Napa Valley Point Resort and Winery was to hotel enthusiasts.

"Somehow," he continued, "I ended up with the ball and I'm fouled, so I'm headed to the free-throw line for two shots. It's my first collegiate free throw and I throw an airball. *An airball.* I couldn't even shoot the ball fifteen feet.

So, when it came time for my second free throw, I was still reeling from the embarrassment, and I overcompensated my shot and it went clean over the backboard, which happens to be thirteen feet high off the ground. My second shot looked more like a field goal than a free throw."

His wine-stained shirt faded from my focus as his story and the passion in his voice transported me somewhere else.

"So, as a result of that first fateful game, I will forever hold the title for the player with the worst consecutive free throws in basketball history. To break this down for you, in case basketball is as much an anomaly to you as wine is to me, the total difference between my first and second free throws was an improbable twenty-eight feet for a fifteen-foot shot when nobody was even guarding me."

Alone in the cave with him, I stood silently, not knowing what to say.

"Anyway, as my buddy Dan reminded me, it was the first game of the season. I was still finding my footing."

"Did you?" I asked.

He tilted his head.

"Find your footing?"

His smile was pleasing and reassuring at the same time. "I did."

"Okay, then." I turned to retrace my steps out of the cave, and he gently tapped my shoulder. I glanced at him over my shoulder.

"You're not out of the game yet," he said.

"It's finding my footing that seems to be the hard part," I said.

"It usually is, but you will." A broad smile made his brown eyes almost disappear, which was actually really cute. "Heck, if I can—anyone can."

"Thanks, Tony."

"Anytime. I'm taking a long-needed break, so I'm booked here for the month. If you find yourself tipping off-balance, give me a shout. My room has a balcony so you can literally give me a shout."

"A modern Romeo?"

"More like a crotchety old man sitting in a rocking chair on his balcony yelling at kids to stay the hell out of his yard."

When I laughed, the smile in his eyes was impossible to ignore. Tony had done the one thing I didn't think was possible—he made me forget about my wine mishap and looking like a fool my first day on the job.

CHAPTER **TWENTY-ONE**

TONY

"I'm pretty sure I know where the housekeeping department is and where they keep their bags, if you want to wait?" Chloe wrapped her Point Resort jacket around her waist to hide the burgundy splashes on her pants that looked like a Jackson Pollack painting.

"No need. I'm sure there's one in the closet in my room," I said, and headed toward the elevator.

"Tony?"

I turned.

She hurried toward me. "I think I actually have to get you that bag and take your clothes to housekeeping. I haven't read the employee handbook yet, but it seems like the Point is pretty specific about their policies, so…."

"Understood. When you find one, bring it up to my room. I'm in suite 225."

"Got it, 225." It was the first time she relaxed since

Victorine's scolding. But instead of leaving, she remained standing in front of me.

"You okay?" I asked.

"Yeah. It's just, you didn't have to do that."

I cocked my head. "Do what?"

"Cover for me with the wine thief and everything."

I shrugged. "Please. I was going to ask to try it out anyway."

"You were?" She genuinely looked surprised.

"Absolutely." I sounded like one of the Point employees. "I mean, how many times will I get a chance to steal some wine?" I clenched my jaw. *What the fuck is wrong with me?* Granted, I was thinking of switching careers, but at this rate I'd be fired before I could resign. I'd never been this colossally incapable of doing my job. *Wine thief? Why don't I just tell Chloe the real reason I'm here.* I shifted my attention back to her unsuspecting brown eyes.

"I meant, the barrel. It's really hard to use that wine thief on the barrel."

"Agreed. It looks easier than it is," she said, clearly not picking up on my slip of tongue.

"I bet."

"Okay, well, thanks." She extended her hand like we had closed a deal.

Instead of teasing her, which would have drawn more attention to the awkwardness of her handshake, I firmly shook her hand.

"I'll be up as soon as I find housekeeping." Her eyes widened. "Don't tell anyone I said that." She chuckled. "I'm already in enough trouble."

"Lips are sealed." The elevator opened and I stepped inside. "I'll see you later."

The Point only had four floors of suites and I was on the second floor, so it wasn't like I ever had to wait long for the elevator or to get to my suite. I walked into my recently cleaned room. The queen-sized bed was expertly made, fresh towels were stacked beneath the sink, and the snacks I'd grabbed from the minibar last night had been restocked. It was as if I had never occupied the room.

The connecting door in the suite that led to the room Dan and Ty had shared was now closed and locked. I needed a shower, but I didn't know when Chloe would return.

I grabbed my cell phone from my pocket and hit speed dial.

"Hey buddy, how's wine country treating you?"

"Not bad. You and Ty get back okay?"

"Yup, and Lori came to the airport to pick us up, it was pretty great," Dan said, and I could hear the smile in his voice. It happened anytime he spoke about his fiancée.

"So how are things going in your hunt for the mother vine?"

I exhaled and ran my hand through my hair, which was sticky. When the wine thief splattered, it went all out. "Fuck if I know. I spoke to Winters today and, hold up, Dan, I'm going to put you on speaker. I've got to wash my hands."

"Should I even ask?"

I laughed, hit the round speaker button on my phone, turned the volume to the highest setting, and placed my cell on the bathroom counter. "You still there?"

"Yup."

"Remember that time we sprayed the keg hose on Ty because he was being an idiot about something?"

"Back in high school?" Dan asked.

"No, college." I flipped on the faucet, splashed my face, and then ran my hands under the water and through my hair.

"Oh, right, when he didn't want to pledge a fraternity because he considered frats to be haughty and elitist?"

"Yeah, and then he said he was already a member of the most exclusive group on campus," I said.

"Oh yeah, that's why we sprayed him," Dan said.

"When Ty tried to reason his way out of pledging with us because he was one of the twelve men that made up the basketball team at UCLA and claimed he was selected by talent and not by who he knew or was related to or what clothes he wore, which was how he thought all fraternities operated…."

"We put the keg hose on him," Dan said.

"Right, he got hosed," I said.

"What made you think about that?" Dan said.

"Well, if there is karma, Ty just got payback." I grabbed a towel, wiped my face, and tossed the towel back on the bathroom counter. My shirt had dried on me. I peeled it off and tossed it on the floor. The wide black waistband of my Calvin Klein steel-colored boxer briefs rested on my abs above my low-rise jeans. I was no Marky Mark, but we wore the same brand and my abs were getting back to washboard shape.

"Karma? What do you mean?" Dan said.

I grabbed the phone and placed it in the hallway beside the closet. "I went on an impromptu wine tour and Chloe squirted me with the wine thief."

"Chloe, huh? And what the fuck is a wine thief? Or have you reverted to talking about yourself in the third person?"

I laughed. "No, the wine thief is this glass tube that pulls wine out of a barrel for barrel tastings."

"And Chloe got you wet? Isn't that supposed to be your job?"

"Funny." I opened the closet, grabbed my suitcase, and slid it onto the floor in the hallway.

"So, you saw Chloe again?"

"Purely by chance," I said, unzipping the suitcase.

"Was it, though?" Dan's voice had a mocking tone.

"Actually, it was. I was at the back of the hotel speaking to Winters on the phone when the new group of wine educators came out with the corporate trainer."

"How are things going with Winters?"

I stopped rummaging through my suitcase for a clean pair of jeans. "That's the thing, he mentioned something about *his guy*."

"What the fuck? I thought you were his guy?"

I stared at the phone. "Right? That's what I thought too."

***

CHLOE

"Well, as Chris Staple would say, 'That was easy.'" I actually felt a sense of pride taking a housekeeping laundry bag to Tony. Not only were the housekeepers super friendly, when they heard about my mishap in front of Victorine, but they also loaned me a pair of uniform pants. Apparently, Victorine was an equal opportunity offender.

I hadn't read the employee handbook, but I sensed if staff weren't allowed to use the guests' restrooms, the guest elevator was probably off limits. I found the back stairs that led to the second floor. I heard the housekeepers mention a service elevator, but I wasn't going to press my luck. Finding housekeeping buried in the back hallways of the hotel was my win for the day. Now to get Tony Mahoney his laundry bag.

I took the stairs two at a time. I was in new khakis that actually fit better than the one pair I found at the strip mall by my sister's house, and since my red Polo hadn't been stained, I could return to training. My first day on the job was turning around. The emergency exit led to the second floor, but thankfully didn't alarm when I opened it and stepped into the refrigerated air that chilled the hallway.

The doors to the suites were a rich burgundy and the halls were covered in a subtle gold tapestry that made me want to touch them. I did, and the material moved back and forth against my fingertip. The paisley printed in the lush fabric was smooth with a fuzzy grain that changed color and texture with the direction of my fingertip. *That's cool.*

Suite 225 was in the middle of the floor. I walked toward his room and the closer I got, the louder the voices became. I stood outside the suite, checked the room number on the door, but before I knocked, I listened. *Who is Tony talking to?*

***

TONY

"So, what are you saying? Winters has a someone working at the Point?"

I shrugged toward my cell phone that was beside my suitcase next to the door. "I don't know what to think. Only that Winters wants me to find where the Point's mother vine is located and apparently *his guy* will do the rest."

"What the fuck is that?"

"I know, right. It confused the hell out of me. Like it's not hard enough finding where they stash this vine, but if Winters has someone working on the inside, then why have me here? It seems counterproductive."

"Or," Dan said, "Winters wants to ensure that if you don't get the location or a clipping of the Vine that his guy does."

"You think he's doubling down?" I asked.

"Would it be so unusual? Winters is all about having the

corporate edge, so it wouldn't surprise me if he had you and someone else at the hotel to find and steal a section of the mother vine."

"You're probably right. But my job was never to steal the vine, just identify what made the Point's 2016 Cab award-winning. I feel like I've done that," I said.

Dan scoffed. "Buddy, I don't know who you're fooling, but it isn't me. You know how Winters plays ball and it's not by the rules. You weren't sent to Napa to *just* identify the source of their award-winning wine, which was pretty damn good by the way, you were sent there to systemically ruin the Point's product. And the best way to do that is to have someone on the inside who can tamper with the winemaking process and someone on the outside who can funnel the vine out before it's ruined."

"Winters is shrewd, but that seems even a bit extreme for him," I said.

"The guy had you steal a dog food recipe," Dan said.

"I didn't *steal* anything. I gathered the ingredients and manufacturing list for the dog food," I said.

"You stole the recipe," Dan said.

"Whatever. This isn't dog food. This is wine," I said.

"Yeah, and now that Chloe drenched you in it, you have a reason to go visit her. Or at the very least, she's not going to push you away when she next sees you."

I scratched the back of my neck that was also sticky. "Dan, she had a pretty rough start."

"All the better. Take her out to dinner. Or better yet, have her invite you to dinner."

I volleyed my head. "I'm not sure. I don't think she knows anything about the mother vine."

"Not yet," Dan said. "Listen, the ball's in your court now, and all you have to do is use it to your advantage."

"Uh…." I massaged the tension in my neck.

"Tony, you're there for a job. It sucks what happened to Chloe this morning, but she's a tough girl. She's been through worse. She's a wine educator, so at some point she's going to be shown where the mother vine is, and if you're already on good terms with her, you have a better chance of her telling you where it's located."

There wasn't anything Dan said that didn't align with the objective I'd been assigned by Winters. But it didn't align with me.

"I don't like the idea of using Chloe."

"Buddy, you're not using Chloe, you're *utilizing* her knowledge."

"Dude." I laughed. "Semantics, really?"

"Tony, you face this moral ambiguity every time you get sent on assignment."

"No, I don't," I said.

"Then you won't have any trouble gathering information from Chloe, who is merely a source with firsthand knowledge," Dan said.

"But she could lose her job," I said.

"Only if you're dumb enough to get caught, or an unethical bastard who rats her out by giving up your source," Dan said. "Come on, you're smarter than that. You know, my old man was a reporter and he never revealed his sources, even when he faced contempt of court charges. And I'd like to think that a collegiate athlete is a lot tougher than a wimpy writer."

"Listen there's nothing you're saying that I haven't already thought, but utilizing Chloe is basically using her. And I'm literally sick to my stomach of using people. I don't think this is the right job for me anymore. Like you said, Winters doesn't play by the rules. And he hasn't for a while now. Honestly, the money was a huge incentive to suck it down and play by his rules, but I don't think I can do that anymore." I paused, and when Dan didn't jump into the conversation, I continued, "If I could gather the information Winters needs the way I used to, no one would get hurt. But that's not what he wants. If I don't get what he wants, which is the mother vine, he has someone on site that'll do it and I guarantee you that person isn't concerned about Chloe or anyone," I said.

"Buddy, I didn't know this was bothering you so much," he said.

"This isn't on you or anyone. It's on me. I think when Winters told me he had another guy on the job, it clicked. It doesn't matter what intel I gather for him. If he doesn't like the results there are a dozen other guys who will do his bidding," I said, and the reality of my statement settled in my gut like a lead weight.

"Everyone's replaceable," Dan said.

"Yeah, I know, and with that logic, don't be loyal to your company because they'll never be loyal to you," I said.

"Yeah, yeah, heard that one before. But that's not me. I am

loyal."

"Hundred percent," Dan said. "That's why it was an easy choice for you to be my best man."

"Thanks, buddy. I've got to go. Chloe's supposed to drop off a laundry bag pretty soon."

"Enjoy your time with her. And remember she can be a source without hurting her. Talk to you later."

***

CHLOE

Source? It felt like an electric shock zapped through my body, like when my socked feet rubbed against the thick carpet in my sister's house and zinged me. Hearing Tony and Dan's conversation caused a much greater current to course through me. I stood outside the door to his suite and as the shock drained away, numbness took its place.

Utilizing me? Winters? Did I hear that right? What the fuck?

I felt dizzy. But when I heard movement in the suite, I quickly snapped out it and rapped my knuckles against the door. I smiled until I thought my cheeks would burst.

The door opened and a shirtless Tony stood before me. His chest was almost as defined as his muscular arms, which rippled with definition when he held the door. A suitcase was pushed off to the side that I tried to focus on, but my attention drifted back to his bare chest and the dark trail of hair that led from his belly button and disappeared behind his Calvin Klein briefs. My body no longer zinged from anger, but it did prickle with something I couldn't identify. The band of his Calvins hugging his abs was eye candy. I hadn't seen a man's body in three years. Part of me wanted to reach out, feel my way across him and ride him to a much-needed orgasm. Another part of me wanted to push him back into his suite, knock him to the floor, and stuff the laundry bag in his mouth. My rising, raging hormones were offset by a much deeper part inside me. *How can I lust over another man?*

Because you're human, my rational psychologist self answered.

My hormones, which I'd thought had died with Ben, had merely been hibernating, and now the long, cold winter of mourning had ended and I could feel the heat and temperature rising. I took a calm, steady breath the way I encouraged my clients to do in order to operate from my higher self. *Fuck the higher self.*

"Here's your bag," I said, and held the plastic catchall toward him.

"You found housekeeping," he said, as if he was just a regular guest and not some spy sent here by Winters. *Winters? Why does that sound familiar?*

"Oh, my God! Winters wine?" The connection flew out of my mouth before I could take it back.

He leaned against the door, the expression on his face never wavering. "What about Winters wine?"

I could respond one of two ways: confront him with the

truth or avoid it altogether. *Fight or flight at it's best.* But as I stood in front of a shirtless Tony, that deep well inside me, which operated at a physical level long before it ever reached a cognitive one, ached to be heard.

"Tony, I overheard your conversation with Dan."

His gaze shifted and he closed the door. I wasn't sure how I should feel—scared, nervous, calm. But fortunately, the suite had a couch. And if I was half the counselor I thought I was, I'd have Tony on that couch and in tears within five minutes as he told me about his childhood and/ or parents.

"What exactly did you hear?"

"Everything," I said, and then clarified. "Actually, what I heard was a man who is wrestling with inner turmoil and has serious concerns about the off-center ethics of his job."

When Tony's face softened and he motioned toward the chair beside the desk, I knew whatever happened next would be therapeutic.

"May I get you something to drink?"

"Water," I said.

He placed a bottle of water on the desk and sat on the couch across from me. Everything reminded me of my office on campus except his enticingly bare chest.

"Maybe a shirt?" I suggested.

Tony jumped up and grabbed a shirt from his suitcase. He slid it on and resumed his seat on the couch at the foot of his bed.

I pulled a hair band from my wrist and coiled my hair on top of my head. "So, you're here on business, not pleasure."

I started with the obvious.

"I'm in competitive intelligence gathering," he said, and when I didn't comment he elaborated. "Basically, I get hired by companies to systemically gather, analyze, and manage information on their competitors without anyone being the wiser."

"You're a corporate spy," I said with a slight grin.

"It's actually called research and reconnaissance," he corrected.

"Does it bother you when someone confuses what you do with espionage?"

"I get paid the same no matter what anyone calls me, and when I deliver, like I always do, I get paid even more for the next assignment. So call me what you like just as long as the check clears," he said, and when he crossed his arms over his chest, I knew I'd struck a nerve.

I crossed my legs to mirror his stance and gently swung my leg over my knee to show him I wasn't a threat.

"How long have you been in competitive intelligence gathering?" I asked.

"Long enough to know I shouldn't be having this conversation with you," he said. He uncrossed his hands and he pressed the bridge of his nose. His body language screamed that he was looking for relief and if I could just crack his defenses, the release he was searching for would be his.

But I knew from counseling, the only way to achieve that was if I drew him out. And the most effective approach was to reflect back to a situation that echoed his.

"I'm not very good with keeping secrets," I said and chuckled. "For the longest time, I tried to keep the fact that my husband died to myself—as if I didn't mention it, the pain didn't exist. But the only person I was fooling was myself. And even then, I wasn't because my body knew. I carried the grief in my shoulders that were always tense, my jaw that was always clenched, but the kicker was my stomach."

"Why?" Tony leaned forward and rested his arms on his knees.

"My gut always knew. I could swallow enough ibuprofen to numb the tension I carried in my body, but my gut wouldn't let up. It knew that the only way I'd get over my loss was to go through it and not around it," I said. "Now, whenever my gut goes off, I listen because it's usually telling me something that my subconscious wants me to know."

"My gut's been a wreck," Tony said.

I slowly nodded.

"It's bad enough that my level of sloppiness on this assignment is *totally* out of the ordinary, like putting my phone on speaker to talk to Dan about what's going on. *Anyone* could have heard our conversation. But even before that, I was asking the most obvious questions on the Wine Train like I wanted to get caught." He shook his head, and all the questions he asked on the train flooded my sober memory.

He did ask a lot of questions. But I silenced my thoughts. I was the most effective as a counselor when I remained objective and didn't jump onto the self-loathing train with someone.

"I don't know what the hell's going on, but my heart's not in it." He leaned against the back of the bed. "*Fuck. That's it, isn't it? My heart's not in it, that's why I keep fucking up—so I can get caught.*"

"And if you were caught what would happen?"

"Game over. I'd be ejected from corporate intelligence gathering and my firm would fire me. I'd never work another research and reconnaissance again."

"Would that be so bad?" I leaned forward to bridge some of the distance between us.

He tried to look like he didn't care one way or the other, but I sensed that was for show.

"Tony?" I said, and this time he raised a brow.

"I don't know," he said. "I've been doing this for so long that it's become my identity. If I didn't do this, I'm not sure what I'd do."

I met his gaze. "No one understands that more than me." Emotion caught in my throat. "I'm not sure if you could tell, but I'm not exactly skilled with all things wine-related. In fact, my knowledge of wine is dismal at best. But..." I paused, uncrossed my legs, and placed both feet on the carpet to ground me. "What I was doing wasn't working." I slowly exhaled.

"I clinically knew that memories of Ben's death would come back when I least expected it and only time would soften their power over me, but I wasn't giving myself that time." At this point, I didn't know who was helping who. "I left a really good counseling job at the college to be an underpaid wine educator at a resort in a new town because I knew the only way for the sharp pain to lessen was if I did something different."

"Did it work?"

I gently smiled. "Now it's a dull ache, *but*," I stressed, "by removing myself from our old stomping ground, I no longer get blindsided when I pull up to a stop light and remember it's the spot where he first told me he loved me. Now I can have those memories without them paralyzing me. I was half-assing my job because I wasn't happy. I love counseling people but I needed a breather. To use basketball as an analogy, I needed a time-out."

"So you threw in the towel," he said.

"No. I took a time-out. I'll probably return to counseling when I'm ready, but right now I'm taking care of myself," I said and realized my own truth.

"In my industry, it's all or nothing," he said. "And right now, throwing in the towel sounds like a good idea."

"But if you chuck it all in now, what happens to Winters's inside guy?" I surprised myself with my question.

Tony shrugged. "Winters still gets the mother vine and I get the boot?"

"What if you stuck around and pretended to Winters that you're still on the job so that *we* could track down the other spy at the Point?"

"We?" It was the first time a smile lit his face.

"Yeah," I said. "*We.* I'm still a newcomer to Napa, but I don't like the idea of anyone stealing the mother vine and ruining my fresh start." I laughed. "I can ruin things enough on my own, I don't need outside help."

"I won't argue that," Tony said. "So how exactly would we work together?"

"I'm not sure."

"So if I agree to work with you, you won't blow my cover?"

"No, not at all. Telling anyone that you're a spy or corporate intelligence gatherer won't bring us any closer to discovering who Winters's other inside guy is. If anything, it'll burrow him further underground," I said.

"If the guy or gal is worth their salt, that's exactly what they'd do—only to surface later."

"Exactly. But if we work together, we can flush out the inside guy," I said.

"And how do you propose we flush him or her out?"

"I haven't thought that far ahead, but maybe Dan's suggestion that we have dinner isn't so stupid after all," I said.

"I hear the Point has a really great grill on property," Tony said.

I wrinkled my nose. "I don't think I'm allowed on property after hours."

"Of course. Let me talk to the concierge desk and find a place off property. How's tomorrow night?"

"Perfect," I said too quickly, and when I realized it, I blushed.

He laughed. "Great. It's a... date?"

"Yeah, it's a date," I said with a grin.

His eyes softened. "Looking forward to it."

"Me too." I stood and searched the floor for the laundry bag. When I spotted it, I grabbed it and handed it to Tony. "This is my excuse for basically missing the last half of training. If you could just, um, you know, give me your clothes, I'll take it down to housekeeping."

"This isn't dirty… yet," he said, tugging on the clean shirt he put on at my request. His coy smile was enough to buckle my knees. "But who am I to pass up an offer for dry cleaning?" When he slid off his shirt, I turned my back and faced the hallway as if he'd just undressed in front of me, which I kind of hoped he would. *What the fuck, Chlo. You just counseled him onto neutral ground.*

I exhaled and tried to cool myself down, but Tony's body was seriously sick, and those Calvins were practically calling my name. I began counting to focus on anything other than his body… and heard the unmistakable sound of his zipper. *Fuck. Really.* I couldn't help myself, I turned around just as he stepped out of his jeans. His thighs were muscular, his calves were well-built, and I could only imagine how thick his dick was. *Oh, damn.*

The suite narrowed, and no amount of air conditioning could lower my temperature. I reached into the open collar of my shirt and began slowly rubbing my collarbone. I had no idea why, but if I didn't touch something I was less than a foot away from groping him.

"I… uh." I swallowed. Tony stood before me in nothing but Calvins and a devil-may-care grin.

"Okeydokey, I'll just grab those jeans." I was about to get the jeans off the carpet when I realized I'd be bending right into his boxers. *Nope.* I looked up at him and smiled. "Could you get those for me, and your shirt?"

His laughter was sexy and disarmingly attractive.

He stuffed his clothes in the bag and handed it to me.

"Thanks." I swung the housekeeping bag between us like an executioner's ax, hoping to kill the sexual tension and desire. It didn't work. If anything, the swaying made me dizzy. I shook my head to center my thoughts and walked toward the door.

"Thanks for the talk." I reached for the door handle.

"Thank *you,* Chloe. I know you're taking a time-out from counseling, but talking to you helped." His brown eyes never left mine.

"There are some things I don't totally suck at," I said with a smile.

I opened the door, and walked away from his suite, his mesmerizing body, and the intensity I felt in mine. My body stirred with a mixture of bewilderment and passion that was never a good combination. One led to bad choices and poor decisions, and the other to heartache and regrets, which only fueled more confusion, bad choices, and poor decisions. When it came to matters of the heart or heat, I tended to react to what my body wanted and not what my mind warned me against. And when it came to Tony Mahoney, my body desired what my mind told me was nothing more than a sexual attraction. My mind also told me we could work together without the sex thing getting in the way. Sure, because there's bound to be one time in the history of the universe when two young, single, consenting adults in their prime, who were strongly and mutually attracted to each other, refused to let sex or other forbidden fruit get in the way. Just because it didn't happen to Adam and Eve, or any other couple since then, didn't mean that this time it couldn't actually work.

CHAPTER **TWENTY-TWO**

CHLOE

I quietly shut the door to my sister's house and went directly to the guest bedroom. My shit was strewn everywhere, but I knew what I wanted and where it was. I opened the closet, and the neatly built-in shelves where all my T-shirts, sweaters, and jeans were stuffed was another eyesore I didn't want my sister to see. But on the top shelf, all by its lonesome, was a pine box. I grabbed it and headed toward the overstuffed king-sized bed. I hopped on top without pulling back the comforter, something Charlotte would lose her shit about, and emptied the contents of the box on the expensive handmade quilt.

A baggie full of failed pregnancy tests, which was what led us to realize Ben was sick, fell to the bed along with a wooden nickel from our first date at the Orange County fair. A lock of his hair and mine braided together and tied with a blue ribbon was sealed in another baggie. When he began to lose his hair, I shaved mine. Ben had loved my long, wavy hair, but when he touched the stubble across my shorn head, he saw the beauty of baldness. Almost everything that was on the quilt in front of me could trigger a good cry, but I was too revved up to be sad.

I rummaged through old movie tickets, playbills, and the funeral mass card with our picture on the front.

"I know it's in here." I flipped through the pages of one of the many journals we'd kept when he was diagnosed with prostate cancer. His doodles filled the pages, with my penmanship beside his drawings. Each one told a story of his journey with cancer. The heaviness in my chest returned, and I felt my eyes sting.

"Ben, I met this guy," I said, and then laughed. "Yeah, not like that. *Or maybe it is like that.* I don't know. He's at the Point to get the secret location of the mother vine, but he agreed to help me find the other inside guy. And I was thinking about when we went to that vineyard in Santa Barbara, you took notes."

But I couldn't find the notebook.

"I want to copy your notes into my notebook and use that information to flush out the inside guy. Because don't you think if he's there working for another winery and we come into contact, he'll know if my info is bogus and call me on it?" I glanced at the ceiling as if my dead husband would suddenly answer me. "You know, my thought was to lead this other guy or gal in the wrong direction. And don't even try to convince me it's a bad idea," I said, knowing I teetered on a line Ben would never have crossed. "Whoever this inside guy is, deserves it."

I scratched my head, but Ben's notebook didn't seem to be in the pile of keepsakes. What was on the bedspread was a small, gray, brain-shaped object that read "Orange Coast College—Counseling & Student Development Center." It was a stress toy we gave to the students who came in for counseling.

I grabbed the brain and began squeezing it. "I think Tony's a good guy, but…" The more I squeezed the brain, the better it felt. "He's not too good at his job. I mean, what kind of idiot discusses illegal activities on speakerphone? And I'm not a fan of his buddy, Dan. I'm surprised they didn't have a court stenographer in the room for a transcript of the conversation, as well as a notary public to certify the document. Morons."

"Who's the moron? Or morons?" My sister stood in the doorway to the guest room.

"Tony and Dan, who we met on the train."

"Tony Mahoney," she said, and walked into the room.

"I didn't remove the comforter." I confessed the obvious.

"I see that." She picked a piece of lint off the bedspread and sat on the corner. "I thought Tony was only in Napa for a bachelor party."

"Ha!" Charlotte jumped a little at my outburst. "Sure. That was probably just the cover. Or maybe they were actually there for Dan's bachelor party, but that's not why Tony's staying." I tried to squeeze the gray matter out of the brain. "Nope. Mr. Mahoney is staying at the Point for a *month*—as if *that* shouldn't have been my first clue. I mean, who can afford to stay at the Point for a month?"

"More than you could imagine."

"Charlotte, the lowest room rate is eight hundred a night—and if you multiply that by thirty...."

I looked at her and she shook her head.

"No, I meant for you to actually multiply that by thirty."

My sister chuckled. "It's twenty-four thousand dollars."

"See. Who would spend *that* much money under the pretense of requiring a much-needed break?"

"Chlo, people rent houses in Napa for more than that just for a week's stay," she said.

"Whatever. It doesn't matter. Tony's not really staying at the Point for a break." I shook the brain at my sister. "He's working for Winters Winery to find the location of the Point's mother vine."

My sister slowly nodded. "Have you been drinking?"

"No!" I threw the brain at her, which she caught. "I mean I had a few barrel samples, but no, I'm not drunk. I heard Tony and Dan talk on the phone."

"How'd that happen?"

I waved my hand as if the minor details weren't important, when in reality they were. The devil was in the details, and Winters was the devil. I just didn't want to repeat the entire story.

"Suffice to say, I accidentally spilled wine all over Tony, and I had to go to his suite to get his clothes, and when I got there, he was on speakerphone with *Dan*. I heard them talk about how Tony works for Winters Winery and I'm simply a *source* that Tony's meant to *utilize*."

"What?" My sister stretched out on the bed and tossed the brain beside a blue notebook I'd overlooked. I picked it up, flipped through the pages, and recognized the notes from the winemaker Ben and I had met in Santa Barbara. It contained everything to make their Pinot Noir that Ben took a liking to—the winemaker had taken a liking to my bald husband—from when they harvested their grapes to how long they let the wine ferment. I grinned and waved the notebook at my sister.

"Yeah, it's all true. I heard all the details before I saw Tony in his Calvins."

My sister suddenly shot upright. "What? You saw Tony Mahoney in Calvin what?"

"Boxer briefs."

"*Really?*"

I nodded.

"Huh. How'd he look?"

"Really good actually, but that's not the point."

Now she nodded. "And what's the point?"

"That he's here under false pretenses. He only wants the mother vine so that Winters Winery can, I guess, win back their title? I don't know enough about wine, but I heard what I heard. And Tony's a spy."

My sister laughed. "It's called intelligence gathering, and it happens all the time in the corporate world."

"Not at my hotel," I said, and my sister smiled.

"Your hotel, huh?"

"Listen, just because I suck at my job doesn't mean I'm not loyal to the Point. They don't deserve to have someone underhanded try to steal what Rob Erickson and Rich Chambers worked so hard to create."

My sister's professionally threaded eyebrow rose, and her blue eyes locked with mine.

"Chloe, what are you up to?"

I smacked the notebook against my palm. "Well, after I counseled Tony, he agreed to help me flush out Winters's inside guy, because apparently Winters didn't leave it to chance and has two guys working at the Point."

"So what's with the notebook?"

"Well, now that I think it through it was a stupid idea. On the drive home, I thought that once we figured out who the other inside guy was, I could feed him the process for making the wine in Santa Barbara, but I didn't follow my concept through to completion." I tossed the notebook back on the bed. "*Dammit*. Winters is obviously not a complete idiot, even if he lacks morals. But he's probably got an experienced winemaker overseeing his winery—sure, it's his 'hobby,' but making wine for sale on the scale he does is not something you can do on the side while running a large corporation. I've learned that much. So, while Winters might involve himself somewhat, he'd definitely have someone at the winery overseeing the day-to-day operations, and that someone is probably well-versed in winemaking."

My sister nodded. "Agreed. Whoever Winters has at his winery would certainly know the difference between making particular wines, and between conditions in Santa Barbara and Napa. Your idea about giving the inside guy the wrong wine-making formula only works to foil Winters's plot if he has a total newbie making the wine, but that's likely not the case."

"Yeah, it sounded good in my head on the drive home, but it's stupid. So was my idea to give him false info about the vineyard."

"Sorry about that, sis, but yah, neither would work. All Winters needs is a cutting of the mother vine. Any notes or recipe he got would likely be ignored anyway," Charlotte said.

"Crappity, crap, crap. I really wanted Winters to come away with the most expensive bottle of vinegar."

"So, now what?"

I shrugged. "Well, I've got Tony on my side and…."

"Chloe, just be careful. The people who work in corporate intelligence are in that career for a reason—they're good at weeding out bullshit. And they're even better at disguising their motives."

"You think he's playing me?"

"No, just be careful. He may have agreed to help you, but later he may be plagued by doubt. Like is he doing the right thing? Is this really the way he wants to end his career—because make no mistake, what he's agreeing to do *will* end his career."

"I'm usually good at reading people, but if I'm wrong then I'll be prepared. I may know dick about wine, but when it comes to a battle of wits, Tony is virtually unarmed, and my PhD in psychology can be a weapon of mass destruction when it comes to mind games. *No one* can mess with someone's head like a trained psychologist." I leaned back on the stack of pillows behind me and smiled. "Besides, whatever happens with Tony, my focus is on Winters. And when I'm done with Winters Winery and his equally slimy inside guy, 'corporate intelligence' will be nothing more than an oxymoron."

***

I couldn't wait for the alarm to ring. I barely slept, thinking about my dinner with Tony. Even though I knew Ben's notes were useless, I tucked his notebook into the back waistband of my khakis and hid with my shirt like someone would do with a gun. Of course, it wasn't, but I felt armed and dangerous. And if I was going to go head-to-head with a corporate spy, I was going to act like one myself.

I bypassed the breakfast pastries Coach had arranged on a platter and placed on the bar that extended from the kitchen, and headed straight for their espresso machine.

"Have you ever drunk espresso?" Coach asked.

I shrugged. "I've been to Starbucks."

"Okay." He handed me the ground espresso beans, a filter, and a scoop. I bypassed the scoop and sprinkled a healthy amount of the finely ground coffee into the filter that lined the silver attachment, just like I'd watched my sister do countless times.

"There's so many bells, whistles, and chrome on this machine for basically forcing hot water through to make a cup of coffee," I said.

"Actually, it's *extremely* hot, pressurized water, and an espresso machine has a way of pulling out the flavor," Coach said. "And in order to do that, you'll want to tamp it down for tighter-packed coffee." Coach compressed the grounds by tapping the silver cup against the counter. He then reattached it to the machine.

He pushed a button, and a green light on the control panel lit that the water was reaching the ideal temperature of 250 degrees.

"That's just below the boiling point," I said.

He nodded. "It uses extremely hot water to extract the espresso shot, or, in your case," he laughed, "double shots."

Within minutes, a syrupy liquid shot with a foamy, creamy head streamed out of the machine and into my cup.

"Yum."

"Careful, Chlo, it's hot."

I waited a few minutes for it to cool down before I took my first sip. My eyes practically watered.

"That's, uh, pretty stout," I said, and Coach laughed.

"I think the word is strong," he said. "Espresso's the real deal. If you need a pick-me-up, it'll do it."

"No joke." But I didn't have time to waste so I polished off the double shot, grabbed a bear claw, and headed toward my car.

"Uh, where are you going with that?" Coach said.

"What?" I looked around. Had I accidentally picked up something on my clothes?

"The bear claw." His graying eyebrows furrowed.

"Oh, this?" I waved the cinnamon-glazed, buttery, flaky

goodness toward him. "I'm going to eat it on the way to work."

Coach shook his head and grabbed the Danish out of my hands. "Your sister would kill me if she knew I let you drive your new car and eat a sticky bun."

"It's not a sticky bun. It's a bear claw. I took the one that was least sticky," I said, but Coach pointed toward the door that led to the garage like a drill instructor.

"It'll be waiting for you when you come home. Have a good day at work."

"Killjoy," I mumbled under my breath.

"Or I could give it to Zoey and Lana." His voice echoed toward me.

"Don't you dare, Coach! That's my bear claw."

The advantage to driving a sports car was its speed. I made it from my sister's house to the cobblestone sign that announced the Napa Valley Point Resort and Winery in record time.

I pulled into the underground employee parking structure, and parked away from the mass number of cars. My rubber-soled clogs didn't make a sound on the concrete as I approached the garage entrance into the hotel, which was why they never heard me.

"I think they're going to move Chloe to another department," Barry said.

I ducked beside one of the hotel shuttle vans.

"Why? Because she spilled some wine?" Emerson said.

"Spilled some wine? She completely soaked that guest," Barry said.

"Eh, it was her first time."

"And probably her last. You met Victorine. What part of her by-the-book approach seems open to screwups? Plus, I heard her asking if there were any concierge positions available."

"Victorine could have been asking for someone else. Besides, the guy said he did it," Emerson said, and Barry scoffed.

"If you actually believed him I've got a bridge in New York I'd like to sell you." Barry's tone was as sharp as his personality. "Nope. I think Chloe's consigned to the concierge desk where she can't fuck things up."

"Have you ever spoken to a concierge before? That's a completely guest-facing position. Based on your logic, if Victorine wanted to get Chloe away from guests the last place she'd put her is at the concierge desk. The potential to screw things up is huge, especially in a resort like the Point where the concierge deals with expensive guest requests. No, if Victorine wants to ensure Chloe doesn't fuck up, she'll put her somewhere else."

It was the second time I felt zapped by something I'd overheard. *Enough.* I may not have been the best wine educator, but I wasn't going to be reassigned. *Nope.* Besides, we'd all just started. *There's got to be a learning curve allowed.* And if there wasn't, I'd just have to up my game. I stood, tucked my shirt back into my khakis, ensured the notebook was secure, and walked toward them wearing a smile. I was getting good at faking it.

"Hey, guys."

Barry's tan complexion seemed to drain of color.

"What's up, Chlo?" Emerson the poet may not say much, but he wasn't a douche. I didn't like what he'd said, but he wasn't saying it to be mean.

"Nothing much. Just getting into work early to brush up on my wine skills," I said, without making eye contact with the Flash of nothingness next to me. "I had a rough start, so I figure it's all up from here."

Emerson grinned. "Can't get any worse, could it?"

I chuckled. "Now, don't go jinxing me."

He laughed.

"Catch you guys in the cave. That's where we're meeting today, right?"

"The vineyard," Barry said.

"Oh." I glanced at Emerson, who confirmed with a nod. "Okay, see you there."

The only way I'd be able to find the inside guy was by staying employed at the Point. Not knowing where we were supposed to meet for training was not a step in that direction. I slowly inhaled, centered myself with a deep, cleansing breath, and opened the door into the hotel. A long corridor that led from the executive offices to the back hallway and locker rooms greeted me. With my focus on getting to the time clock by the locker rooms, I didn't see him step out of the office. Nor did he see me. Our bodies collided, and to make matters worse I tripped over my clogs and fell smack on my ass. The sudden jolt seemed to kick-start the espresso. The caffeine rushed through my veins like a volt of energy, and like the Bride of Frankenstein, brought me back to life.

"Excuse me, you all right, then?"

Dazed, I looked into blue-green eyes that were as magnificent as the ocean and just as easy to get swept away by. They weren't hazel. They were this blend of something I'd never seen. They almost seemed to change from blue to green as I watched.

I nodded.

"My apologies," he said with an accent, and I thought maybe I had been hit harder than I knew.

"Actually, I think I ran into you," I said.

His long, narrow face held a smile well.

"Yes, but you're the one on the floor, aren't you?" He extended his hand. "May I?"

I slipped my hand in his and he pulled me to my feet effortlessly. I straightened myself out and stood in front of him. "Thanks."

"I don't believe we've met. I'm Rob Chambers." He had this ridiculously hot English accent that made my knees weak.

"Oh, the owner?"

He tipped his head. "One of them. And who do I have the pleasure of meeting?"

"Chloe. Chloe Dorsey."

"And where are you stationed, Ms. Dorsey?"

I stared at him like he was Benedict Cumberbatch, but damn if that wasn't who he reminded me of. And like Sherlock, he had this rich, sexy-as-hell voice. The man could read the phone book and I'd probably orgasm.

"Stationed?" It was all I could say while I stared into his eyes.

"Your position at the Point?" A heap of auburn curls was even messy like his British alter ego.

"Right." He was devastatingly handsome. "Uh, my station's in the cave."

When he laughed, his high cheekbones tinged with color in his otherwise pale face. "The cave? Now, we can't have that."

"Oh, no. I mean I'm a wine—"

"Please excuse the interruption," Victorine reached for my forearm, but he intercepted her.

"Victorine, is Ms. Dorsey one of our new wine educators?" He spoke to her, but looked at me. His eyes seemed to shift colors again. I didn't have an accent fetish, but I could if he kept talking. *Damn.* Listening to him was like a binge marathon of Sherlock.

"Yes, Chloe was recently hired. She began her wine training yesterday."

"How'd that go?"

I felt the heat rush to my face. As much as I thought I was a good liar, I wasn't. "Uh, well...."

"We began with barrel tasting," Victorine said, and I cringed.

"Bit rough, was it?" The lilt in his voice made everything he said, including his spot-on description of my performance, sound eloquent and not like a complete and utter fuckup.

"A bit," I said.

"Nothing that can't be amended," Victorine said, placing a gentle hand on my shoulder. "Chloe's skill sets may be better suited for a position in the back of the house."

It was the only time I broke eye contact with the owner and looked at her. "Like the concierge desk?" *Like what Barry said is true?*

The curt shake of her head made my stomach fall. "No, the concierge desk is in the front of the house, which is a highly visible position." Her eyes widened. "However..." She smiled at Rob as if delivering bad news was something she enjoyed. *Bitch.* "I had the opportunity to speak with the human resources department, who thought you might be better positioned in the inventory and stock room, which requires organizing, loading, and unloading materials."

"Inventory? My life is such a mess, do I look like I can take stock of anything?"

Rob's laughter made me smile.

"Well, we can discuss this later," Victorine said, trying to usher me away from the owner.

"Actually, I'd like to finish the discussion now." It had to be the espresso giving me a shot of courage.

"All right, well, there are other BOH jobs that may interest you," she said.

"BOH? What is that?" I glanced at Rob.

"It stands for back of the house." He crossed his arms but when he did, it didn't come across as rude or standoffish. It was more like he was striking an elegant pose.

"Back of the house? As in the opposite of the front of the house?" I said.

Victorine held up her hand in a defensive position, as if she was blocking everything I had to say or would say. "Back of the house employees are vital to the success of the Point Resorts. Our back of the house staff members work behind the scenes where all the magic happens," she said, and I think she actually believed her own hype. "The Point Resorts wouldn't survive without the back of the house staff, because without the BOH crew there'd be no services to upsell."

"So, you want me behind the scenes." *This can't be happening. I'll never find the inside guy if I'm not in the wine cave. Or in the vicinity of the wine-making process. I can't be stuck inside the hotel.*

"There are many BOH jobs to choose from. If inventory isn't a good fit, there's also a porter position available. Our porters come in at the end of the night to help clean the kitchen."

"Would that be in the housekeeping department?" My chest tightened and my breathing felt clipped—all the signs of an impending panic attack. "Was I that awful yesterday that now you want me to clean the kitchen *after* everyone's left?" It sounded as pathetic as I felt.

"No, a porter is assigned to the kitchen department, not housekeeping."

I had to laugh because there was no other option, save crying. "*Or* you could combine the inventory clerk and porter and I'll be half-assed at both and together that will make me *almost* a halfway decent employee." I didn't care that I was in the presence of one of the owners. If anything, it gave me the strength to speak my mind.

"Victorine," I kept my voice calm, "I didn't pack up my life, place most of it in storage, and move from Southern California to Napa to be a porter or an inventory clerk. I'm sure those are fine positions and extremely valuable to the hotel. However, I *chose* the Point because they offered me the chance to," I thought of Dan and took a play from his unethical playbook, "*utilize* my educational background in an industry I'm extremely interested in." *And the Point was the only interview I've had in three years.* But she didn't need to know that.

When neither she nor Rob said anything, I did.

"I realize I didn't get off to the best start yesterday, but surely there's a learning curve to any new position at the Point?"

Rob smiled, and Victorine slowly nodded. "There is. It just seemed like you weren't as interested in the winemaking aspect as the others."

"It was my first day," I said without apology.

"Victorine," Rob interjected, "for weeks, the corporate office has hounded me to do my part with the Train the Trainer program that the Point Resorts mandate of all their owners." He paused and directed the conversation toward me. "It's a corporate mandate where owners learn every aspect of the hotel so that they can assist in a pinch. I've already learned the wine educator job, so," he pivoted toward Victorine, "why don't you let me train the trainer with Chloe?"

My heart raced, and I wasn't sure if it was the double

shot or the offer.

"It's highly unusual for an owner to train line staff," she said, as if the pecking order was lost on me.

"Agreed. But I think it would be quite brilliant to see how much I remember from my wine training with you," he said, with just the right amount of edge that Victorine lightly tugged on the bottom of her black blazer, which seemed to straighten out not only the jacket, but her place in the hierarchy.

"I realize how limited your time is, so perhaps Ms. Dorsey could train with you in the mornings and save her afternoons for the more mundane tasks, like setting up the wine cellar room for dinners and wine pairing events," she said.

"Brilliant idea." Rob turned toward me and propped his elbow out as if I'd slip my arm through his and skip merrily on our way. Or maybe his stance was just some weird British thing. "Shall we?" He was cocksure and polite at the same time, which was another dangerous combination.

I practically bowed toward him. "Yes, we shall."

I didn't look back at Victorine or wait for her permission. I simply took Rob's cue and left.

CHAPTER **TWENTY-THREE**

TONY

"Good morning, Mr. Mahoney, this is Trista, how may I assist you?"

I knew it was standard operating procedure for the hotel operator to greet me by my registered name, which made me imagine what happened when guests registered under an alias. Through my research of the Point, I discovered an online board from former employees willing to spill the secrets of the five-diamond resort. One discussion link claimed Keith Richards, who was a frequent guest of the Point's New York property, went by the name Mr. Big Stuff.

"Trista, I was hoping you could point me in the direction of a restaurant in Napa for a," I thought to how I'd phrased it to Chloe, "date."

"Excellent," Trista said. "I think our concierge desk could best serve you. If you don't mind holding, I'll transfer."

"Actually," I spoke before I was transferred. "I'd rather

have a referral from a local for a place that only the locals know about."

"Okay, well, is this a first or fifth date?" she asked, and I laughed.

"Uh, it's a first date, why?"

"Rocco's is a great first date place. It's not in Napa, but it's in Yountville, which is a small town just ten minutes north of the Point. It's one of those sneeze while you're driving and miss it places. But Rocco's is worth it. It's a wonderful Italian restaurant with a huge menu and private booths. It's where my husband took me on our first date," she said.

I smiled. "Sounds perfect. Can you make a reservation for me, or is that something the concierge desk can do?"

"A few of the best things about Rocco's are they don't take reservations, they serve great beer, and they won't close if people are still waiting for a table and it's midnight."

"My kind of place." I grabbed the pen and pad of paper on the nightstand beside the bed. "So how exactly do I get to Yountville?" It sounded like the name of a town in one my niece's Dr. Seuss books.

By the end of the call, I had directions, no need for reservations, and everything lined up for a first date—except the date. *Why didn't I get Chloe's phone number?*

I picked up the phone again and pressed the button for the operator. Before Trista could finish the standard greeting, I cut her off.

"Hey, Trista, it's Tony Mahoney again."

"Hello. How can I assist you?"

"Would it be possible for you to *discreetly* get a message to one of the new wine educators?"

"Absolutely. What message would you like me to deliver and to whom should I deliver it?"

She was good. I jotted Trista's name to include in the tip envelopes they provided at the end of my stay.

"Trista, her name is Chloe Dorsey and as I said she's one of the new wine educators. I realize the Point policy is against guests and staff fraternizing, however, before Chloe began working at the Point we met on a wine train."

"Wonderful," she said.

"It was, actually." I thought back to Chloe's soft touch when her fingers strolled down my arm in the train's corridor.

"What message would you like to get to Ms. Dorsey?"

"Could you please tell her that I found the only place in wine country that doesn't serve wine, and if she'd like to meet in the lobby at seven I'll be waiting."

Trista broke from her script and laughed. "Excellent. Chloe Dorsey. Seven o'clock—and in respects to the meeting place, may I offer a suggestion?"

"Of course, please."

"The Point Resort lobby is well occupied by guests and hotel staff," she said, and I knew immediately she was protecting Chloe from a rule infraction. "However, our west-end vineyards are open to the public."

"Thank you. Would you please change our meeting place to the west-end vineyards?"

"Wonderful. I'll personally ensure Ms. Dorsey gets the

message," she said.

"Thank you, Trista."

"My pleasure, Mr. Mahoney. Enjoy your date."

"Thank you, I will." I replaced the cordless phone back in its charging station, grabbed the basketball out of my carry-on gym bag, and headed toward the outdoor courts I had spotted on property.

CHAPTER **TWENTY-FOUR**

CHLOE

"Would it be an accurate assessment that the barrel tasting presented difficulties?"

Rob Chambers stood with his hands behind his back and leaned toward me to bridge the space between us. We were in the hallway in front of the time clock. I placed my card into the mouth of the machine and waited for it to spit it out.

"That would be a kind assessment of my dismal performance." I placed my timecard in the elongated steel file rack that hung on the wall.

Rob extended his arm toward the executive suites where the owners and general manager had offices. But instead of going straight into the executive offices, we turned left into the den of administrative assistants, bookkeepers, and copiers. The room buzzed with electronics and the smell of a strawberry-scented air freshener.

"The good news is you can only go up from here." He opened a side door that led from the hotel to an area of the resort grounds I hadn't seen.

"This isn't the cave." I blocked the sun from my eyes.

He laughed. "No, this isn't the cave." He extended his arm toward a narrow pathway.

I took the lead even though I didn't know where we were headed. The cobblestone footpath provided a route that I followed.

"This is the west-end vineyards, which are open to the public." He walked behind me.

I leaned toward one of the vines and smelled the rich fruit. "If it's open to the public, that must mean it doesn't contain the mother vine." I stood and continued walking. "*Or* it does because the best place to put something you want to hide is out in the open because no one ever sees it. Refrigerator blindness at its best." When I no longer heard his feet behind me, I turned around.

Rob's face looked aghast—even for a Brit.

"What?" I brushed from my nose down to my chin. "Do I have something on me?"

"That's extraordinary," he said.

"What? What's extraordinary?"

"Rich and I have operated this winery for nearly a decade, and no one's ever made that connection," he said.

"What connection?"

"That the mother vine is located out in the open in the west-end vineyard for just that reason."

"Nuh-uh." My eyes widened and I glanced at the vine I had just sniffed. "This is"—I looked around the vineyard, but no one else was in it. Still, I lowered my voice—"the *mother of all vines is here?"*

The smile on his face was like the one Coach wore when his football team won. Rob was as proud of his grapes as Coach was of his players.

"Wow." I stood in stunned disbelief. "Really?"

He nodded. "Really."

"And it's open to the public?"

"It is." Rob walked toward me. "You referred to it as refrigerator blindness?"

I nodded.

"Rich and I call it 'selective sight.' People tend to miss what's right in front of them."

"I couldn't agree more," I said, and then returned my focus to the rows upon rows of vines. "Still, I can't believe this is it?" I gently touched a leaf. "Amazing."

"Even when we tell the wine educators that the west-end vineyard contains the mother vine for our cabernet sauvignon, they don't believe us. They think we're still hiding its location and that only a *select few* know where it *really* is on the property."

"Denial is a very powerful emotion." My response was instinctual.

"How do you mean?"

"Well, emotions are both powerful and complex. And an emotion like denial can exert a strong influence over someone's ability to interpret facts." I thought of an example I always used in the undergraduate classes I instructed.

"We're taught from an early age to control our emotions—stop crying, don't be afraid, quit overreacting—

so, over time, we begin to substitute what we're told to believe for what we know."

Rob's changeable eyes were as blue as the sky above us.

"So," I continued when he didn't seem bored, "when we're told that the mother vine is as protected as the gold at Fort Knox, and then we're shown that it's kept out in the open, the facts don't align with what we've been conditioned to believe—so we reject or turn to denial, thinking this isn't right. The mother vine would *never* be available to the general public."

"Interesting. How is it that you know so much about denial?"

I laughed. "Well, besides having some experience with it, I also have a background in the psychological dynamics of how people control their emotions." I rolled my eyes. "Sorry. That's a very passive-aggressive way of saying I'm a licensed psychologist. I just learned early in my career not to reveal I was a shrink because everyone seems to think it's license to unload."

"Fascinating." He was standing with his hands behind his back again, which made me wonder what he was afraid he'd do with his arms when they weren't restrained. Or perhaps his stance meant nothing, and as Freud would say, sometimes a cigar is just a cigar.

"Did you have your own practice before moving to Napa?" he asked.

"No, I chose to teach and offer my services at the college counseling center."

"You seem young to be a psychologist."

I smiled. "Not really, although a lot of people think that. My husband used to say that if we had a dollar for every person who said it, we could go on a world trip."

"You're married?"

I noticed the subtle glance at my left hand. My ring finger was bare, a conscious decision I made shortly after Ben died. Our wedding bands were in the pine box along with all my favorite memories.

"I'm widowed," I said, putting it all out there. At this point, what did I have to lose?

"I'm sorry."

"Me too."

"You've had some life-altering experiences thrown your way."

"The same could be said of you," I said. Rob couldn't be more than five years older than me. Maybe ten, but still.

"Being in the right place at the right time had much to do with my success," he said as we walked around the maze-like vineyard, me still in the lead. "I'm still fascinated by the topic of denial."

I nodded.

"If I'm understanding you correctly, you believe that denial is the reason why people never believe the mother vine is where we say it is located?"

I turned around. "Those who don't believe the mother vine's location are most likely denying the facts, which allows them to keep spinning their wheels rather than stopping to face reality."

"I'm not sure I'm following."

"Okay, if a wine educator is shown the west-end vineyard and told this is where the mother vine is located, then the entire secrecy of its location is for nothing. That doesn't fit with what they believe, which is we must protect the mother vine at all cost. So, denial comes into play. It's easier to deny reality than accept it. If the vine is so readily accessible, how can it be protected? People will want to believe it's a lie because they don't want to think it could easily be stolen."

"We have video monitoring and guards," Rob said.

"I believe you, but when a wine educator or winemaker challenges you, that may be why."

"Denial," he said.

I slowly nodded. "The upside is that denial doesn't work long-term. Reality always wins. However, when reality does set in, the reaction to the truth often turns to blame. So, when a winemaker or wine educator actually comes to grips that the west-end vineyard contains the mother vine, and a section is—God forbid—stolen, their first reaction will be to blame... you."

"I'd be blamed if it rained at our summer staff picnic," Rob deadpanned.

"Blaming the boss always eases the pain when reality bites," I said, and he laughed.

"I think Victorine may have been correct about your skill set," he said, and it felt like my heart plunged to my stomach.

"Really? You want me in the back of the house."

His smile was as warm as the sun that bathed us. "No.

Your talents wouldn't be utilized in the back of the house."

I exhaled. "Okay, so where? I really wanted to work with wine."

"And you will. In our marketing division."

"Marketing? Uh, I'm not sure if you missed how poorly I did with the barrels yesterday, let alone the wine thief. The only thing I know about wine is how to spill it. And drink it."

"Making wine is the easy part." His arms relaxed by his side. "Creating new approaches to entice people toward wine is the real challenge." He gently touched my shoulder. "Ms. Dorsey, you know how people operate—how they think and why they react the way they do. Your background is a perfect fit for us as we explore and develop new techniques toward reaching the next generation of wine lovers."

Huh. Vines with plump, juicy grapes surrounded me, and the owner of one of the most award-winning wineries in Napa stood before me offering what would amount to a career. It would mean making Napa my home, not just a layover.

"Please join our team," he said. "I oversee the marketing division, so you already know who you'd report to." He gently smiled. "I think it would be a splendid opportunity, with a salary that would more than compensate for your recent move. I'd have you begin as a wine educator because the exposure to guests is invaluable. And in that position, you can begin to hone your skills for what people are drawn to at our winery."

The sun seemed to shine even brighter as I looked into

his green-blue eyes. Accepting Rob's offer would center on moving forward, not looking back. What Winters did or didn't do with the mother vine wouldn't break the Point, because they were already centered on future wines. I offered a smile of my own. "Thank you."

"Is that a yes, then?" His inquiry sounded even sweeter with his accent.

"It is. I mean, yes. Yes, I'll join your team." I held out my hand, and he pulled me into his side for an unexpected, awkward embrace.

"Ms. Dorsey, I think you'll be as wonderful an addition to our winery as when we transplanted the mother vine. I expect great things to happen."

CHAPTER **TWENTY-FIVE**

TONY

Who is that guy and why is he hugging Chloe?

I palmed the basketball that had bounced against an edge of the backboard and rolled off the court. Just beyond the court was a vineyard we hadn't toured during our Wine Train stop. I glanced at the sign beside the entrance. "Westend Vineyard—Open to Public." Beneath that in italicized print it read, "Grapes are sensitive! Please stay on the path."

Grapes are sensitive? Whatever. I stared at the dude with his arm around Chloe. The sun made her black hair shine, and even from a distance I could tell she was smiling.

Who the fuck is he? I bounced the ball on the packed dirt that lead to a rock path. The bounce on the dirt echoed among the rows of vines. Chloe and the guy looked in my direction.

I cocked my head and gave a noncommittal wave, like I was just some guy shooting hoops while they were getting their hug on. I was at least eleven feet from the basketball hoop, but I was determined to pull a Steph Curry and crush it.

I dribbled into the dirt and spun to face the back of the basket. Feet planted, arms elevated, wrists snapped. I took a leap in the gravel, and the shot was not only successful, but, like Curry, it wasn't anything I'd ever be able to replicate. The ball sailed over the backboard and dropped into the net. *Swoosh.*

***

CHLOE

"Someone's peacocking for you," Rob said.

I nervously laughed. "I don't think that was for me."

Rob arched an eyebrow. "Would that be another example of denial?"

I felt heat rush to my cheeks. "Okay, yes, that shot may have been for my benefit."

"Do you know him?" Rob walked us toward the basketball court that Tony occupied.

"His name is Tony Mahoney. We were on a wine train together, and he's a guest of the Point. He has an interest in wine…." I didn't finish the sentence. I gave Tony my word that his cover wouldn't be blown. Besides, I was about to help create the next award-winning wine. I didn't know how, only that for the first time since Ben died, I felt like

I had purpose. Rob positioned himself at the corner of the court. I took my place beside him like the shadow I would become to learn and absorb everything I could about the hotel and wine business. It was time for change.

Tony turned, looked at me, and smiled. "Can I interest either of you in a game of horse?"

"Playing horse is the only time I can letter in basketball," I said with a hint of laughter. "But no, thank you."

He chuckled. "The hoop's not regulation height, but it's a great venue for horse." Tony hoisted the ball toward the basket. It hit the backboard, circled the rim, and effortlessly dropped through the net. If he was showboating, his muscles flexing in his sleeveless tank was impressive. The ball rolled toward his feet. He bent over and palmed it like an athletic god.

"Horse? That's when you shoot hoops and miss one letter at a time?" Rob asked.

"If you miss the shot, you get a letter," Tony said.

"I'm more of a croquet man," he said, and I almost laughed until I realized he was serious.

Croquet? Really? Bummer. But it did explain his lanky, buggy-whip-like arms. Rob had no definition to him. What he lacked in physicality, he made up for with style and grace.

"From the looks of it, I'd be out of my league," he said to Tony. "But thank you for the offer." Rob approached him, but stopped short of connecting with Tony on a handshake level. "I'm Rob Chambers."

Tony tucked the ball under his arm, and his forearms bulged. "Tony Mahoney."

I waved toward Tony. "Hey again."

"Hello, Chloe." He took a step toward me, and the odor of man sweat hit me. I wished I was embarrassed to admit it, but I wasn't—the aromatic scent of man sweat drove me crazy. My sister would think I was crazy, but male sweat was hot. From graduate school, I knew my penchant for man sweat was in my genetics. I could also cite research that linked male sweat and female arousal, so I wasn't alone, but still, try explaining to anyone the chemical reaction of male sweat as a turn-on, and it fell flat. The closer Tony got to me, the more I inhaled him—his sweat had a woodsy scent with a hit of vanilla. *Aaahhh.*

He had a manly man scent that made me want to whiff more of him. Some guys' sweat was gross, but Tony's wasn't. My heart rate increased, my mood, which was already good, got even better, and when I eyed the sweat running down his neck, my arousal spiked along with my body temperature.

He wiped his hand on his shorts and shook hands with Rob. "You're one of the owners of the Point," he stated with confidence that made me want to push him to the court and mount him like some sex-starved animal. *What is my problem?*

"One of them, yes," Rob said, and his accent redirected me.

I vacillated between two men, who were both hot and jumpable for different reasons. I brushed my clog against the court to ground myself. *Get a grip, Chloe. Tony's a spy about to turn rogue and Rob's your boss.* I was beginning to act like the women I used to counsel on campus. They'd come in and claim to be instantly in love with someone.

I called it "insta-love," and it was misleading. Those women weren't instantly in love; they were, however, instantly attracted to someone. But women had been conditioned to believe that sex without love was slutty, wrong, and shameful. Slut shaming was almost as big an issue as body shaming on campus. So, when women had sex with a guy and feared it was too soon, they deflected by claiming "insta-love." I tried to show them an alternative view—insta-attraction. And that's all it was with Tony—an attraction. An instant attraction, and his manly sweat didn't tame the pull toward him.

"Mr. Mahoney, I was told you recently enjoyed Napa's local Wine Train."

"From what I remember," Tony said laughing.

"Well, if anything that you discovered about wine is a bit blurry, shall we say…," Rob's demeanor was as wrinkle free as his suit. "I have an open-door policy. So please stop by. Anytime we can encourage a devotion and following to our wine, we will." Rob reached into the front pocket of his dress shirt and handed Tony his business card. "It has my cell number too. Don't hesitate to phone or text with any questions. Have you joined our wine club yet?"

Smooth. I watched Rob work Tony into a corner.

"Not yet." Tony stood in a broad stance, but it didn't thwart Rob.

"With each shipment, we include a little history about the wine and the process that went into its development."

Rob glanced at me. "I'll have a shipment sent to your house so you can see how it's packaged when it arrives."

"Wonderful." My heart skipped a beat. My sister would be thrilled. I didn't pay rent, but having an unexpected shipment of wine arrive from the Point would more than make up for being a mooch.

"I see you found our basketball court," Rob said.

"I did," Tony replied.

"Mr. Mahoney is staying with us for a month," I said, looping myself in with the Point and in turn with Rob, which decisively left Tony on the outside.

"I trust you are enjoying your stay so far?" Rob asked.

"So far." Tony's hold on the basketball looked pretty tight, but if he didn't want me to blow his cover, I couldn't fawn all over him. Or indicate that we were working together. I wasn't even sure we still should be working together. *What have I gotten myself into?*

"Excellent." Rob gestured with his head. "We won't keep you any further from your game."

Rob pivoted on the heel of his expensive-looking black dress shoes, and I followed. Part of me wanted to look back at Tony, but I didn't.

***

TONY

What the fuck was that? I tossed the business card to the

side of the court. I gripped the ball and hurled it toward the basket, where it slammed into the hoop and made the whole thing shake. I repeated the play over and over until my arms burned and my shoulders ached.

What would one of the owners of the Point want with Chloe? The only vineyard owner I knew well was Winters, who thought he was scrupulous but was too dishonest to have any moral high ground.

The most obvious answer was that Rob was "an owner," but more specifically, he was the owner of the place where Chloe worked—her boss. For all I knew, Chambers made a habit of having a personal chat with every new hire, to foster team building or some crap, even if he then never spoke to them again.

It didn't align with how Winters operated, but maybe that's why the Point was leading the charge in wine-making.

I bounced the ball off the backboard, caught it, and shot from wherever my feet landed. I repeated the drill, moving all over the court.

Still, if Chambers made it a habit of getting to know every new hire, why did he choose Chloe to start with? Something wasn't adding up.

If this was Winters's winery, he'd only seek Chloe out for what he'd want from her. *So, what does Chloe have that Chambers wants?*

I was at the midcourt line, took the shot, and missed. I couldn't feel my arms anymore, but my mind was still jumping. I grabbed the bottle of hotel water beside the basketball pole, twisted off the cap, leaned against the cold steel post, and chugged it down.

Chloe was a wine educator. A teacher. And a widow. *What am I missing?*

She's single, educated, and… alone? *I got nothing.* I reached for Rob's business card, which was about as exciting as one of Winters's. I understood why Winters was flat, he was a financier. The only things that turned him on were numbers. But Chloe? She was all fire and go. So, what was it about her that Chambers wanted? Or saw?

I thought of her attributes—Chloe was a good listener, she seemed to genuinely care about others; when Dan had extended an apology, she'd accepted it. She could talk to anyone, and her inquisitive personality didn't put people off; if anything she got people talking. *Hell, she got me to admit to someone other than Dan that I wasn't happy at my job.*

I leaned against the basketball pole. *That's it.* She got people talking. She was a counselor. And who better to have in your arsenal than a trained therapist who could use their analytical skills to explain human behavior. In the wine industry, hell, in any competitive industry, understanding consumers in an ever-changing marketplace was essential. Chloe was an untapped goldmine. *Why didn't I see that before?* My gut tightened. I hadn't seen it because I hadn't looked at Chloe as a corporate asset or liability. She was this fresh-faced, vibrant woman who had the ability to make a missing tooth look beautiful.

I'd bet money Chambers had discovered Chloe's credentials and jumped on the chance to have a psychologist in his resort and winery. *The fucker's brilliant.*

Shit. Where does that leave us? Will she still want to work with me after meeting the owner? Now it's personal. It's one thing to offer to help when it's simply a concept, but now Chambers has a face and most likely a connection with Chloe.

I glanced around the court and realized I had nothing but time on my hands and no one to spend it with.

Chloe was the wild card I hadn't anticipated. She may have proposed dinner to figure out how we could find Winters's inside man, but now it no longer felt like a date, but an assignment. *Or worse, obligation.* The only thing I had was a heavy heart, a gnawing gut, and a headful of doubt.

CHAPTER **TWENTY-SIX**

CHLOE

The line that led to the time clock was about two feet long with people, and whoever was at the time clock clearly didn't know how to operate the machine.

"It's probably Barry," I said into Rebel's ponytail.

"No doubt." She turned and her hair almost whacked me in the face. "You got any plans tonight?"

"I had dinner plans, but…." I cringed as soon as the words left my mouth.

"But?"

"I'm not so sure it's a good idea. Or if it's still on the table," I said, thinking of my distance toward Tony and the stunned look on his face when I left the court with Rob.

"Chloe Dorsey? Is there a Chloe Dorsey here?"

Rebel raised her hand and pointed toward me.

A twentysomething-year-old with strawberry-colored hair that complemented her hunter green PBX uniform approached me. "Are you Chloe Dorsey?"

"Yes, is everything okay?"

She grinned and leaned toward me. "I have a message from Mr. Mahoney."

"You do?" My body fired with a burst of adrenaline, which just didn't make sense.

She handed me a slip of paper that I opened. *Please meet Mr. Mahoney in the west-end vineyard at 7 pm.* I glanced at her. "Uh? The west-end vineyard?" My stomach knotted. *There's no way he could know that's where the mother vine is—could he? Did he hear us? Is that why he wants to meet me there?* Suddenly, my whole plan to team up with Tony to find Winters's mole seemed careless, stupid, and career-killing.

The woman, whose name tag read Trista, smiled. She leaned into me. "I actually suggested the west-end vineyard because it's off the radar from peering eyes. You know, so you can meet him there without anyone seeing you guys."

Shit. How many employees think that? The west-end vineyard was probably watched more closely than Area 51.

I slowly nodded. "Is there any way you could get a message to Mr. Mahoney that I won't be able to—"

"She'll be there," Rebel jumped in, and I immediately shook my head.

"Rebel, I can't."

"Yes, you can. And Trista here isn't going to tell anyone either, are you?"

Trista's wide blue eyes grew even larger. "No. I think it's romantic."

I waved my hands through the air. "Nope. It's not. Mr. Mahoney and I are... well, I proposed we have dinner because...." I raised my shoulders and thought of my new job offer. I had no business getting involved with catching a thief. "There's really no reason to meet him."

"But does *he* know that?" Rebel's name and nose ring didn't lend toward someone I would think of as pragmatic, but damn if the little renegade wasn't sensible.

"Uh, it's complicated," I said.

"So you didn't cancel?" Trista's face scrunched up like she had tasted something sour.

"No, I didn't cancel our dinner. But, it doesn't matter, because I'm not meeting him at the west-end vineyard."

"Why?" Rebel stared at me.

"It's just weird." *And God only knows who monitors that video feed.* I turned to Trista. "Is there any way you could reach out to him and cancel for me?"

Her strawberry curls sprung with life when she tilted her head. "Oh, bummer. He seemed excited about it. He said it was a first date."

I rolled my eyes. "It wasn't a first date, it was just a meeting." My body reacted to my betrayal with a sharp jab in my stomach. *Fucking gut.*

"Where food and beverages would be served?" Rebel said.

"Yeah, so?" I said.

"I get that you're from So Cal, but here in Northern California we call that a date," Rebel said. "Did Mahoney make dinner reservations with you?"

We both looked at Trista.

"No. I suggested Rocco's, which is in Yountville and doesn't require reservations," she said. "I'm about to end my shift, but I could ask him to meet you there?"

"Yes. Do that," Rebel said, and then looked at me. "Just go. It isn't like you have any better plans." She didn't even try to phrase her dismal assessment of my private life into a question.

"It's only Thursday," I said.

Rebel saw right through me. It wouldn't matter if it was Thursday, Friday, or Saturday. I sighed loudly. "Yeah, I don't have any plans."

"Excellent," Trista said. "I'll log back on to the computer and call him. We also have his cell number in the FrogKiss system so I can text him if he's not in his suite."

"Yah." I raised my fists in the air like pom-poms and feigned enthusiasm.

Trista left, and we inched forward in line. By the time we did clock off, I'd have an extra half hour on the books. Not that it would soon matter. Rob had made it sound like my salaried position would start as soon as I passed training.

Rebel glanced at my uniform. "Do you have time to go home and change?"

"My sister doesn't live *that* far away. It's about a twenty-minute drive."

"Without traffic," Rebel said. "And then you have to get back to Yountville. Everyone in Napa is clocking off. Come to my house and borrow something. I'm five minutes away *with* traffic."

I knew it was pointless to argue. When we finally reached the time clock, Rebel grabbed our cards and punched us out. While I followed Rebel to the parking garage, I texted my sister.

Chloe: Having dinner out. See you later.

CHAPTER **TWENTY-SEVEN**

TONY

I waited at a corner table beside a red-painted wall. The restaurant's patio section was slowly filling with couples and families. The hostess had found a table for two tucked beside the wood fire stove that crackled and hissed. Thin-crust topped pizza was pushed into the hearth with a large aluminum paddle that slid the pies effortlessly in and out of the oven.

I still wasn't convinced Trista's text message was real. *But who else would have sent it?* No one knew about our dinner—except Trista, the Uber driver who picked me up from the hotel, and Chloe, who showed about as much interest in seeing me as a root canal. The outside seating gave me a long view of the restaurants and bakeries that lined the street in Yountville.

Trista was right. Yountville could easily be driven past, but the atmosphere of the town was already worth the detour.

A line wrapped around the pastel-painted bakery across the street. Every time the front door to the pastry shop opened, someone departed with a coffee in one hand and a pink box in the other.

"*Yum*. Good things come in pink boxes," I said, and her laughter caught me off guard.

I glanced up, and Chloe stood there in a short, flowy dress that a good evening breeze would kick up and get things started for a guy. The style reminded me of something that may have been worn in the sixties. It had this funky green paisley print against a burgundy fabric that looked like it might be silk. It was flirty and retro and totally fit her personality. Damn if Chloe didn't wear it well. Her silver-painted toes popped out of strappy sandals that wrapped around her slender ankle. The shoes added three inches to her, and when I stood I smiled into her chocolate-colored eyes.

"You came," I said, and pulled out her chair.

She sat with a smile that didn't seem forced. "I did."

"I wasn't sure...." I took my seat across from her.

"Yeah, I'm sorry about that, but when I saw you on the basketball court, I didn't want to show any favoritism." She shook her head. "Anyway, Trista and Rebel were pretty insistent I show up."

"Rebel, she's one of the wine educators, right?"

"The only other female besides me," she said.

"And after you leave, she'll probably be the only one left," I said, and wished I hadn't.

"What makes you think I'm leaving? I just started yesterday."

"I guess it was seeing you with Rob Chambers." There, it was out in the open.

But Chloe's lips remained pursed behind wine-colored lipstick that made me want to part them and taste her with my tongue. Her black hair was pushed off her face with a silver band that reflected the twinkling lights strung along the patio and made it seem like she was glittering. She was lethally pretty. The more I stared into her brown eyes, the closer I came to wanting to kiss her.

Instead, I handed her the drink menu. "Since you're the wine expert, I thought perhaps you could order a bottle for us."

"I thought this place didn't serve wine," she said with a raised eyebrow.

"It's the only thing Trista got wrong," I said.

Chloe's eyebrows furrowed with confusion.

"Trista was right about Rocco's having a great menu, open seating, and being the best place to take someone on a first date," I said without apology.

Chloe's lips curved into a mischievous smile behind the drink menu. When the waiter, a guy named Austin, arrived at our table, she looked at him.

"May we have two pints of amber ale with two shots of your best whiskey?"

"Two boilermakers," Austin said, and headed to the bar.

I rapped my hands on the edge of the table. "Beer and shots? I'll drink to that."

"It's almost summer, and beer really hits the spot. Besides, I'm not a fan of high-end cocktails that look pretty but don't always taste good." She laughed and reverted her focus to the menu.

Austin returned with two rust-colored shots that almost matched the amber ale. After he placed them before us and left, I raised my shot. Chloe set down her menu and delicately picked up the shot glass.

"To…." I completely lost my train of thought.

"Beer!" She briefly made eye contact, threw the shot back, and chased it with the ale. Her eyes squinted and mouth puckered, but all I saw was her beauty.

Fuck. I'm in trouble.

"So, what *were* you doing with the owner?" I asked.

"Working," she said, avoiding eye contact.

That damn menu was her go-to when she didn't want to look at me, and no amount of beer was going to change that.

"Chloe," I said, and the tone in my voice made her set down her menu. "It's my responsibility to find Winters's other guy. I think it's incredibly sweet that you offered to help, but this entire debacle is mine to sort out."

Her hands interlaced together on the table.

"You don't owe me anything. And just for the record, that whole wine thief thing in the cave, and covering for you, well, that was selfishly for my benefit so I didn't have to watch your spirit get knocked down a peg by someone as wretched as Victorine."

Chloe's eyes looked glassy, and I didn't think it was the whiskey. "Thank you."

She was about to resume reading the menu, but I reached over and placed my hand on the appetizer section. She set it down.

"I owe you a better explanation." I drew a deep breath, looked at her directly, and let honesty be my guide.

She didn't move. Her hands remained poised in front of her.

"As I told you, I'm on assignment for Samuel Winters, who owns multiple corporations and Winters Winery."

She slowly nodded, so I continued.

"As a corporate intelligence gatherer," I said without breaking eye contact. "What that actually means is that I infiltrate targeted corporations to gather information on their products, their portfolio, their business model, and anything else necessary to analyze their performance in the marketplace to basically systemically hinder their effectiveness with what made them a threat."

"You turn their strengths or assets into a liability or weakness," she said.

"Exactly."

"And you're at the Point to do that with their 2016 Napa Valley Cabernet Sauvignon?"

I pushed back my shoulders, grabbed the pint, and took a long, slow drink. I waved the empty glass toward Austin.

"Other than Dan and Ty, you're the first person I've ever told the full extent of what I do."

"That must feel liberating," she said with a gentle smile.

"You have no idea. It's like I live this double life, and for a while it didn't bother me, but over time it's just weighed me down."

"When we aren't authentic, it affects our physical and

mental health.”

“There’s the therapist side of you again,” I said, suddenly embarrassed. “But I don’t want you to feel obligated to help me because you listened to a disenfranchised employee.”

“I don’t.” Her words hinted at unspoken emotions that had her reaching for the menu again.

“Chloe. What’s going on?”

I saw the steadiness in her gaze and knew she wanted to talk but something was holding her back. *Is it Ben? Or has Rob already tainted the waters with rich talk and promises?* Chambers may not be like Winters, but my gut said otherwise.

“I was offered a *really* good job, well, career today,” she said. “And now….”

“And now you’re not so sure that helping me is in your career’s best interest.”

“Exactly.”

“Then don’t. Really. It’s okay. You’re off the hook. Shit, you were never on the hook. I started this assignment and I’ll see it through, but,” I held up my hand to allay any fear, “my focus will be on identifying the other inside guy to shut down his operation.”

“You’d do that?” The surprise in her voice saddened me.

“Of course I’d do that. I may be many things, but I’m an honest thief.”

Her laughter brought Austin to our table.

“Sounds like someone’s having fun,” he said.

Chloe smiled. “Actually, we are.”

“Wonderful. Are you ready to order?” he asked.

I glanced at Chloe, who nodded and asked for cheese ravioli and minestrone soup. I ordered the meat lasagna, which I would regret tomorrow on the court, but the smell of garlic from the pizza oven made me salivate.

"Austin," I asked before he left. "Can we get some bread?"

When a small loaf arrived, I held it over the wicker basket and broke it in half. The dry crust crumbled into the paper lining.

"So, back in the day, I may have been an altar boy," I said with a grin. "And I've never forgotten Father August, who told us that breaking bread with your enemy was a sign of forgiveness and moving forward." I extended a piece of bread toward her. "Chloe, you were never my enemy, but I betrayed your trust."

"And in turn, I caused you to question my motives about dinner." She accepted the bread.

"Besides serving as a symbolic sign of forgiveness, breaking bread with someone can also mean the start of friendship," I said, and she raised her eyebrow at me. "Scout's honor."

"You were a Boy Scout too?"

"It's a Catholic thing. Altar boy, Boy Scout, football, basketball, bingo—basically anything the school needed us to sign up for, we did."

She laughed and held the bit of bread toward mine. "To friendship."

I tapped the edge of her bread in a makeshift toast. "To friendship."

As Austin cleared our dinner plates, Chloe reached into her purse and placed a notebook on the table.

"Whatcha got there?"

"It was my husband's," she said. "It has notes from a wine tour we went to in Santa Barbara. Stupidly, I thought the notes would help flush out Winters's inside guy, like he'd notice I knew nothing, which let's be honest, I don't need notes to help me sell that."

When she laughed her entire face brightened.

"Then I thought if that harebrained idea didn't work, I considered feeding him *or her* the wrong wine-making process, but neither of my ideas are very solid."

I didn't even mask my laughter. "Yeah, it's probably a good thing that I'm doing this on my own."

"Actually," she tapped her pen against the pad, "this notebook has *a lot* of blank pages that I can write on with new ideas, and since I gave you my word that I'd help, and I don't break my word, I'm going to see this through." She paused. "And, Tony."

I looked at her.

"I want to."

I pressed into the table. "Are you serious?"

"Yes."

"What about your new job? I'm not sure I feel right about this."

"I hate to quote your buddy, Dan, but when I heard your conversation, I remember him saying something about utilizing me and that I wouldn't get caught if you didn't rat me out. Or something to that effect."

"I'd never involve you. I mean, if it ever came to that, I'd take the fall. And no one, not even Winters, would know you ever helped."

"I believe you."

How is it that those three small words—I believe you—spoken by Chloe, carry a mantle of responsibility I have to meet?

"Tony, you mentioned that you're an honest thief and I appreciate your willingness to sort through this Winters thing without me. But, *I wouldn't feel right* not helping you after you've been so truthful and showed me your hand, so to speak."

"Well, I did bare my soul in my hotel room," I said, to her amusement.

"Okay then! Since we're back on the case together, I'll take notes like a *real* detective. So, where do we begin?"

Her voice held the most adorable amount of enthusiasm. I wanted to lean across the table and kiss her. Instead, I lowered my voice and conspicuously glanced around the restaurant as if I was scouting the place. When I shifted my attention back to her, her brown eyes widened with interest. I steadied her in my sights like I was about to reveal top secret information that would put her life in peril because it came from a classified file that had led to the premature death of everyone who had ever read it. None of which was even remotely true, but it just showed the overly dramatic effect she had on me. She wanted to be on the case and I wanted to be the man her gaze convinced me wasn't lost. A man with integrity, honor, and a dose of fun. Then I could make my case that we should be together.

202

CHAPTER **TWENTY-EIGHT**

CHLOE

"How is it when you're with someone you like, the hours fly by like minutes?"

When Tony was no longer undercover or on assignment or whatever he called it, the man who emerged was much more relaxed and carefree than I first experienced. It wasn't like he wasn't fun on the Wine Train, but I realized he was guarded. Since I knew why, I also understood how hard a balancing act it must have been for him.

"I'm having such a great time," I said. "I don't want to go home."

"Then don't. Hang out with me," he said.

I didn't shake my head or verbally disagree, but I also didn't say yes. I just sat in the moment of being wanted.

"Do you smell that?" Tony leaned into the table, and I tucked my notebook, which was filled with brilliant strategies to flush out Winters's inside guy, into my purse.

"We've *got* to go to that bakery." He cocked his head to a building behind me and across the street. It was the color of butter, and when I inhaled, the scent of freshly baked deliciousness pulled me out of my chair.

Tony glanced at the bill, left two hundred on the tray, and pocketed the receipt.

"May I help with dinner?" I asked on our way out.

He waved away my comment. "Please. That was cheap."

"I think it was the bottle of wine I ordered," I said.

"It was a good choice." He gently placed his hand on the small of my back and led me out of the restaurant and across the street. It was a simple gesture, but the presence of his hand on me felt so natural.

The bakery had a line, but unlike the wait at the time clock earlier in my night, everything in the air here smelled yummy. When we finally advanced through the door, the sweet and savory aroma of desserts, pastries, and bread floated through the air like an adult version of Candy Land. And the child in me emerged. While we waited for the bakery attendant to approach us, I lightly elbowed Tony.

"How 'bout we just order one of everything to go, please?" My joke was met by a nod.

"Another good idea," he said.

"Don't you just love it when a place lives up to their reputation?" a woman behind us remarked.

"What's their reputation?" Tony and I asked at the same time, and grinned at each other.

"This bakery is renowned for its breads, and its delicacies will make you feel like you died and went straight to heaven."

I turned to Tony. "I don't know 'stop' when it comes to sugar."

He slowly nodded. "Are you telling me this as your friend or potential workout coach?"

"Friend, definitely friend."

"Well, as your friend, everything's good in moderation."

I scoffed. "That's what every addict says."

"Then as your future basketball buddy, eat whatever you want tonight and we'll deal with tomorrow when it gets here."

"I think I like the basketball buddy better."

When the bakery attendant appeared with an open pink box, I really wanted to ask for one of everything. Instead, I pointed to a peanut butter chocolate-chip cookie that was as thick as the brownies. I then pointed toward a tray of gingerbread cookies with pink sugar sprinkles, and tapped the glass. "Two, please."

"Cookies?" Tony truly looked perplexed as he ordered tiramisu, an éclair, and a cinnamon roll.

"They're my weakness. I *love* cookies—like need-a-twelve-step-program-for-my-addiction love cookies. And I haven't seen a gingerbread man like this since I was a little girl."

"Can we get a dozen gingerbread men, please," Tony said, and I practically did a happy dance right in front of the baker. "And a double-shot, two-pump, no-whip mocha." He turned to me. "Coffee?"

"Yes, please."

"Make that two."

We left the bakery with two pink boxes wrapped with string, and portable hand warmers that held the promise that the night was going to end well. The aroma of chocolate mocha opened my senses as we strolled through Yountville's main street. Hotels, restaurants, and a small winery dotted the landscape.

"It's not Napa," Tony said.

"No, but I like it."

"Me too," he said.

The streetlamps along the road lit our path. Tony stopped beside one, placed his coffee on the sidewalk, and gently cupped my face.

"Thank you." The touch of his lips against mine was light, sincere, and warm.

I didn't stop the kiss, but when it was over, I gently pulled away. "I usually don't kiss my friends."

"Really?" He picked up his coffee. "Dan and I do all the time."

Tony respected my boundary even if he used humor to acknowledge it. We turned to walk back toward Rocco's where my car was parked. There wasn't another kiss or move to kiss me.

"Where'd you park?" I asked.

"I didn't. Uber did," he said.

"Do you need a ride?" I asked while he stood on the curb.

"I can text for a ride. It's no big deal." He grinned. "See, good things come in pink boxes." He placed both our bakery boxes on the passenger seat.

"Aren't you taking yours?" I looked at him across the roof.

"Right, my goof." As he leaned into my car, I attempted to toss my purse on the seat beside the boxes, but missed. The entire contents of my bag tumbled to the floor. I groaned.

"I've got it," he said.

But I quickly met him on the passenger side of my car. God only knew what my purse contained beside lipstick, tampons, and my absurd little statue of Buddha. Ben loved to collect the oddities, so I had one for my dash and one for my purse. Even though I was Catholic, I figured karma never hurt. I just wasn't sure what Tony would make of all the other crap I carried around.

As I stuffed mechanical pencils, Chap Stick, and my wallet into my bag, Tony gathered the slips of paper that littered the floor. I was sure most of them were gas and food receipts, but when he handed me a couple of index cards stapled together, it felt like my heart stopped. I teetered on the heels of my sandals and almost fell when Tony gently placed his hand on my back.

"You okay?"

My reply was a vacant nod. I held the index card that contained Ben's penmanship. I absently sat on the curb beside my car.

"Where was this?" I asked.

Tony shrugged. "I'm not sure. It was beside your notebook and the receipts. What is it?"

"It's from Ben."

"Oh." Tony remained crouched beside my car. "Would you like me to go?"

I shook my head and glanced at the card that had an asterisk at the top.

*Read this first.

I wrote this on an index card because after a lifetime with someone, that's what you do. There's no card, floral arrangement, or even singing telegram that could tell someone what I had to say, because I already checked. I thought about a spoof on the Poltergeist *movie, but even I'm not that macabre. "It's back."*

So instead, I wrote what I had to say on index cards and thought about placing them in your cookbook where I knew my wife would never find it.

Oh, Ben. I laughed, and Tony gently sat quietly beside me.

Instead, I decided to tuck them into one of our journals and trust it would find you when the time was right.

My eyes burned, I blinked away the tears and flipped to the next index card.

Chloe,

The cancer is back. In fact, I don't think it ever left. Remission is just a three-syllable word for pause. Are you smiling? Please smile for me, Chloe. One smile from you could offset the worst chemo had to offer. Prostate and now colon cancer. Pain in the ass. Am I right?

I smiled while tears streamed down my face.

But I know that this new chemo cocktail isn't strong enough to rid my body of this poison that has decided to take residence; to invade and take over. I'm sorry. I'm so terribly sorry to leave you.

My chest shook and my hands trembled. Tony's arm around my back made me feel like I wouldn't drift away.

I'm not that much of a religious guy—this you know. But even I know I have fought the good fight. I have finished the race. Now it's time. But before I go, I have one last thing I need you to do for me. I know what you're thinking, "are you kidding me?" Nope. Not even a little.

I need—no, I want you to do what we always talked about doing before the Big C entered our life. Before oncologists and surgeries. Before radiation and chemo. Before sunburns from the inside out. Before hair loss. Before bedsores and nausea. Before diarrhea and adult diapers. Before I became someone you nursed and took care of, I was your king and you were my queen. And together we were going to rule the world—or at least Orange County. We had a dream of a life together, and sometimes that's all that's required.

I flipped to the next card.

So, my sweet, beautiful Chloe, what's gotten me through these last awful months is knowing that you will carry on in my absence.

Chloe, just show up. Show up for life. And be happy. Not alone. I don't have anyone picked out for you, only I know your life is meant to be shared with someone. Smile, Chloe. Oh, just once while you read this. Smile for me. Please.

Your happiness is all that matters to me. And that isn't by yourself. Okay, I know how you'll respond—so do some of that shrink stuff. Stop. Pause. Breathe. Look at me. Okay, maybe you can't. But imagine me. My eyes. I don't want you alone—ever. I don't want you unhappy or sad, ambling through life by yourself. I want you the way I met you— alive. Passionate. Energetic. Crazy. Reckless. Zany. Klutzy.

The cancer has stolen everything else. Please don't let it steal your spirit too. Or your giggle. It can't take both of our lives. I won't allow it.

My chest felt heavy as I turned to the last card in the small deck of Ben's final words to me.

So please, one last request. For me. Live your life—be happy. And when you find a man who makes you smile or laugh, or maybe someone you can't stop thinking about, let him in. Don't push him away. Don't shut him out because you think it's betraying me or us or what we had. I know how you think. But being happy and finding happiness with someone else honors what we had. It's what I want for you, more than anything I've ever wanted.

Chloe, I will be with you in the sunrise every morning when you wake. But the nights belong to new love.

Chlo, I have loved you for a lifetime and I will love you throughout eternity. This is not goodbye. It's simply I'll see you at sunrise.

Ben

I placed the index cards against my chest, lowered my head, and began to cry. I didn't know how much time passed while I cried. *How could he have known?*

"I wasn't expecting this." I covered my face with my hands and lowered my head.

"Chloe." His hand warmed my back. "What can I do?"

I shrugged and handed him the index cards. When Tony read the stack, his face held the emotion I felt in my heart. "I'm so sorry."

"Me too." It was what I always said. My stomach tightened and shook. I dropped my hands and looked at him.

"He's never coming back."

"No, he's not." His voice was as compassionate as his dark eyes.

I brushed my chin against the collar of my dress, but the tears streamed down my face too fast. Tony gently pulled me into him, and I didn't turn away.

"No one could ever replace Ben." He tucked me into an embrace. "But I can't stand to see you hurt. Chloe, it's breaking my heart."

I cried against him, and just when I thought I couldn't cry anymore, the last three years of living in limbo rolled out of me. "I can't wait anymore for him, and he doesn't want me to," I sobbed. "I guess it's just real. He's never coming back. He died. And I've waited. Our time just went so quickly."

"I can't imagine," Tony said in my hair.

"I've been *so* lonely."

"Oh, Chlo."

"Tonight, at dinner, I finally felt—*something*." I pulled away slowly and looked into his eyes. "I didn't think I would ever feel anything other than pain. But now, it feels like I can breathe without it tearing me apart."

"I didn't know your husband." Tony cleared his throat, and hearing him refer to Ben as my husband made me aware that he recognized just how important Ben was in my life. Tony wasn't someone who would diminish my pain or the love I shared with Ben. Nor was he someone who would want me to get over it when a memory or emotion blindsided me.

"I didn't know him, but from reading this," he handed me back the card, "he doesn't want you to suffer like this."

When I smiled, my eyes felt swollen and heavy. "Ben never wanted this for me."

"There's no timetable for what you're going through." Tony gently pressed his lips to my forehead.

I tilted my head toward him until our lips found each other's. His lips were warm, gentle and safe. He brought me into a world I'd left three years ago. A world of love, passion, and feeling alive.

Each kiss reawakened me to the here and now. The

present and the future, not the past. Ben wasn't in my mind or on my mind when I kissed Tony. He vanished into a pocket of a memory where he'd always be. When our lips parted, for the first time in a long time, I knew what I wanted and I was staring right into his eyes.

"Will you drive us back to the hotel?" I asked.

"Of course."

"Where are we going?" Tony walked beside me as I led him from the hotel lobby toward the employee entrance to the wine cave.

"Only wine educators have access to the cave," I said, the index cards in one hand and my employee key card in the other.

"Oh-kay." I heard the hesitation in his voice.

"It probably doesn't make any sense, but there's something I've got to do."

"Try me," he said.

"The last time I dreamt about Ben was on the day of our wine tour," I said.

"I see."

I gently smiled. "It's not like that. I was lost—in all my dreams I'm lost, which doesn't take a licensed shrink to figure out is a metaphor for my life. But I also believe that those who die never really leave us." I swallowed the knot in my throat. "I think Ben was trying to lead me toward… I don't know, finally letting go. And finding my way out of the darkness, which is what it feels like to be lost."

"Sure," he said, but uncertainty remained in his voice.

"I just wanted to go back to where I had the dream." I slid my access card into the entrance door and the light turned from red to green. I pushed open the door.

"What about private parties?" he asked. "I remember Chris saying that they rent out the wine cellar room for events."

"If there were any private functions happening tonight, one of the wine educators would be working it. We all clocked off at five. And the more senior wine educators left for the bar before we even clocked off." The lights in the cave twinkled and it felt like I was walking beneath stars. I reached for his hand. "It's okay. I just want to go to the barrels."

But I couldn't remember where I had fallen asleep. All the racks of barrels were identical. I glanced at the security camera perched in the far corner of the cave and the distance between the camera and barrel seemed right. I knew from training that the camera's range wasn't great and I would only be a blur.

"Well, this seems as good a place as any." I carefully placed the stapled index cards between the barrels until they were hidden and closed my eyes. *Thank you, Ben.* I let the emotions wash over me—the heaviness of sorrow that weighed down my chest, the ache of loss that wrapped around my throat, and the purity of love that burned my eyes with the memories of my life with Ben. But then something else happened—my body flushed with warmth as I felt something I hadn't in years—peace. Beautiful, calming, all-encompassing peace. I opened my eyes with a smile. *Closure.*

I pivoted on my heel and turned right into Tony.

I pressed into him and he pulled away from me slowly. "Uh, maybe I should drive you home."

I slowly shook my head. "No."

"Chlo."

"Please." It wasn't a plea as much as a declaration of renewal. "A weight has lifted from my body that is indescribable. I have no doubt about moving forward." I looked into Tony's eyes. "Be with me."

His face softened. "There's nothing I want more."

My eyes welled and he kissed my eyelids. "Chlo, I don't know if you're ready for this."

I softly giggled. "So, you're saying I'm in for a big treat?"

He smiled. "God, you're so beautiful. But you don't have to make this okay for me."

I shook my head. "I'm not. I'm making it okay for me. And there's *no one* I could ever imagine being with for the first time other than you."

Tony brushed my hair away, cupped my face, and kissed me gently, opening my mouth. Our tongues moved in a dance of exploration that in every way felt right.

My body responded as my hands roamed across his back feeling the muscles that led to the dip in his back. I felt the waistband of his boxers or briefs, I wasn't sure which, only that I wanted to know what he looked like without his jeans.

I reached for his belt buckle and cinched it off in one snap. He stopped kissing me and smiled.

"I guess I haven't forgotten everything," I said.

When Tony laughed, it was this deep, masculine huff that signaled to my body that I was with a man. That laugh and his lips rekindled desire. I unbuttoned his fly, he kicked off his running shoes and his thumbs dipped into the side of his jeans as he hiked them off. His shirt was over his head and on the floor in a matter of seconds. Boxer briefs that looked like the pouch for his cock wasn't large enough as his erection stretched the fabric.

I unstrapped my sandals and pulled off my dress. I stood before him in a pink bra, panties, and an open heart.

***

TONY

I never knew how gorgeous gutsy could be until Chloe stood before me. My desire for her grew stronger and stronger. She was surrendering more than just her body, she was offering me her heart. God knew there wasn't anything more that I wanted, yet I felt like this moment was the most important in my life. It was Chloe.

She reached behind her and unhooked her bra, which fell to the floor. Full, ample breasts that hadn't been touched in years beckoned me to her as she abandoned herself to the moment. Yet I didn't move.

So many thoughts whipped through my mind like a tornado, until she walked toward me and looked up at me through her lashes. The whirlwind funneled to a single thought—nothing mattered more than Chloe. Guarding her heart with mine meant giving her my all.

I tipped her chin toward me and kissed her before I reached for my wallet in the back of my jeans. I withdrew a condom and placed it in her open hand. She draped her arms over my neck as I bent down and swept her in my arms. As I carried her toward the room where we had lunch during the Wine Train tour, her breasts bounced and my cock throbbed.

The twinkling lights cast a soft glow to the room. The massive round table wasn't what I wanted, but the stack of chair pillows stacked in the corner was perfect. Or perfect for us.

I gently kicked the stack and pillows tumbled to the floor, which caused Chloe to giggle. I lay her on the scattered arrangement. She placed the condom beside us. With the arched ceiling lined with lights and the pillows strewn around us, I gazed into Chloe's dark, dark eyes and felt like I was given access to her soul. I removed my boxers, slowly slid down her pink lace panties, and lay on top of her. She wrapped her legs around my waist as we began moving against each other.

The heat from her directed my cock toward her wetness. I rolled away slowly, ripped open the condom, and covered my cock.

Being with a woman for the first time was usually heated, rushed, and filled with anticipation that ended all too soon. But not with Chloe. I had no warning for the emotions I felt when I gently slid inside her. Her head leaned back, her eyes closed, and the sensuality of her open mouth was surreal.

She murmured beneath me while her legs guided me deeper inside her. I kissed her neck and as I made my way to her breasts; her back arched as she rose toward my mouth. Her body responded to me, her eyes opened, and when she looked up at me, I felt like she was peering into my soul.

There was no hiding with Chloe. She saw right through me. The beauty of her body against mine was unlike any I'd known. There wasn't any music, but I swear I heard a melody, or maybe it was her heart beating against mine. She rocked against me and the heat between us turned to sweat. Her legs dug into my ass, thrusting me into her. Our bodies slid against each other until she turned us to take the top position. I raised an eyebrow and smiled.

"What? I know what I want," she said.

I slowly shook my head. "Probably the sexiest quality about you."

She straddled me and glided herself up and down my cock in a rhythm that slowly increased as her clit rubbed against me. Once she found the sweet spot, she moved faster and faster until her thighs tightened around me, her head fell back and all I heard was her moan in pleasure.

I kept moving beneath her while she rode out her orgasm. When her thighs stopped trembling, she slid off me and pulled me back on top of her. I outlasted her and that's all that mattered. But I knew if she kept grinding against me, I wouldn't last much longer.

She reached up and touched my face. I leaned down and

gently kissed her. She wrapped her legs around me and that's all it took. Our lips remained pressed against each other as I thrust into her and practically shouted into her mouth when I broke the seal of our kiss when my cock exploded.

I collapsed on her and rested my head on a pillow beside her head. Her voice was in my ear.

"I always wondered what it'd be like." Her lips brushed my skin. "I never knew it could be like this."

Chloe had exposed herself at a level I didn't know existed. I'd loved other girls, but there was something so much stronger going on between us. *What's stronger than love?* Chloe.

CHAPTER TWENTY-NINE

TONY

I tucked Chloe beneath my arm and shielded her from the overnight front desk manager as we made our way to the elevator. Beneath my other arm was one of the pink boxes we grabbed from her car. We were quiet in the elevator, lest the security cameras have sound. I opened the door into my suite and she entered like she didn't have a care in the world. The feeling of pride that made my chest swell was unlike any I'd had. It wasn't ego, but happiness. Chloe was genuinely happy. And I wanted to keep it that way.

"So, what I want to know is who goes into a first-rate bakery and orders cookies?" I grabbed her hand and the pink box and led her to the bed.

"Don't knock it till you try it," she said.

I raised an eyebrow. "Uh, think I already have and I liked it."

Her laughter that had always sounded forced now flowed

naturally and spontaneously.

"Do you mind if we watch ESPN?" she said, and I almost fell off the bed.

"Do they now broadcast soap operas on ESPN?"

"No!" She swatted my leg. "I like ESPN."

"Seriously?"

"Yah, since living with my sister and her husband, Coach, it's kind of become my nightly ritual," she said.

"If ESPN is your nightly ritual then I'll give up my nightly needlepoint and Bible studies to watch sports with you—because I'm *the kind of guy* who sacrifices for women just to make them happy."

"Mahoney, shut up and turn on the TV."

A woman after my own heart. There was no way to hide my smile. I grabbed the remote from the nightstand and clicked to ESPN. The highlight reel started as I popped open the lid to the box to find a dozen gingerbread men staring up at me. I was about to offer Chloe a cookie when she grabbed a gingerbread man dusted in pink sugar and bit off his head.

"Okay then." I followed her lead and was surprised to find the gingerbread man was soft in the center and crisp on the edge. I took another bite, and was hit with the sweet flavor of molasses and sugar. "Not bad, but it's missing something."

Her eyes searched mine for an answer.

I reached for the phone and ordered two glasses of cold milk. When two chilled glasses arrived with a carton of milk stuck in a bucket of ice, I knew I had the makings to end an already perfect evening.

I bit off the head of another gingerbread man and dunked the headless cookie into the milk. The flavor of cinnamon left a savory taste in my mouth.

"Milk is to cookies what cheese is to wine," I said. "I know you missed that part of the wine tour and I'm sure Victorine already gave you the spiel, but the Point's next marketing strategy should be pairing cookies with milk."

"I don't know about the Point, but after we remove Winters as a threat, cookies and milk may be the only thing he'll be able to market."

"No argument there." I polished off one gingerbread man and worked through the team of smiling, spicy, wake-up-my-mouth goodness.

When I reached the last cookie, I held it toward the light of the TV. "Gingerbread man and Chloe, respect. This midnight cookie-palooza was worth the extra calories. You've both earned a place in my heart and my stomach."

Chloe's eyes looked tired, but the smile on her face wasn't. "My grandma always told me that one was the path to the other. And I guess the pile of crumbs you left in what was once a box full of cookies is proof positive to her platitude."

CHAPTER **THIRTY**

CHLOE

Who knew the wiry, spindly, inhuman Victorine would be the key to discovering Winters's inside person? But Tony was convinced if anyone knew something was amiss with the staffing, it'd be her. And since only the hotel owners, winemakers, wine educators and the trainer knew the location of the mother vine, Tony's money was on one of the new wine educators. So my mission was to befriend the heartless, twiggy trainer. *Lucky me.*

It was one thing to get Tony to talk in his suite because I reinforced what I overheard from his conversation with Dan. Tony was disenfranchised and questioning his career choice. All I had to do was reflect back his feelings. *Counseling one-oh-one.* But as Victorine stood tall beside Rob, with nary a hair out of place nor a wrinkle in her linen suit, I sensed cracking that nut was going to be a bit tougher.

"Vic, I'm sure you've already read my memo regarding

Ms. Dorsey joining our marketing division after the completion of her wine educator training," Rob said.

I was still stuck on *Vic*.

"Yes. I read that." The flat tone in her voice was customary.

"Right, so today during my allotted time with her, I'd like Ms. Dorsey to spend time with you going over the key marketing points we formulated last quarter," Rob said.

"I have the other wine educators to train," she countered.

Suddenly I felt like an unwanted child tossed between two warring parents.

"I was under the impression that you had two existing wine educators in your orientation class—a Mr. DeLorme and Mr. Staple?"

Barry and Chris. I did not know Barry was already a wine educator. Interesting. The plot thickens.

When Vic didn't answer, Rob raised an eyebrow. "Was I misinformed?"

"No, that's correct. Mr. DeLorme and Mr. Staple were required to attend a refresher orientation course for wine educators," she said.

"Then it's perfect. While I'm sure their standards aren't up to your snuff," Rob said in his English accent that was just yummy, "I am certain these two gentlemen are more than capable of training those in your orientation class who don't possess the same level of experience as they do. And, as you're always teaching me," a subtle Sherlock-like grin crossed his face, "experience is the best teacher."

Victorine interlaced her hands together like she was

being schooled by her own rhetoric, which she was. I purposefully kept a look of neutrality. While my instinct about not liking Victorine was quickly formed, I needed to appear open and accepting. I offered a warm, gracious smile while I kept my ill will and malicious thoughts buried behind my toothy grin. I had to be her ally. And by the way Rob just right-sized her, I had the perfect inroad to gain her confidence, and hopefully, the information I desperately needed.

When we left Rob's office, I walked beside her and waited until we were alone in the back hallway before I spoke.

"So," I slowly segued into the conversation. "I'm kind of wondering how you feel about having your schedule flipped like that?"

"It's nothing I can't handle," she quipped.

"Of course. I would imagine you can handle quite a lot. Still…" I let my voice trail off so doubt could subtly creep in. I mentally counted to three before I resumed. "I imagine it's a bit jarring."

"Jarring is an accurate description," she said curtly.

Progress. When I had reticent clients who weren't very communicative, I had to do the work and invite them to talk. And the best approach to draw out a clammed-up client was with open-ended questions.

"Victorine, I've always wondered what is it about the hotel and winery that you like?"

Her brisk pace became brisker and her lips remained pursed in her taut face. If I ever wanted to test Einstein's assertion that time was relative, I simply needed to take Victorine on as a client. Her ability to let the clock tick by through avoidance was second only to a troubled teen's.

But this was probably the one chance I had to question her about the staff. My palms began to sweat with worry, coupled with a burning desire to get her to talk. I reverted to a technique many in my field would question.

"I suppose you'd need to see the hotel as a safe, supportive environment for you to really like it," I said, answering the question for her.

She stopped dead in her tracks.

There's nothing quite like feeling misrepresented to get someone talking.

"I don't have a problem with the hotel." Her first real connection.

"Of course. It takes time to feel supported in a male-dominated industry," I said.

Her arms crossed over her pale pink linen suit. Even when people aren't talking, they still communicate. Her posture, the hardened expression, and the spike in her breathing were all speaking to me.

"I'm sure you'd feel happier more often if you felt like you were part of the group and *for certain* accepted by the all-boys management team," I said.

Albeit controversial, my slanted assertions about Victorine got her to pull me aside in the hallway where our backs were to the security camera's lenses and far enough away from eavesdroppers.

"The hotel may be driven by men, but there are many

powerful women behind them," she said.

The human drive to be perceived correctly is powerful.

"So why aren't you happy?" I continued throwing out falsehoods until one took hold. The fact that Victorine thought she was powerful wasn't groundbreaking.

"What? I am happy."

"Oh." I purposefully feigned surprise. "I guess the only time I've *really* seen you happy is when you're training staff."

"Well, of course," she snapped. "When I'm training the staff I'm doing what I was hired to do and was trained to do. My position as a corporate trainer was hard-earned. It's not like I started in one position and then was promoted because the owner liked me."

Ouch. I knew that little dig was directed at me, but when I maintained a look of impartiality, she continued.

"I had to cross train in every department before I was even considered for the position. I spent *years* at the Point's property in New York, then southern California before I was even considered a promotable candidate." Her shoulders dropped and her face suddenly softened. "I've never been prouder than when I was offered the corporate trainer position at the Napa Valley Point Resort and Winery."

"You must have been over the moon," I said.

She rolled her eyes. "If the Napa Valley Point Resort wasn't attached to a winery with a spoiled child at the helm, then I'd be, as you said, over the moon."

"I haven't met Rich yet," I said of the other owner.

"You'll like him. He's very professional."

And I immediately knew the spoiled child in question was Rob.

"It's bad enough that wine educators begin providing tours before their training is finished, but some of the staff they've hired are questionable." Anxiety pinched at her forehead. "They'd never be hired at any other Point Resort."

I had to know who "they" encompassed.

"Is it more to do with their lack of wine knowledge, absence of hotel experience, or overall skill set?" I simply rattled off every deficiency I had as an employee.

"It's more to do with personalities," she said.

Bitch didn't pull any punches. Sure, okay. As with any problematic client, I knew my reaction was being tested. "Victorine, that must be frustrating," I said, reflecting back her disappointment.

"Chloe, you have no idea."

Bam! I'm in. When she reflected back my name, she made it personal to her.

"It's as if they don't care who they have representing the winery as long as they're young, attractive, and single," she said.

I quickly mentally inventoried the wine educators: Barry, Chris, Emerson, Rebel, and me. All single. *Interesting.* I didn't personally know the other, more senior wine educators, but from Tony's research the four had a nightly watering hole and the bartender had indicated they were long-time employees devoted to Rob and Rich.

"All that *and* then to have to retrain them...." I threw that resentment into the conversation.

"The winery could probably get somewhere if we weren't constantly taking one step forward and two steps back. Both Barry and Chris were put on the floor too soon and now it's come back to bite us."

I nodded as if I knew the how and why, which I didn't. But I was getting closer. Victorine was no longer sparing her words or discontentment.

"Funny, I was under the impression Barry and Chris were still relatively new to the Point."

"Barry's been here the longest with ninety days, and Chris is shortly behind him with seventy-something days."

Great. If one of them had just been hired, it'd be more obvious.

"Ah yes, the Flash."

"Barry's actually very knowledgeable about wine. But it's retraining his approach to the guests...."

I tilted my head and the question was on my lips when Victorine answered.

"When we inherit an employee from a previous winery there's an entirely new training element in place," she said.

"That's right," I lied. "Barry said he was from—" I snapped my fingers like the name was on the tip of my tongue.

"Winters Winery."

Bingo.

"He does have a thing for their 2012 Summerset." I dropped the award-winning wine into the conversation like a seasoned pro. *That's right. Who's the spy now?*

"Yes, it would be a welcome relief if he remembered

that the Point's 2016 Napa Valley Cabernet Sauvignon practically erased the taste of Summerset from wine connoisseurs' palates."

"It's almost as if he's still loyal to Winters Winery," I said.

She shrugged. "With the Flash, who knows." She straightened her jacket and clasped her hands together. "I suppose we should head to my office at some point and discuss marketing points."

I lightly laughed. "Of course. Thank you, Victorine." I gently placed my hand on her arm. "I really appreciate you taking the time to share your knowledge with me."

She smiled like I had just bestowed the highest compliment on her, when really I hadn't done anything more than pay attention to her. *Tony has his methods and I have mine.* Getting the needed information didn't involve money or force, whether through bribes or blackmail, because it never cost a dime to pay attention.

CHAPTER **THIRTY-ONE**

TONY

Tony: Did Rob ever send u the Point's cab? From 2016?

I texted Chloe, who was finishing a training shift in the cave.

Chloe: Yup. My sister's stoked.

Her reply was instant. Chloe had found the one spot in the cave that had cell reception.

Tony: Got any plans tonight?"

Chloe: Would 2night be any diff from last 2 wks we've spent 2gether?

I grinned.

Tony: So, you're telling me I've got a chance.

I threw in an amended quote from *Dumb and Dumber*.

Chloe: Mahoney, just tell me the plans.

Tony: Ur sister's house after work. Meet u there.

Chloe and I had been careful not to be seen together, which meant we spent a lot of time at her sister's house.

Or in Yountville at Rocco's, our favorite restaurant. But no matter how we spent our evenings, our nights always ended in my hotel suite. I'd meet Chloe by the stairwell and tuck her under my arm like the best-kept secret. And she was.

I grabbed my gym bag like I was headed toward a pick-up game off property, which the front desk had come to expect when I passed them on the way to the valet. The downside to a five-diamond hotel was that they did everything for guests—including enlisting Uber on my behalf. The upside was that I had different drivers each night so my whereabouts remained unknown in case Winters's inside guy was watching me.

Charlotte's kitchen was a chef's paradise. Instead of mixing and matching brands and styles, her kitchen consisted of a stainless-steel appliance suite. The convection oven and gas range were top of the line. The built-in French-door refrigerator was large enough for the hotel's kitchen inventory. But I think what impressed me the most was the dishwasher and over-the-range microwave that never hummed or made a sound when they were in use. Like everything in her home, Charlotte had the best.

So I knew asking her to part with the Winters Summerset 2012 Cab that she'd finally secured was not going to be easy, which was why I brought a pink box filled from the bakery in Yountville.

Charlotte and Chloe were so different, yet shared many similarities. And I knew from grabbing a glass from the cupboard in her kitchen that Charlotte hid her "nummies," as she called the box of boutique chocolates she placed on the shelf above the glasses. As if the artfully filled truffles laced with creamy coffee, hazelnut, and pralines wouldn't be discovered.

If she really wanted to stash her sweet-tooth cache, she'd be better off putting them in an undesirable location, like the vegetable crisper or in the bathroom behind the feminine hygiene products. Two places no male thief would ever look.

Charlotte liked designer sweets, but something told me she could be enticed by a good old-fashioned pink bakery box of nummies. And if that didn't work, I also had aged cheese and charcuterie from Rocco's.

"Chocolate, cheese, or meat," I said to Charlotte with a grin. "The perfect trio of offerings that any wise man not heading to Bethlehem would offer."

She surveyed my offerings with a raised eyebrow. I couldn't tell if she was impressed or pissed.

"Chloe tells me that Rob sent a few bottles of his 2016 cab," I said, hoping that she'd have an easier time parting with Winters's award-winning cab if she remembered she had multiple bottles of the Point's award-winner.

Charlotte eyed me suspiciously. "Yes, it was very generous of Mr. Chambers."

I knew Chloe had told her sister that we were working together, but I sensed she wasn't too happy about the prospect.

Even though I was on assignment for Winters, he didn't

know I was working against him. I was so off my game, I hadn't even tried his wine to know what I was up against. *That's corporate intel one-oh-one—know your product.* And time was running out. I still didn't know who his inside guy was, and I didn't want to risk being spotted buying Winters's award vintage. I only had one chance to make the perfect shot at convincing Charlotte to agree. If I pressed too hard, I risked fouling out.

"So…." I clasped my hands together realizing my food enticements failed.

"Relax, Mahoney," Charlotte said, and I heard her sister in her voice. "I've already got Coach bringing the Winters cab from the wine cellar."

Dan and Ty always said I didn't have a good poker face, and when Charlotte laughed, I relaxed.

"Thank you," I said.

"It's no secret that I've wanted to taste the Winters Summerset 2012 since Martine mentioned it on the Wine Train," she said.

"Yes, you made a big point on the train that you were unimpressed that there was an acclaimed wine that you hadn't tasted," Chloe said. "So it seems kind of obvious that you'd want to try this ASAP."

"Sometimes you let a wine wait," she said.

Chloe rolled her beautiful brown eyes. "Sure, sell that to someone who'll buy it. You've been looking for an opportunity to taste it and now we've presented you with one."

As if on cue, Charlotte's husband, John, who both women

referred to as "Coach" surfaced from their wine cellar.

"This does look good," he said and handed the bottle to his wife.

We were gathered by the marble island in their kitchen with four crystal wine glasses positioned strategically in front of each of us. Charlotte uncorked the wine expertly and allowed it to breathe before she poured a sampling into each of our glasses. I remembered what Chris said about twirling the wine, which I did. Once Charlotte placed the glass to her lips, we all followed suit.

The cab was velvety smooth, but the look on Charlotte's face was not impressed. She paused and took another sip. Again, dissatisfaction crossed her brow.

"What's wrong?" I asked.

She turned to her husband. "Would you mind bringing up one of the bottles of the 2016 Napa Valley Point cab?"

"Of course."

Coach disappeared and Charlotte remained mum. I glanced at Chloe who shrugged. "Tastes good to me."

Charlotte placed four new stemware in front of us and repeated the process with the Point cab.

"Again, tastes fine to me," Chloe said. "But I'm not the wine expert."

"Chlo, you don't have to be a wine expert to know they taste the same," Charlotte said.

"Really? I didn't get that," Chloe said.

"Therein lies the difference between a connoisseur and a commoner," Charlotte said with a feigned smugness. "One knows the difference and similarities in the vintage, and the other only knows how to uncork the bottle."

"Hold up there, sister, I can do more than uncork a bottle. I'd like you to know that I am getting rather skilled at using the wine thief," Chloe said, and I leaned over and planted a kiss on her head.

She glanced up at me, and for a moment, everyone disappeared. That's what it was like with Chloe. The world vanished when she looked at me.

Charlotte swirled the Point's cab in her glass and took a sip. She cleansed her palate with a small piece of cheese. Then shifted her attention and taste buds to the Summerset. Before the glass parted her lips, her white-blonde hair shook. "How can wines from different vineyards taste so similar?"

Coach and I mimicked her process.

"They are similar," I said.

"It's almost like they came from the same vine," Coach said, and Charlotte pointed toward her husband.

"Exactly," she said. "I knew something was familiar about the Summerset."

"Did you try the Point's cab before this?" I asked.

The look on her face made me feel like a dumbass for asking.

"We were sent a case by the owner. It would have been rude not to open one," she said, as if everyone knew proper wine etiquette.

Chloe laughed. "So that's a passive-aggressive yes."

I was still stuck on the two wines tasting similar. "Winters's wine came first, so…." My brain worked through the puzzle. Two wines, from two different wineries, with similar taste. "Could Rob and Rich have somehow stolen their vine?" I said. "They both worked at Winters Winery."

"Oh my gosh, my dentist said that he worked at a winery with Rob, but I didn't know it was Winters Winery," Chloe said.

Charlotte reached for four more crystal wine glasses. "Coach and I are going to step into the foyer," she said. "Chlo—you and Tony fill our glasses but don't tell us which wine is in which glass."

"A blind taste test?" I said.

She nodded as she slipped her hand into Coach's and they disappeared into the entryway.

Chloe and I went to work without saying a word. We didn't need to. No one read me as well as she did.

Charlotte and Coach returned and each tried the wines placed before them.

Any suspicions about the similarities in the wines were confirmed when neither wine connoisseur could distinguish between the two cabernets.

"Tony, keep in mind that neither my husband or I are truly qualified to tell the difference since neither of us are certified sommeliers, however, I do think it's safe to say that something's not adding up," Charlotte said.

"So now what?" Chloe looked at me for the answer.

"Now, we determine if there's a wine thief."

After we finished two bottles of wine, Chloe opted to

remain at her sister's. And I opted to tuck her into bed. I pulled the blankets up to her slender, delicate chin and gently kissed her.

"Sweet dreams," I said, and wished I never had to be apart from her. But we both knew Winters had someone else at the Point, and not returning to my suite would raise suspicions.

She gently pulled me on top of her. "I wish you could stay."

"Me too." We kissed and our lips lingered until I gently, reluctantly pulled away.

"Tomorrow?" she said.

"And the next day and the next," I said.

Charlotte sent me off in the Uber with the box of nummies we hadn't eaten. When I opened the door to my suite, it was dark.

I thought I left a light on?

I was palming the wall for the hall light with one hand while I carefully guarded the pink box with the other. Her voice broke through the darkness.

"Why ruin the mood with bright lights?"

Ginger.

I'd recognize her come-on-let's-fuck voice anywhere. The hall light flicked on, and the first thing I saw was that the door to the connecting suite was ajar. The second thing I saw was Ginger in a white T-shirt and black leggings that cupped her perfectly shaped ass.

I walked past her, set the bakery box on the desk, and

nodded toward the door. "I'm not sure who you convinced to give you access to my suite, but it's time for you to leave."

"Oh, Tony, why the long face?"

"I don't know, because you're in my suite without my permission?"

"Winters said you asked for my assistance." Her lips were as shiny as her blonde hair, which swept her shoulders when she crossed her arms over her ample chest.

"No, I didn't ask your father for your help on anything," I said.

"I really thought you were expecting me." Her tone shifted, and it sounded like she was honestly surprised.

Embarrassment turned her cheeks red. "You honestly didn't ask for me?"

"No." My tone was probably harsher than it needed to be, but with Ginger I felt like I was a walking in a minefield. One wrong step and one of us could be destroyed and it wasn't going to be me.

She turned toward the door that connected our suites. "I'm sorry, Tony. I don't know why Winters sent me here."

To get under my skin. Or his guy's been following me. But when she glanced at me before disappearing into her room, the expression on her face wasn't rejection or even confusion, but something I'd never seen with Ginger – hurt. She seemed truly saddened that I would think the worst of her or that her father sent her here unnecessarily. Still, it was the only time I was grateful that Chloe wasn't with me. When she was in her room, I turned the dead bolt and then placed my luggage in front of the door.

CHAPTER **THIRTY-TWO**

CHLOE

"We're supposed to be on the lookout for a woman named Ginger," Rebel said to our group.

"Why?" Barry asked.

"Apparently she's a guest and requested a tour of the caves, but all the tour openings with the experienced wine educators were filled, so the concierge desk arranged it with Victorine that she shadow us," Rebel said.

"Cool." It was the extent of Emerson's input.

We were in the third week and final day of training in the cave, and I'd be happy to be above ground. However, in these last three weeks I'd spent nearly every night with Tony. I never had the perfect name or body to be James Bond's love interest, but I certainly had an interesting time with this spy. Thoughts of Tony burned in my mind, but it still didn't take the chill from the air. It was cold as fuck in the cave.

We were huddled together in the entrance to the cave when a willowy woman in black leggings, a gray sweater, and pink Converse high tops approached. Her blonde hair was pulled back in a messy bun that looked effortless and elegant at the same time. Her makeup appeared natural, which, when I tried that approach, took hours to pull off. Some women just made looking beautiful effortless, and she was one of them.

"Are you Ginger?" Rebel asked.

She held out her hand. "I am."

"I'm Rebel, and that's Chloe, Emerson, Barry, and...." Rebel looked around. "Chris was here, but now he's not."

Where is Chris?

"Thank you for letting me join you today. The concierge desk said that their customary tours were booked and since they are short-staffed on wine educators, when they offered this option it seemed like a win."

"The cave is pretty cold. May I get you a jacket?" It was the most Emerson had spoken in weeks.

Granted, he was following training protocol by offering Ginger a jacket, but still, the timing of his initiative wasn't lost on me. Even Barry seemed to lose his edge. He stood with his hands on his hips like he was actually the Flash, but the smile on his face was the most genuine I'd seen from him.

"No, but thank you for the offer," she said, and Emerson's cheeks turned red.

"All right, wine educators, let's begin." Victorine approached with Tony beside her and it felt like my heart jumped to my throat. Tony was in a blue hoodie that had UCLA Bruins emblazoned in gold on the center of his broad chest. His jeans were relaxed, which matched the loosened shoelaces on his high tops. He wasn't sweaty, but I knew his scent as well as I knew my own.

"We have two guests joining us today." Victorine extended her hand to Ginger. "You must be Ms. Fraser."

"Please, it's Ginger. Ms. Fraser is my mother."

I still hadn't identified what it was about Victorine that tightened my gut, but when she shook hands with Ginger, the handshake seemed to last a bit longer than normal. It was like Victorine recognized her—or perhaps she was admiring her flawless makeup. I knew I was.

"I'm sure you all remember Mr. Mahoney from our first day of training. He decided to finish where he left off— without any spills this time." Vic directed that comment toward me. *So much for our little hallway chat.*

Ginger extended her hand to Tony. "I'm Ginger."

"Tony," he said flatly.

Huh.

"Okay, wine educators, today each of you will perform a part of the wine tour that is offered to every guest at the Napa Valley Point Resort and Winery." She clapped, and my nerves jumped.

Fuck, I was okay until she did that. Which I knew meant I wasn't okay.

"Why don't we begin with Ms. Dorsey," Victorine said. *Of course.*

When I wasn't with Tony, which was rare, I'd practiced

every part of the tour on my sister while she ate the nasty cream-filled chocolates Coach kept in ample supply.

I posed myself in front of Tony and Ginger. "Hello, and welcome to the Napa Valley Point Resort and Winery. I'm Chloe." I thought to how Rebel phrased it, and then put my own little spin on it. "Chloe or Chlo, either way, I'm you're go-to." It was so lame, but Ginger smiled so I breathed a bit easier.

"We'll start with barrel tasting, so if you'd like to follow me."

I knew Victorine was gauging how well I interacted with all the guests, so I tried to make eye contact with both of them. Together they looked like one of those annoyingly cute, good-looking couples.

Ginger looped her arm beneath Tony's and said, "I guess we're the guinea pigs."

He laughed, and my heart fell from my throat to my gut. I knew we couldn't let on that we were together, but seeing him with another woman sucked.

"Uh, yeah, so, um, we'll just go to the barrel tasting room," I said.

The other wine educators followed behind Tony and Ginger. I glanced for Chris, who remained missing. I wanted to signal to Tony that Chris went AWOL after Rebel announced that this Ginger woman was going to join us. I didn't know if it meant anything, but the timing seemed odd.

But what could I do? If I tried to get his attention by jerking my head, raising my eyebrows, or winking, he'd probably think I was having a spasm, stroke, or seizure. Besides we had our nightly meeting spot in the stairwell. I'd have to wait until this evening to tell him my suspicions about Chris.

I positioned myself by the barrel that had caused so much trouble before. I was determined to make that round, wooden bitch mine.

"What I find interesting about the winemaking process here at Napa Valley Point Resort and Winery is that wine cannot be contained," I said, and watched the confusion cross everyone's face, which was what I had expected.

I patted the barrel. "The winemakers at the Napa Valley Point Resort and Winery are never satisfied. They will never say, 'This wine is perfect,' because a winemaker can never satisfy their desire to achieve true perfection. For that reason, the winemakers will spend their lifetime trying to perfect the process, and in turn their wine. It's what makes them the best in their field." I remembered the winemakers we had met during training, and my brief time with Rob. What I was about to say was 100 percent true. "You *would not* believe the level of passion in Napa Valley. Wine is our livelihood, so in good times and bad times, whether a winery is in a boom or a bust, the constant is our passion. That passion is what you taste when you open a bottle from the Napa Valley Point Resort and Winery. And since we all know passion is hard to contain, we keep ours in a barrel."

When Tony and Ginger laughed, I knew I had nailed it. My counseling at the college had focused on positive psychology, which followed Aristotle's definition of human nourishing. Basically, doing the right thing felt good. And right now, I felt good. There wasn't anything I'd said that wasn't true.

I presented everyone in my group with a spotless wineglass before I approached the barrel and carefully uncorked it. I gently held the wine thief, placed it in the center of the barrel and withdrew rich, red wine.

I took a long, deep breath, and grounded myself before I approached Ginger.

"May I offer you a sample of our cabernet sauvignon?"

"Please." She held her glass toward me. I slowly released my thumb and the wine flowed into her glass. When it hit the midpoint, I pressed my thumb over the top, and the wine stopped. I cautiously moved to Tony. The moment of truth.

"Sir, may I interest you?"

Tony raised an eyebrow. "Interest me in what?"

I felt my cheeks flush and temperature rise. "*Wine*. May I interest you in some wine?"

His elbow playfully bowed out, and I backed away from the gesture.

"Have you forgotten how well it went the last time I tried to use this thing?" Everyone except Ginger laughed.

He held his glass toward me, and I was immensely relieved when the wine got to the intended target, which wasn't Tony. I turned to Victorine. "I don't know about you, but that right there is as good as it gets."

Despite herself, she laughed. After I filled everyone's glass including mine, I replaced the leftover wine in the barrel and raised my glass. I thought about the lock I'd secured to Love Lock Bridge.

"To Napa." I turned my attention to my group. "The land of dreamers, believers," I made eye contact with Tony, "and second chances."

"Cheers!" Rebel said from the back of the group, and I smiled.

The wine had the taste of victory. Rebel approached me, and I grinned.

"I did it," I said, smiling so wide it hurt. I snuck a glance at Tony, whose gaze seemed to follow me everywhere. He had done the same thing during our Wine Train tour, but now it was different. Tony was mine and I was his. And the energy and connection between us couldn't be contained no matter how hard we tried. "I actually mastered the wine thief."

"The wine thief?" Ginger didn't miss a beat.

"Oh, yes, it's this." I held up the wine thief. "It's called the wine thief because you're stealing wine from the barrel."

"Interesting." She slightly shifted her head to the side. "I'm glad I asked."

It was a passive-aggressive reminder that I had failed to explain to the group the wine thief.

"Ms. Fraser raises a valid point." Victorine referenced Ginger by the name Ginger associated with her mother, which was when I realized what it was about her that made my gut tighten. When Victorine found a person's Achilles' heel, she pressed.

"However," she said, approaching me, "your progress this time is exemplary."

Good enough for me. I thought of Tony's comment at dinner and tipped my glass toward Victorine's. "I'll drink to that."

Rebel hip-checked me. "Nailed it."

I hip-checked her back. "Like a hammer."

I fell in line with the other wine educators when Emerson was chosen to lead us to the fermentation room. I waited until Victorine's attention was on Emerson before I discreetly stepped away from the group. I didn't know why Chris suddenly vanished or where he went, but I intended to find out.

"I think Chris is our spy," I said when I met Tony in the stairwell after my shift.

Tony continually looked over his shoulder.

"You okay?"

He shook his head and cornered me against the wall, which normally would be a huge turn-on, but his vibe was all wrong.

"Winters's daughter, Ginger, showed up last night," he said.

"*She's* Winters's daughter? So Fraser isn't really her name?"

"No, it is," Tony said. "She uses her mother's maiden name."

"Is she in corporate intelligence gathering too?" I asked when I really wanted to know if Ginger was a spy.

"She has helped on a few projects."

"She's helped you." I didn't even pose it as a question and Tony didn't disagree.

"It's Winters's punishment. Anytime I don't deliver or he thinks I'm not delivering, he sends Ginger."

"Is that why she went on the wine tour?"

Tony leaned against the wall, but kept me blocked from view if anyone entered the stairwell. "You don't miss a beat." His brown eyes looked intent, but not angry. "If this wine thing doesn't work out for you, you should really consider a career switch. You'd fit in nicely in my industry," he said with a grin.

I thought of what Rob said about his success with the winery. "I think it's just about being at the right place at the right time."

His eyes twinkled. "Cute."

"What?"

He squeezed my arm. "Oh, come on—like you didn't know that was Winters's motto for W. Enterprises—Corporate Solutions. *We're In The Right Place At The Right Time.*"

It felt like all the blood drained from my body. "You're kidding, right?"

"Nope." Tony's face mirrored the confusion that coursed through my body. "Why?"

I shook my head. "It's something Rob said. And while I know he worked at Winters Winery, don't you think that's a bit odd to basically paraphrase the competition's catchphrase for the reason why his winery was successful?"

"Yeah, that's not smart and I never got the impression

that Rob was dumb." Tony reached and tucked a strand behind my ear.

"So, what do we do?" My energy level was off the charts. "I haven't been able to locate Chris, but it's looking more like he's our guy, right? I mean, he disappeared when Ginger arrived on the scene, which would make sense if he works for Winters and Ginger is Winters's daughter." I widened my eyes. *"Oh my gosh, that's it, isn't it?"* I could barely contain my enthusiasm. "Chris vanished because he was afraid of being recognized by Ginger!" I clapped and drew in a large gulp of air at the same time. I wanted to pace, but Tony was in my way. "Add to it, now we have Rob somehow in the mix—not to mention Ginger. It's like drowning in a sea of suspects and I can only swim after one of them." When I came up for a breath, Tony was smiling.

"Chlo, this isn't an individual race, we're a relay team. We'll double our chances and cut the lists of suspects in half."

"That's an excellent plan," I said, pushing past him for the stairs and his suite.

"Uh, no," he said, and I practically got whiplash looking back at him.

"Uh, no?"

"Ginger has the connecting suite to mine and she already manipulated or bribed some dumb doorman or housekeeper to unlock the door, so we can't go to my room," he said.

I grabbed his hand. "If we can't go your suite, there are a few other spots on property that don't have cameras. And I know Ginger will *never show up* where I'm taking you."

"I didn't think we could use the basketball courts because of work," Tony said when I led him from the back of the hotel to the courts.

I nodded. "That's correct."

"Mysterious," he said, and I smiled.

"Listen, I'm not going to let Ginger or Winters or anyone ruin what's become our thing." Although I already knew our thing was changing. Tony didn't live in Northern California, and eventually, he'd have to return to his home in Southern California. I squeezed his hand and felt my eyes sting. I turned away from him and bit the inside of my mouth. *I can't be sad.*

I suddenly thought of the Laughing Buddha on my dash and in my purse. *Ben.* He brought us together. I knew that now. His index card was the final piece in my grief recovery. The sunrise reminded me of Ben, but he no longer consumed my every thought. And my nights hadn't been lonely since meeting Tony.

Don't go—ever. The words remained stuck in my throat. We walked in the moonlight toward the dimly lit corner of the court. What I couldn't say, I expressed in my touch. I moved my hands up his back and into his hair. Our kissing elevated the art of romance. Each time we kissed, Tony's lips brought me into a world where loss and heartache hadn't touched me. There was a purity and beauty that made it so easy to surrender myself to him. From our first time in the cave to every time.

***

TONY

Chloe's touch was magical. It relaxed and stimulated at the same time. Her hands were in my hair and we were in our own universe. Her passion had a purity that made leaving her unimaginable.

The lights were on a timer, which I turned off. Alone in the dark with the moon as our guide, I would be with a woman I never expected and now couldn't imagine not seeing daily.

She slipped her red polo shirt off and let it fall to the court. Her khakis were next. I pulled off my hoodie and stepped out of my jeans. She lay on the pile of clothes, her hair fell from her face, and I stared into her big brown eyes that knew me so well.

I slid off her black panties and reached behind her back to release her lacy bra. I knew this body and yet every time I was with her, it felt new. Her breasts pressed against my chest and her legs wrapped around my waist. When Chloe was in, she was all in. There were no half measures. Her body responded to me and my cock throbbed to be inside her. But I waited. I always waited. I wanted to take my time with Chloe, so when I gently pulled out of her embrace, I inched down her body and her legs parted. I knew her taste and as she rose toward my lips, my mouth slowly, tenderly savored her. My tongue gently moved her clit back and forth in a pattern that I knew drove her crazy, but did the job. I took longer, slower licks and her hips rose. Her hands in my hair, her ankles braced against my legs, her thighs tight— she was close.

I placed my finger inside her and she began to scream. I gently cupped her mouth with my hand, but she practically bit me. While I had ensured that we wouldn't be watched in the corner of the court, she didn't seem concerned with who heard us.

I kept one finger inside her, my mouth massaging her clit and my other hand on her mouth. Her breathing intensified into my hand. Her body shook and her legs gripped me. Her orgasms were as strong and passionate as she was.

She pulled me toward her.

"I've got to get a condom," I said.

"Don't stop."

"Chlo." I reached beneath her for the pocket of my jeans and grabbed my wallet where I had stashed one. I ripped open the package, slid it down me, and entered her.

Her pussy tightened around me and felt like a perfect fit. I slowly moved in and out of her. Our bodies were in sync. The moonlight cast its warm glow on her face. *This woman.* I didn't want to let her go.

I held her face and stared into her eyes. She wrapped her legs around my waist and pulled me deeper, further into her. We were one. I felt her heart beat against my chest. My lips met hers, and I pressed into her with the force of a man lost in a woman's touch.

She rocked us toward climax and I held on to her. Heat flooded my cock. When I knew she had hit her second orgasm, I moved toward mine. Her heels dug into my ass and I responded. No one loved on me like Chloe. *Damn.*

I looked directly at her when I exploded inside her. Sunrise would come too soon. I lay beside her and pulled her into me, never wanting to let go.

CHAPTER THIRTY-THREE

CHLOE

A full moon lit the sky when we left the basketball court. When we reached the sign that announced the west-end vineyard, Tony laughed.

"Grapes are sensitive." He shook his head. "That's as lame as the first time I read it. *Please stay on the path.* What do they think we're going to do?"

"Steal the mother vine."

Tony stopped and looked at me.

"This is where?"

I slightly nodded.

"You're kidding me, right?"

I shook my head. "Not even a little."

"Why are you showing me this?" Even if his voice hadn't revealed his shock, his eyes did. His face was so expressive. I'd miss that when he returned to Huntington.

"Listen, we're a team. And…"

Suddenly, Tony grabbed my hand and pulled me into the corner where the basketball court and the west-end vineyard met. Alone in the dark, I was about to either giggle and ask for a few minutes to regroup before we hit it again or yell at him for yanking my wrist so hard. I wasn't able to do either, because the moonlight illuminated two people kissing. I squinted and the profiles came into view. Tony covered my mouth with his hand as if he knew what my reaction would be. *Oh, my God! Ginger and Rob?*

I didn't have to be a trained therapist to read the shock on Tony's face and the way he closed his mouth like he was actually trying to swallow something. Winters's daughter and the Point's owner was definitely news to him, and as hard to swallow as it was for me.

My heart raced and my adrenaline spiked. *If Rob spots me with Tony anywhere even near the mother vine, I'm screwed. What was I thinking?* Oh, clearly I wasn't. The clinical side of me surfaced but it did little to settle my writhing nerves. *I am not good at this spy game—at all.*

Tony was calm, cool, and collected, as if trouble was miles in the distance and not a stone's throw away. Whereas I was sweating, shaking, and about to shart my pants. I was beyond relieved when he quietly led us through the shadows to the basketball court. Neither of us said a thing. *What was there to say?* I was more confused than ever.

CHAPTER THIRTY-FOUR

TONY

"Go directly to your car and drive to your sister's house. I'll meet you there."

"What about Ginger, Rob, and Chris?" Chloe's face remained ashen and her eyes were filled with worry.

"The person we need to talk to is Chris, and I think I know where I can find him," I said.

"Then I'm coming with you," she said.

"Chlo, it's not smart," I said. "We still don't know if Barry or Chris are Winters's inside guy, but my money's on Chris."

"Mine too," she said. "So, let me go."

I hesitated. Deniability only worked if I kept Chloe removed from whatever I discovered. But Chloe shook her head as if she had just read my thoughts.

"Nuh-uh. We've been a team this entire time. I showed you, or rather pointed toward, the mother vine. That's a career killer—not to mention aiding and abetting in a felony if you were to steal it. I wouldn't have betrayed my employer and risked my job, and the possibility of prison, if I didn't believe in what we were doing. Something's not adding up here—from the Summerset's and the Point's cabs tasting so similar to Rob and Winters's daughter making out by the mother vine. What the fuck? You can't bench me now. I'm in too deep."

As usual, Chloe made a solid argument. She had beauty, brains, and no shortage of moxie, and I'd be a fool to keep a triple-threat All-Star on the bench.

"Okay. Meet me in Yountville at the No Winers or Minors bar."

The No Winers or Minors bar lacked the pretentiousness and priciness of Napa. Nothing but kegs and hard liquor, and if someone requested a wine list, they were asking for a brawl. In short, it was a working man's place. It was also the hangout for the Point's senior wine educators.

The lanky blond sat on a barstool beside another wine educator I recognized but not by name.

"Chris Staple?" Chloe approached him before I could. "Where'd you go? One minute you were at our last training session and the next you suddenly were a no-show. I looked all over the hotel for you and it's like you just disappeared from the resort altogether. What's going on?" When Chris didn't respond, Chloe leaned in on him like I'd only seen Dan do on the court and lowered her voice like she was about to talk smack and didn't want the ref to hear.

"Listen, asshat, are you working for Winters or not?"

He stood, grabbed his beer, and walked to a corner table. Chloe doggedly followed on his heels like she was about to make the steal of the game. When he was safely out of earshot, I knew he was our guy. He held out his hand toward Chloe like they'd never met.

"Uh, hello?" she said.

"It's Chris Winters," he said.

She withdrew her hand. "What?"

"You're his inside guy," I confirmed.

He nodded. "I *was* the inside guy."

"I'm so confused." Chloe pulled out a chair and sat.

I continued to stand even after Chris sat beside her.

"Winters?" Chloe said. "Like Samuel Winters?"

"I'm his nephew, which is why when Ginger showed up on property and wanted to join our final training session, I had to leave. I couldn't let my cousin see me."

"Didn't Ginger know you were there?" I asked.

A grim look crossed his face that was a younger version of his uncle's. "Samuel sent me in undercover months before you arrived."

"Why? For the mother vine?" Chloe asked.

"That's part of it," Chris said. "But also to keep an eye on Chambers and what direction he had for the hotel operation."

Chloe massaged her forehead. "Rob? Uh, it's been a long night, so you're going to have to dummy this down for me. Your uncle, Samuel Winters, sent you to the Point to find the mother vine, keep an eye on Rob Chambers and the hotel, but Ginger never knew?"

"That's right," he said.

I crossed my arms over my chest. "Winters didn't want his daughter to know you were there because you weren't watching the hotel's operations, you were watching Rob."

Chris nodded.

"Why? Because Rob and Ginger are a thing?" Chloe looked from me back to Chris.

"Uh, my cousin has a thing for Rich," Chris said.

"*The other Point owner?*" Chloe's voice drew the wrong kind of attention. I stood beside her to block any unwanted eyes or ears.

"It happened a long time ago, but yeah, Ginger's crazy about Rich," Chris said.

"Are you sure?" Chloe said.

"Yeah, pretty sure. It started when Rob and Rich worked at Winters Winery. It's actually where they met. They were both right out of college and headed to Northern California to be wine bums."

"Would Rich have taken Winters's mother vine?" Chloe asked.

Chris shrugged. "We don't know. I thought Rich had a very strict moral compass but it may have changed. When Rob and Rich worked for my uncle, Rich began dating Ginger. They were *crazy* about each other and everyone thought those two would end up together, but when Winters refused Rich's request for his daughter's hand in marriage, Rich backed off. It was crushing to my cousin." Chris took a sip of his beer.

"So, instead, Ginger started working her way through her father's staff and when that didn't get the reaction she wanted, she moved on to the competition?" I said.

Chris curtly shook his head. "Ginger's very purposeful. Everything she's done has been decisive."

"Or *derisive* toward her father," Chloe said.

"Exactly," Chris said.

"What was your assignment?" I asked pointedly.

"Winters suspects that Rich stole his mother vine. After all, it doesn't take a sommelier to notice how similar the taste of the Point's cab is to my uncle's Summerset. So, my mission was actually to steal the Point's mother vine and have it analyzed so my uncle could prosecute if it is his stolen vine."

Chloe tucked her dark hair behind her ear. "So, Winters suspects that Rich is at the heart of this, but what about Rob?"

Chris shrugged. "Until you told me that Rob and Ginger were a thing, I didn't know."

"The only certainty is that the two cabs taste similar and Rich is the likely suspect because he was denied the woman he loves," I said.

"Yah, and the only way to prove it was to get to the mother vine, but when Victorine put me back into training mode, my opportunity to work undetected was shot down," Chris said.

"Because as a wine educator you know exactly where the mother vine is," Chloe said.

He nodded. "Right out in the open."

I ran my hand through my hair. "I still can't believe they do that."

Chloe laughed. "It's actually quite brilliant. Keep things out in the open and no one sees it."

"It'd only be brilliant if I had a sample of it," Chris said. "But now I *really* can't go back. If my cousin has a thing for Rob, she'll spot me for sure."

"Yes, but I can," I said.

"We can go back and steal a sample tonight," Chloe said, which I shook my head against.

"Listen," she said. "If Rob, who hasn't done anything but be a mentor and friend to me, has been screwed over by his business partner, then I'm all in," she said. "And after the way he and Ginger were kissing in the west-end vineyard they're probably either in her suite or his house on the hill. Either way, tonight's the perfect time to take a cutting."

Damn, if I couldn't argue her logic.

"Deal, but Chris can't go," I said. "If Ginger saw him, everything would be for naught."

"Agreed," Chris said. "I won't tell my uncle about Ginger and Rob until we have the vine."

I grinned. "Yeah, I'm not sure that's going to go over very well."

"Once you get the vine, text me." Chris reached for his phone in his back pocket and within minutes my cell buzzed with an incoming text. "I've had your number and now you have mine. We'll meet at Winters Winery."

CHAPTER THIRTY-FIVE

CHLOE

I directed us toward the west-end vineyard. I knew the cameras were positioned in each corner of the vineyard and recorded continuously. The live feed looped into the security office and the monitors. When we were shown the feed in security, there appeared to be one row that wasn't captured in the frame. I was kind of banking that what I saw was accurate. I hadn't spent much time above ground. The last three weeks, I had been assigned to cave tasting tours, honing my skills and taking notes on what wine Point guests preferred. Rob periodically checked on me, but our work together hadn't fully commenced. I was grateful. My time was free to spend with Tony, who I led away from the camera's focus and stood in front of a small row of vines.

I held up a cautionary finger. "I know what we're doing is for the greater good, but all I ask is that you are careful with the vines. They are sensitive and somehow I think they've already been through enough."

Tony pulled me into an embrace. "Chloe."

I reached around his waist and tucked my hands into his back jean pockets to bring him closer to me. "I'm trying to be strong, but…" My eyes filled with tears. "I also know that once we figure this all out, you'll be reassigned to something new. Or at the very least, will have to return home to Huntington."

He tipped my chin toward him. "I don't want to think about that." His lips touched mine in a soft embrace.

***

TONY

When our lips parted, I bent down to tie my shoe, gently pulled one of the vines from the soil and stuffed the entire thing into my high top. Then I reached behind the vine to the next row and grabbed another sample that I put in my other shoe. I spoke to Chloe as if I was tying my shoe.

"Okay, right now would be about the time security would come. They have to have this placed watched more closely than Pamela Anderson's cleavage during a *Baywatch* episode, so if they arrive…."

She laughed. "We'll share a jail cell together."

But no one showed up. I casually pressed the tip of my high top in the dirt, like I was putting out a cigarette when really, I rearranged the dirt to cover my tracks. I stood and tucked Chloe under my arm and spoke quietly into her hair.

"Okay, go back to your car and I'll text you the address of Winters Winery and meet you there," I said.

"I can Google it. But why don't we go together? We parked behind the basketball courts—no one's going to see us."

"It may seem lame, but I'm still officially working on Winters dime and I'd rather not show up dressed like this when I present him with what he's been after," I said.

"Right." Chloe glanced at her uniform. "Huh. Maybe I should change too?"

"We don't have time." I squeezed her hand and walked toward the hotel while Chloe headed toward her car.

"I've got a contact at UC Davis who will rush our samples through," Winters said as soon as we stepped into his office. Chris stood off to the side of his desk like a scolded child. I figured he either told his uncle about his daughter's involvement with Rob or he had told him I was finishing what he was sent to do.

"That's great." I was about to sit in the chair in front of his Cherrywood desk when he wagged his finger.

"It'll be great once I see the taillights on your car heading toward Route 128," Winters said, never one to mince words.

"You want *us* to drive the samples to UC Davis?" I asked.

"I think it's a fair trade," Winters replied, and I felt my jaw tighten. "After all, I've waited nearly a month for you to deliver."

I stood my ground. "No, that was your nephew's assignment." I glanced at Chris. "Sorry buddy, but when Chris couldn't deliver because you sent Ginger in, *I* had to."

"Well, the bottom line is we have the Point's mother vine and our mother vine, which is the only way to determine what I already know—Rich stole from me and has been profiting ever since." Samuel Winters was physically younger than his aged temperament. He was probably in his late fifties, with a thick shock of black hair that didn't have a hint of gray. Ginger had his blue eyes that had an icy stare directed at me. "I just feel sorry for Rob."

And I didn't have to glance at Chris to know he hadn't been the bearer of bad news.

"Speaking of Rob, there's probably something you should know," I said, and shot a look at Chloe, who had remained uncharacteristically quiet.

"Sir," she said, stepping into the conversation. "I work for Rob Chambers at the Point or I will if I don't get fired, but while I've been on property, I discovered that Ginger and Rob are engaged in an intimate relationship."

Chloe's direct approach was met by hardened, cold eyes.

"With all due respect, Ms. Dorsey, I think your intel is wrong. Or perhaps tainted by your own secretive relationship," he said and I knew Chris had brought him up to speed about Chloe and me.

"This must be difficult to hear," she said in a calm, steady, therapeutic-sounding voice. "However, intel that doesn't support your preconceived notions doesn't mean it's bad. My intel of a stolen kiss in the moonlight is an objective reporting of a firsthand observation. It's your subjective interpretation of the kiss being nothing that's bad."

That's my girl.

Winters's face puckered and I knew he was furious.

"Did you know about this?" Winters turned his fury to Chris, who vehemently shook his head.

"I assumed Ginger was still hung up on Rich," he said.

"Brilliant," he said in a stern tone. "Not only did you fail at securing the Point's mother vine, but your skill in gathering information about the owner is abysmal. Why would I ever place you in charge of anything?"

"Sir," I said. "The Point's security is top shelf. I only secured the mother vine because I was with Chloe. When security approached me to ask if everything was okay when I entered the hotel, I had her as an alibi. They clearly saw me on video, but not her or she would have been approached either by phone or in person. This allowed me to say my girlfriend dropped an earring when we walked through the west-end vineyard and we had gone back to look for it. Chris was working alone."

"I loathe excuses," Winters said. "If my nephew spent more time at the hotel and less at that bar, he would have been able to report my daughter's interactions with Chambers."

I knew when Winters began referring to people by association or last name, he had distanced himself from them.

Still, Chris was green to this industry. He didn't know

what he was doing. That was obvious when Victorine placed him back into the training rotation. I had to redirect Winters energy.

"Who's expecting us at UC Davis?" I asked and grabbed a pen and paper off his desk.

"Dr. Ferman. He's the head of the department and he'll run the test himself." Winters handed me an empty, gallon-sized plastic bag.

"I'll need two," I said, opening my duffel bag.

"Two samples?" he said.

"From my research, the Point started as a varietal vineyard, so I chose two random samples from the west-end vineyard that contains their mother vine," I said, and placed one vine into a bag. Winters wrote *A* on the outside of the bag. He handed me another bag that he marked *B*. Then I was handed his clipping that he marked with *C*.

"Three total samples," Chloe said.

Winters looked at me. "I want you to personally hand these to Dr. Ferman and wait. Their backlog usually takes three to four weeks."

"You want us to stay in Davis for three or four weeks?" Chloe grabbed her red polo. "Uh, I'll need to change and grab a suitcase."

Winters grinned.

"That was your humor," she said.

"It was." And if anyone could get Winters to smile it was Chloe.

I grabbed the three bags. "How long will it really take?"

"Dr. Ferman assures me he'll have it processed by the

end of tomorrow."

"On it." I glanced at Chloe, who began toward the door.

"Ms. Dorsey."

Chloe pivoted on the heel of her black work shoes toward Winters, who reached into his bottom drawer and threw her a Winters Winery jacket. "It gets cold in Davis."

"Thank you." The jacket was black, lined, and embroidered with the burgundy and gold Winters Winery logo. I didn't even have one of their jackets.

Winters shooed us out of his office. "Get to UC Davis and wait for them to open. I want you to be the first ones there."

"Will do." I grabbed Chloe's hand and headed toward her car.

CHAPTER **THIRTY-SIX**

I sat in the driver seat of Chloe's car, amazed at how things were working out. Chloe's head rested on my lap. The seatbelt was stretched across her Winters jacket, which like everything else, she wore well.

The distance between Napa and UC Davis was under fifty miles, but it wasn't well lit. I took our time while Chloe slept.

The exit for UC Davis glowed in the distance. I gently touched Chloe's shoulder. "We're here."

She rose and wiped the sleep from her eyes. "I'm so tired."

"We can get a hotel room," I said, and she vehemently shook her head.

"Your heard Winters. We have to be there when they open. Let's find where the viticulture department is and park outside the building."

"Okay." I handed her my charged cell phone. "I have the campus map bookmarked—I think the Foundation Plant Services building is what we want."

Chloe's face glowed when she scrolled through my phone. "FPS?" She looked at me.

"That's it."

"Okay, it's right on campus."

We found the building and I parked in the first spot I saw. I reached into the small back seat for my duffel bag and pulled out my hoodie, put it on, and cranked up the heat.

Chloe lay her head against me. We were the only car in the parking lot.

"I'm glad you're here." I kissed the top of her head.

Eyes closed, she smiled and wrapped her arms around my waist. "Me too."

The tap on the side window made me flinch. I opened my eyes to find a campus security guard. The horizon looked like it was about to break with sun. Chloe turned toward her side door and continued to sleep.

I hit the automatic window button. "Good morning. We're waiting for the office to open. We have an appointment with Dr. Ferman."

"Dr. Ferman's already in. He gets in at five every morning."

"Oh, okay. Thanks."

The security guard returned to his car and I gently nudged Chloe. "Babe, Dr. Ferman's in."

She bolted upright and grabbed the three baggies from the back seat. "Let's go."

The reception desk was empty and a door that led from the lobby into the back office was open. Chloe walked through in her oversized coat and sensible shoes. Dr. Ferman's office was tucked in a corner away from the lab that we passed through in search of the early riser.

Dr. Ferman looked like he was still in high school.

"Is there a senior Dr. Ferman?" I asked, thinking maybe his mother or father was the department head.

He held out his hand. "Are those the samples?"

Chloe handed them to him. "Yes, and we were told to wait."

"That's fine. There's a lobby out front or the college has a cafeteria. Write your cell number on the entry log on the reception desk and I'll text when I'm finished." Dr. Ferman did not believe in small talk. I supposed if I dealt with vines all day, my social skills would probably suffer too.

Chloe and I sat in the lobby. I think we were both too afraid to leave. Hours passed before Dr. Ferman's assistant called us to her desk.

"Dr. Ferman has finished the analysis, which he sent via facsimile to Winters Winery," she said.

"We were supposed to bring the report back with us for Samuel Winters," I said.

But the assistant shook her head. "The report was returned to Winters Winery."

Chloe leaned her elbow on the reception desk. Her jacket fanned out behind her like a cape. Her hair was heaped into a bun on the top of her head and she stood with one ankle crossed behind the other. Even in her work uniform and Winters jacket, all she needed was a pair of large, dark sunglasses and a cigarette and she could pass for Audrey Hepburn in "Breakfast at Tiffany's." And like Holly Golightly, she had an innocent, nonthreatening appeal that drew people to her.

"I'd love to thank Dr. Ferman, would that be possible?"

The receptionist pressed a button that released the door beside her desk. Chloe smiled in her direction. "Thank you."

Chloe headed toward the door before it locked again. I followed closely behind her.

"I'll keep him busy," she said, aiming her sights toward Dr. Ferman's corner office. "You check the lab for the fax and print a copy of whatever he sent."

I looked at her. "You're serious."

Her expression and voice was grave. "Tony, that report is the only thing that can clear both of us of being charged with theft. And the fact that we're being sent home without it isn't good."

"Right." I walked into the lab while she veered toward his office. I scanned the lab, but I didn't see a fax machine, laptop, or even a copier. *Shit.*

I crossed my arms over my chest and took a step back. *If I was Dr. Ferman, where would I keep my copy of the report?*

There was one window in the entire lab. But if Ferman was an early riser, he'd want to see who he beat to the office.

Didn't matter that he was the department chair, he was young enough to still be competitive.

I walked toward the window where a file holder that was shaped like a silver hashtag held manila folders. I skimmed through the tabs until I found one labeled "Winters." I shook my head. "Sonovabitch."

I opened the file and took pictures of the report with my cell phone. I placed the papers back into the file and set it back in the hashtag when I heard Chloe laughing.

I spotted an emergency exit and hoped and prayed it wouldn't alarm. I took my chances and slid out the back undetected. I headed toward the car and hopped in just as Chloe walked out with Dr. Ferman beside her.

"I was telling Dr. Ferman about that bakery," she said. "What's the name of it?"

I snapped my fingers. "I always forget," I lied. "But you can't miss it. Big yellow cottage-like house in Yountville."

"Sure," he said. "I can find that."

"Hey, thanks for everything," I said with a casual nod. It was enough to appease a punk like Ferman. He might be the department chair, but playing favorites with wineries wouldn't keep him in that position long.

"Listen, next time you're in Napa, you've got to call me." She reached into her purse and handed him a card. "It's the main hotel, but they can reach me in the cave. The cell reception is crap down there."

"Don't have to tell me," he said, elbowing my girl. "I've been in one of Napa's wine caves. There's no cell service."

"Right." Chloe rolled her eyes. "Well, then you know

it makes trying to communicate with the outside world impossible!"

He grinned toward her. "Thanks again for the tip. I love gingerbread cookies."

"Anytime. Take care and thanks again." Chloe squeezed his arm. "Okay, you can drive me home now."

Chloe slipped into the front seat and I gritted my teeth toward Ferman, put the car in reverse, and slowly pulled away. When we were a half mile from the university, Chloe leaned toward me.

"Oh, my God! Did you hear that? He's been in a wine cave!"

"Yes, Ms. Daisy, I heard that. He may even have been on a wine train, too. That doesn't tell us anything. I would imagine someone in his position visits Napa a lot."

"You're right." She lightly tugged on the sleeve of my dress shirt. "Did you get the report?"

"I did."

"Where is it? I want to read it." She looked around the front seat.

"It's on my phone." I handed her my cell.

"Oh, you're good." She scanned the pictures stored on my phone.

"*We're* good. I wouldn't have been able to find the file if you hadn't kept him preoccupied with… what exactly, I'm not sure and I don't think I want to know."

She grinned with her head pointed down. She scrolled through my phone.

"What does it say?" I asked and looked over my shoulder

to merge onto the highway.

Chloe sat back against the seat. "I don't believe it."

"What?"

"The bag labeled *A* was the clipping we got, right?"

"That's correct. *A* and *B* are from the Point winery."

"DNA revealed that the wine-grape variety in bag *A* was a direct offspring of a classic cabernet sauvignon, while the wine-grape variety in bag *B* was considered so mediocre that the report suggested that the plant no longer be planted."

"What?" I glanced at Chloe.

"But wait, it gets better. Bag *C* that we brought from Winters Winery was discovered to be the highly esteemed cabernet sauvignon wine grape that is the offspring of the cabernet franc and sauvignon blanc varieties. Ferman's analysis identified additional DNA marker sites that confirmed the very high probability that these two varieties were indeed the parents of the wine grape in bag *A*."

"What was the probability that he reported," I asked.

She magnified the report on my phone. "Ferman gave the wine grape analysis as more than 99.99 percent sure that the original parents for wine grape *A* was wine grape *C*."

"That basically means that there is less than one chance in a million that Ferman's wrong."

I rolled my shoulders to release the tension. "What else does it say about the wine-grape variety in bag *B*?" I glanced at her. She looked dejected. I knew she liked Rob and imagining his partner had screwed him wouldn't settle well with her.

"Chloe, read me the part about the vine in bag *B*."

"It doesn't say much more than I read. Okay, it says that while the appearance of the grape seems related to the wine grape in bags *A* and *C*, DNA testing uncovered that the wine-grape variety in bag *B* was considered so mediocre that the plant should be banned from further propagating."

"Wow. They don't even want that vine around the others," I said.

"Right. It must have been one of the first varieties Rob and Rich planted," she said. "But it still doesn't answer the question of how Winters's mother vine ended up in the Point's vineyard. There's no way to prove who took it and planted it there. All this report proves is that the parents of the Point's mother vine are Winters's vines."

"Unless Winters is right and Rich stole the vine when he worked there," I said, and pressed on the pedal. "The faster we get to Winters, the sooner we may be to resolving this."

CHAPTER **THIRTY-SEVEN**

CHLOE

"I know you want to go straight to Winters, but if I don't get out of this uniform soon…."

"Hey, no one's stopping you from shedding your clothes. In fact," Tony raised an eyebrow and his brown eyes sparked, "if you'd like some help, I could pull over and we could…."

"Romeo, I think we both need a shower first," I said, and his eyes widened.

"Oh, no you didn't."

I wrinkled my nose. "While I like your man sweat *and I do*, it's kind of turned from sexy sweat to sleeping in a car all night stank."

"The honeymoon's over," he said, and I laughed.

"It'll never be over," I said, and his face broke with a smile.

"So, your sister's house, then?"

I nodded and texted my sister that we were on our way.

My eyelids were swollen from lack of sleep and mascara-streaked my face. I started the water in the Jacuzzi tub in the bathroom off my sister's master bedroom. When the water level was high enough, I hit the button for the jets and poured honeysuckle body wash into the tub. Bubbles rose and I dipped my toe into the water. *Perfect.*

I stepped into the tub and submerged myself under water. Steam rose off the water when I resurfaced and washed my hair. I massaged my head, but it didn't stop the throbbing headache that began behind my eyes and radiated to the back of my skull. With clean hair that swum around my face in the water, I placed a warm washcloth across my eyes.

"Hey, goober girl." I smelled my sister's perfume and thought of our mom, who wore a similar scent—it had this beachy aroma, like coconuts and baby lotion. It was the scent of good memories.

The washcloth lifted from my face and her blue eyes shone down at mine. "Chlo, what happened?"

"Just tired." I scooped an armful of bubbles toward me as if they would magically comfort me.

"Chlo." Charlotte sat on the ceramic tiled side-splash next to the tub. She used to do the same thing with flash cards growing up. My lack of attention drove our mom crazy, so she'd send in Charlotte to teach me my vocabulary words. Charlotte didn't have any more patience than our mom, but she was determined her little sister wouldn't flunk first grade. I learned to read and sound out words in a bathtub. And now my sister sat calmly and waited for me to answer.

"It's a conversation I had with Winters."

"From Winters Winery?"

"Same one."

Her white-blonde hair shook. "What?"

I exhaled. "Last night Tony and I took two samples of the Point's mother vine and brought them to Winters."

"Oh, Chloe."

"It's okay. I wanted to," I said. "If Rob's getting screwed by his business partner he has a right to know. And then Winters wanted a DNA analysis performed of the Point's vines and his."

"That's what I would expect Winters to do."

"Right. And the results show that the Point's mother vine is a near match to Winters's mother vine. What I didn't expect was to see Rob and Winters's daughter, Ginger, trysting in the west-end vineyard."

"Huh. Didn't see that one coming," Charlotte said.

"I know. And I was the one that told Winters his daughter was most likely sleeping with the enemy, or rather, competitor."

"That was useful information for him to have." Charlotte's thinking was pure corporate.

"Okay, but one of the biggest rules of ethics in my profession is confidentiality, and I feel like I crossed that line."

"Chlo, from what you've told me, confidentiality only

pertains to your clients. And it can only be broken if your client is in danger of harming themselves or someone else."

"That's right."

"So, were either Rob or Ginger one of your clients?"

"No."

"Did you discover this information from a private session?"

"No, not unless you consider having a private session of intimacy by a grapevine where I saw more than I ever expected."

"Then what you were doing was acting more as a friend," she said, and before I could interject that Samuel Winters wasn't my friend, nor would he ever likely be my friend, she wagged a manicured fingertip at me. "Tony's been working with you against Winters, who hired his firm to gather intel. By serving as the bearer of bad news you took that off Tony's plate and created a necessary professional distance between Tony and Winters. No man wants to hear from another man that his daughter is screwing the competitor. So what you did was help Tony, who besides being your love interest is also your friend."

The water lapped against the tub. "Thank you."

"So, what now?"

"Well, Tony and I have to return to Winters Winery and give him the results of the DNA analysis, *which* was already faxed to him, but Tony wants to see this through to the end."

"You're kidding."

"Nope." Tears stung my eyes. "I'm so fried from all this spying, the last thing I want to do is go to Winters Winery."

My sister grabbed the lush gray towel hanging on the hook behind her. "Actually, Winters Winery is *exactly* where you need to go." She held up the towel and waited.

I emerged out of my cocoon of sudsy water that I never wanted to leave.

"Winters Winery? That's where I should be?"

My sister wrapped me in the full-length towel that could double as a blanket.

"Exactly. Chloe, I know you. And if *you* don't see this through to the very end you'll always wonder. Even if Tony relays what happens, you are a finisher."

"Charlotte, I'm not a spy. I had to have Tony take the mother vine from the Point. Can you seriously see me strolling into the Point's vineyard with a pair of pruning shears in my bag? Not going to happen. I'd probably trip on the grounds and impale myself."

"Deflection? Isn't that what you call what you're doing?" She handed me her bottle of makeup remover and a stack of circular cotton pads. "You used to steal cookies out of the cookie jar without making a sound. I always sent you to get them because no one was better at mastering that ceramic lid. What I know about you, Chloe Michelle, is if you want something badly enough you can do anything. But lucky for you, Tony already did. And now you're going to partner with him on this to the very end. Consider it closure."

"I've created a monster." I stood in front of her vanity and began to take off my makeup. My sister handed me a washcloth and her facial soap.

"Do you remember what Dad always said about fighting,

and then when we became older he called it conflict?"

I nodded while I scrubbed my face. "Yes." I looked at her in the mirror. "Choose your battles."

"Right. And the trick was knowing when to be soft and when to be strong," she said. "And we don't know if Rich or Rob drew first blood against Winters. I know how much you like Rob, but one of the Point's owners stole from Winters. It's the only explanation that's plausible. But simply because you don't want to know which of the two is the wine thief, that doesn't mean you quit and walk away. This is when you show your strength."

I stared at myself in the mirror, and without makeup, I looked worse. "If I'm going to even have a chance in hell at accomplishing this, I'm going to need a large glass of water, a handful of ibuprofen, a shit ton of concealer, and one of your knockout business dresses from your fat days that would actually fit me."

My sister kissed the back of my wet head. "I'll get the water, the ibu, and the dress. The good makeup that covers wrinkles, pimples, and age spots is in the top drawer. Go wild."

I plugged in her high-end, overpriced ceramic curling iron, grabbed the hair dryer, and began to get myself into fighting shape.

"You clean up well," Tony said. I sat beside him while he drove my car and turned from Highway 29 in Oakville into the long driveway and drove beneath an arched sign that announced Winters Winery.

"My sister's closet helps," I said, feeling refreshed and energized for whatever unfolded.

The winery looked different in the daytime. I glanced out the window at the older, blue-washed farmhouse that had a homey, historic feel. A matching picket fence framed the manicured lawn. A tandem swing hung from a large oak. It was 180 degrees from what I had imagined.

While the Point's cobblestone winery gave the hotel a sense of European history, Winters Winery was pure Americana, including the flag that flapped in the wind. If I were a bed-and-breakfast kind of traveler, this would be ideal.

Lights were strung from the branches of the towering oaks. In the evening, they would look like lightning bugs.

I stepped out of the car in a form-fitting coral dress and braided, espadrille-style Jimmy Choo platform wedges in antique gold with crisscross straps that hugged my ankle. My sister promised the shoes would give me my Cinderella moment, and like my fairy godmother, my sister reminded me that being the bearer of bad news didn't mean I had to dress poorly. The soft texture to the dress made me feel confident despite my hunger and lack of sleep. The cork-filled wedges were like walking on clouds. I knew my sister's shoes cost more than a wine educator made in three months at the Point. However, if style was contagious, dressing like my sister was catching.

Then I spotted her. In a simple, sleeveless black dress, blonde hair swept into a side ponytail and a gold cuffed bracelet wrapped around her forearm that accentuated her toned, slender arms, Ginger stood in a pair of pointy heels, owning the lawn as she stood beside her father.

Guilt needled my side. And then I remembered what my sister said about how I served as a buffer between Tony and Winters with information we obtained from simply being at the right place at the right time—ironically Winters's motto.

Tony placed his arm around my waist and pulled me into a side hug, and my focus shifted to the job at hand.

"Your dress is screaming to come off," Tony said in my ear.

I turned toward him. "Well if either of us are still standing afterward, I'm game."

If I had learned anything in my thirty days at the winery, it was that the passion winemakers possessed was driven by a thousand forms of doubt and insecurity. Everyone wanted their wine to be well-received. Each vintage was a reflection of the winery and in turn the team of winemakers. It was a cut-throat business masked by families like the Winterses who craved the appearance of normalcy among sharks.

"Ms. Dorsey, it's good to see you again," Winters said as if we had met under different circumstances. "So I was recently told you came to Napa with a tragic history."

My stomach tightened and I tried to keep my hands relaxed when I wanted to take my sister's clutch and backhand Tony with it. *What the fuck?*

"What history is that?" Tony said, and then glanced at me and I knew he hadn't told a competing winery or his client about Ben.

"Oh, well, I was told that Chloe, is it?" He waited until I confirmed what he already knew.

"Yes."

"That Chloe is a widow," he said.

Tony slowly nodded as if he was trying to determine how to proceed.

"That's correct," I said, figuring Chris was most likely the source of Winters's intel. I was sure he was doing his utmost to get back into his uncle's good graces. "My late husband, Ben, died three years ago."

Tony's response was the same as the first time I told him—sincere. "I'm so sorry."

But for the first time since Ben died, I didn't respond with my pat, "Me too." Instead, I looked into Tony's eyes that were as dark and stoic as the oak tree beside us. "Thank you. We had a beautiful but much too brief marriage."

"I'm a widower," Winters said.

I didn't respond.

"Ginger's mother died when she was three." He reached and squeezed her hand. "We've been on our own ever since."

Explains so much. Ginger wasn't here as his daughter, but as a surrogate spouse. There was nothing worse than a parent emotionally leaning on a child. A three-year-old wasn't equipped to step into the role Winters had assigned her. And the real tragedy was that the thirtysomething-year-old Ginger was still standing in for his lost spouse.

"I don't know what I'd do without Ginger," Winters said with a look her way. He shook their interlaced hands. "With all the colors in the world, all she wears is black."

She's still in mourning. You haven't allowed her to move on.

"Do you have anyone?" Winters asked.

There were so many things I wanted to say—like, I get that nature abhors a vacuum so when a space as large as a mother becomes vacant, something or someone will unconsciously want to fill it. *I get it. It happens a lot. But how 'bout you let Ginger have her own life and stop making her live yours. The burden is too great.* She would eventually crack and do something to harm herself or someone else. I stared at Ginger and saw the child who would do anything for her father to maintain a sense of balance. But I silenced the counselor and instead answered Winters's question, which he already knew the answer to, and offered a nonthreatening laugh.

"And here I thought it was obvious," I said and reached for Tony's hand. "I've been seeing Tony since, well, you assigned him to the Point to uncover their mother vine." I continued to hold Tony's hand and waited to see who would react.

Ginger dropped her father's hand and I wasn't even sure he noticed.

"I'm glad you're both here," Winters said as if he hadn't directed us to return to his winery after the DNA analysis at UC Davis was performed. "Ginger and I have some wonderful news." He paused as if he were looking for a reaction, so I raised an eyebrow and feigned interest.

"We're ready to unveil our newest single-vineyard cabernet," he said.

"Single-vineyard?" I asked.

"We sought out a unique grape to make these new specialty wines that we're naming Ginger Wines."

That woman has no chance. Children who don't have *their* emotional needs met because they're taking care of a parent's needs tend to grow up to be adults with little or no self-esteem.

Tony smiled. "Congratulations." And then he took a step toward Ginger. "Creating wine seems to be your specialty," he said. "Didn't you offer to help the Point begin its winery?"

"Just in the beginning," she said with a look of neutrality.

"Mahoney, I read the report that UC Davis faxed," Winters said. "And it's clear that Rich stole a clipping of our mother vine to start his winery. Whether my daughter helped in the initial stages amounts to nothing other than goodwill on her part."

Ginger looked so pale I thought she was going to faint.

"What did the analysis show—" she stammered.

"That the Point's mother vine is a clone of ours," Winters said. "So it was Rich as I suspected all along."

"Yet during my conversation with Rich Erickson earlier this morning, he not only assured me that he did not steal your mother vine, but when the west-end vineyard was planted, he was out of the country," Tony said.

Winters arched an eyebrow. "It's unlike you to place trust in an undocumented fact."

"No, it's documented. A buddy of mine is a parole officer who can access TSA records. I pulled in a favor and he conducted a flight history of Rich's travel. Rich was out of the country when the west-end vineyard was planted," Tony said.

"This still isn't adding up," I said. "If Rich didn't steal the mother vine from Winters, then who did?"

Tony closed the space between him and Ginger. He was close enough to kiss her, but when he leaned forward, his energy was anything but sexual. Tony was pissed.

"Did you steal Winters's mother vine and give it to Rich?" he asked her.

I shook my head. *What?*

"I thought about it," she said. "When Rich worked here, we harvested the vines to find the perfect varietal for Winters Winery."

She didn't answer his question.

"Of course it had to be perfect," Tony said. "Because we both know how competitive your father is, which is why *if* he ever discovered that his mother vine was anywhere outside this property, he'd have his team of attorneys in Federal court filing a trademark and unfair competition claim with the aim of shutting the Point or any winery down immediately."

Ginger remained stoically silent, but Winters's hands clenched over his stomach.

Bingo. His body language was symbolic of someone exercising self-restraint. The more Tony zeroed in on his daughter, the greater Winters's body tensed and his face filled with anxiety.

"Or?" I looked at Tony, who hadn't relaxed his stance in front of Ginger.

"Or what?" Winters asked.

"Or you knew it was your vine all along and you've been protecting someone," I said.

"As a business owner in Napa, I would never allow a competitor to steal from me," he said.

I slowly nodded. "Which is why it must have been so hard for you when you read the report from UC Davis, which noted the age of the vines. As a single dad, I'm sure you kept tabs on Rich so you would have known he was out of the county when the Point planted their vines."

"Which leaves Rob," Winters said. "As soon as Ginger and I announce our new wine, I'll notify my attorneys to deal with him."

I grimaced. "Yeah, see that's the problem. Rob is an excellent salesman. I've seen him in action against one of your best inside guys," I said with a nod toward Tony. "Hell, Rob almost sold Tony on a monthly wine package. But we both know Rob isn't the brains of the operation. He's the sales guy, the image man—the closer. His focus is on marketing. But Rich—Rich is the science side of the industry. It's why he and your daughter fell in love—they had a shared interest." I hadn't been the only one to do my research. A quick read on Ginger's LinkedIn profile while I dried my hair revealed she had a degree in viticulture from UC Davis, which was where Rich earned his Master's degree in viticulture.

"As usual Chloe raises a valid argument. If Rich couldn't have stolen your mother vine because he was out of the country when it was harvested, and we both know you don't just let anyone harvest your first vines, so Rob isn't smart enough to do it, that leaves one person who would have had access to the vineyard *and* the knowledge and ability to graft it offsite," Tony said, looking at Ginger.

"Enough!" Winters's voice raised. "My daughter would never jeopardize what I've worked so hard to establish."

Ginger's laughter was unexpected. "What *you* worked so hard to establish?" Her blonde ponytail swayed on her shoulder. "You didn't do anything to build this winery. Rich and I did *everything* and then when we made Winters Winery a success you had the audacity to *forbid us* from marrying." Her blue eyes burned with intensity. "The one man I actually loved more than you and you ran him out of my life."

"He wasn't good enough for you," Winters said.

"He made me happy," she said, and her father grunted.

"Happy? Happy only lasts so long," Winters said.

"Well, I guess no one would know that better than you," she said. "I understand why Mom stopped fighting. She couldn't battle leukemia and your incessant need for attention, so she let the disease win."

Winters's hand came swiftly up and slapped his daughter's cheek.

A smile tugged at her trembling lips. "Guess what, Daddy? When you call your attorneys don't forget to mention that I'm your wine thief. *I stole the mother vine.* The same vine I harvested, cultivated, and brought to life—I planted it in the west-end vineyard at the Point when Rich was out of the country and Rob needed help." She turned and walked toward a black town car and driver that was waiting.

"Rob is only with you for what he can get from you, he's going to ruin you," Winters called after her.

Ginger turned with the elegance of a seasoned socialite and glanced at her father. "Being ruined by Rob would be an upgrade from the devastation and destruction of me that you left in your wake."

I watched in stunned, though admiring, silence as Ginger disappeared into the black car that whisked her away from Winters and the winery.

CHAPTER **THIRTY-EIGHT**

CHLOE

"Why did Winters want to talk to you privately?" I asked when Tony and I were in the seclusion of my car.

"He was still ready to have Rich and Rob arrested, until I reminded him that by prosecuting them it would drag Ginger into it because the Point owners could claim deniability," Tony said.

"Could they?" I asked. "Don't you think one of them realized their 2016 award-winning cab was eerily similar to Winters 2012 Summerset—especially since they both worked there?"

"Of course, that argument could be made," Tony said, turning the ignition. The engine purred. I loved this car but I loved it even more when Tony drove and I could enjoy the Napa Valley scenery. "Winters isn't going to let his daughter's reputation be tarnished—even if she is the wine thief."

"Winters has been dependent on Ginger, which is why he prevented her from having her own life. But now...."

"Now, he's devastated and has forbidden his staff from allowing his daughter to ever set foot on *any* of his properties, in Napa or at his corporations in Southern California. He basically disowned her."

"She's finally free," I said.

Tony glanced my way for oncoming traffic and then pulled onto Highway 29 where he pressed on the gas as he shifted quickly from first to second and seamlessly into third. My car responded, showing off its mettle. My thoughts turned back to the last twenty-four hours.

"If Winters excommunicated his own daughter, Rob will do far worse to me if he finds out I helped steal two clippings of their mother vine. And you know Ginger is set to tell him what just happened." I slowly exhaled. "Well, it was a fun run."

"Actually, Winters sent Chris to talk to Rob on our behalf," Tony said. "He's going to broker a deal that if Rob doesn't press charges against us, he won't have his attorneys try to stop the Point from making their award-winning wine. He may not want to drag his daughter through the mud, but he could hold things up in court for years. He's vindictive that way."

I kicked off my sister's shoes and tucked my feet beneath me on the heated seat. The story that was unfolding in front of me was better than any television drama. But like a TV drama, I sensed there was a cliffhanger on the horizon.

"You mention that Winters is vindictive, so it seems out

of character that he would drop *anything* that easily," I said.

"Well…," Tony began, and my gut tightened. "Winters did have two conditions."

"Which are…?"

"First, our knowledge about Ginger's involvement in any of this is to be forgotten," he said.

"What involvement?" I said, and Tony laughed.

"That's my girl."

"And the second?" I looked at Tony. The length of his neck was visible and I wanted to lean over, begin nibbling and inhaling his masculine scent.

Tony flipped on the turn signal and I glanced through the windshield. The Wine Train was loading passengers. The beauty of Napa was that everything was within a five-minute drive. Still, when he turned into the Wine Train's parking lot, I shook my head.

"Why did you take us here?"

Tony navigated around the potholes, parked, and hopped out of the car. Within seconds, my door opened. I tucked my feet into my shoes and slipped my hand into his.

"Where are we going?" I asked.

"You'll see." He led me over the small pedestrian footbridge that connected the train station to the boarding platform. The bridge fence was adorned with locks.

"Love Lock bridge," I said.

Tony squeezed my hand. "Do you remember when Martine told us that lovers leave locks decorated with their names, initials, or a date that they hooked to the bridge fence? Or sometimes," he said, "there were stories where someone left their lock and a message for their future love."

"Yes." I looked at Tony, whose hand suddenly felt clammy, and I knew he was nervous.

"And then Martine presented each of us with a heart-shaped lock and key, remember?" Tony said.

"Yes, I remember."

"Well, Martine also said the key could either be tossed below the bridge or saved as a keepsake."

He directed me to a section of the bridge where it seemed every lock looked alike—except one.

"When I put my lock here, I had a message to the universe inscribed on the back, not knowing if it'd ever be answered or if I'd be back here again. But I'm hoping both have just happened," he said.

A lock with a red heart drawn on the side of the padlock drew me toward it. I gently lifted the lock and turned it over to read his simple inscription.

Who will unlock my heart?

I fought the tears that filled my eyes and hoped I could speak without losing any composure I had left. But before I could utter a word, Tony reached into his jean pocket and withdrew a key. It felt like my heart jumped to my throat.

"The answer to your question"—I reached for the key in his hand—"is me." I looked into his dark eyes with mine. "I will unlock your heart."

His face lit with an equal measure of joy and relief.

I unlocked his heart and then led him to where I had placed mine. I hooked his heart onto mine, locked them together, and tossed the key over the fence where it landed on the train tracks, like so many other lovers had before me.

"Now our hearts are locked. So whenever you return to Napa…." I couldn't finish the sentence because I didn't want to breathe life into his goodbye. I'd never be able to say goodbye to Tony, who swept me into his arms and spoke into my hair.

"Winters's other condition," he began, "was that I seriously consider a change in careers."

I pulled away. "Did he offer you a job at his winery?"

"Well, Winters *is* looking for a new director for the winery."

I blinked away the tears. "Oh my gosh. Did you say yes?"

A smile tugged at his lips. "Well, let's just say I didn't say no."

"So, you're moving to Napa?"

"That's the plan." His brown eyes almost disappeared when he smiled.

He drew me closer into him and it felt like it always did—I was safe, protected, and loved. After losing Ben, I never thought I'd ever feel anything but sadness. Tucked in Tony's embrace, all I felt was happiness. Tears streamed down my face.

He tipped my chin toward him. "Oh, Chlo, don't cry."

"I can't believe you're not leaving." I blinked away the tears. "After everything we've been through—it's finally over."

He used the sleeve of his shirt to wipe my cheeks. "No," he said with a tender kiss, "it's just beginning."

ACKNOWLEDGMENTS

Wine Thief was always written for my sister, Suzanne Billiter Cragin. Suzi, I've never been a fast learner, but you've always been a patient teacher. You helped me start this book after your husband told me to "Drive it like you stole it! Drive it like you stole it." I knew it was the opening line for a really great book and it was. I've thought of you so often during the different stages of *Wine Thief* and I hope you love it as much as I love you. xoxo Your Favorite Sister

To John "Coach" Cragin—you started something when I got behind the wheel of my sister's swanky car. Thank you. Every yin needs a yang, and Coach, you are my sister's. xoxo Your Favorite Sister-in-Law

And to Chris Purdy, Wine Educator at Pine Ridge Vineyards in Napa—thank you for answering *all* my questions during our wine tour and then following up with e-mails when I had repeated questions! When you drew wine from a barrel and introduced the tool of the trade as a "wine thief," I knew I had the title for a fun romance. Thank you for making this book possible!

So, my motto for this year is "Choose to Shine," and I am surrounded by people who help me shine—like my publisher, editor, and my family.

To *MY* editor, Olivia Ventura, there are no words. You get me—and that alone means everything. Thank you for your steadfast support and belief in me and this series. I continue to grow as a writer because of you. Thank you. Xoxox *(P.S. you deserve a case of wine after this edit.)*

To my publisher, Becky Johnson & the Hot Tree Publishing Family, there are publishing houses and then there are *publishing families*—I have found mine. Your encouragement is a ray of sunshine. And it is only with sun that we grow—thank you for always focusing on the good. EVERYTHING you do and how you support writers matters. Thank you. xoxoxo

To the one writer I reached out to when the edits in front of me looked greater than my ability, Trysh Thompson, thank you. You reminded me to breathe and to find the fun in writing. I did, and I am forever grateful to you.

Ron Gullberg, you chase me across the bed to hold me at night and remind me what it feels like to be fully loved. You are my muse. Since you entered my life, I discovered happily ever after.

To my stepchildren, Dylan and Max, and to my children, Austin, Kyle, Ciara, & Cooper, thank you for the laughter, card games, and hugs that center me. You are my everything.

And to my brothers, Stephen Billiter and Patrick Flanagan Billiter, you've never stopped believing and teasing that I would be the "Stephen King of Romance" and I plan on making that happen! Just wait, brothers!

To my readers, my Resort Romance series is a result of *your* support and continued love of my work. Thank you. I wouldn't be here without you.

ABOUT THE **AUTHOR**

Author Mary Billiter followed in the footsteps of her father, an award-winning journalist, by earning a Bachelor of Arts degree in Journalism from California State University at Northridge. She earned her Master of Arts degree in Adult and Post-Secondary Education at the University of Wyoming.

Mary teaches fiction writing courses through the Life Enrichment program at Laramie County Community College. When school's out, Mary can be found on a bike discovering new trails with her husband and children.

Mary resides in the Cowboy State with her unabashedly bald husband, Ron Gullberg, her four amazing children, two fantastic step-kids, and their runaway dog. She does her best writing (in her head) on her daily runs in wild, romantic, beautiful Wyoming

Connect with Mary:

WWW.MARYBILLITER.COM

WWW.TWITTER.COM/MARYBILLITER

WWW.FACEBOOK.COM/MARYMBILLITER

ABOUT THE **PUBLISHER**

Hot Tree Publishing opened its doors in 2015 with an aspiration to bring quality fiction to the world of readers. With the initial focus on romance and a wide spread of romance sub-genres, we envision opening up to alternative genres in the near future.

Firmly seated in the industry as a leading editing provider to independent authors and small publishing houses, Hot Tree Publishing is the sister company to Hot Tree Editing, founded in 2012. Having established in-house editing and promotions, plus having a well-respected market presence, Hot Tree Publishing endeavors to be a leader in bringing quality stories to the world of readers.

Interested in discovering more amazing reads brought to you by Hot Tree Publishing? Head over to the website for information:

WWW.HOTTREEPUBLISHING.COM

www.ingramcontent.com/pod-product-compliance
Lightning Source LLC
Chambersburg PA
CBHW032104180726

48284CB00002B/442